Coming Ho.

Readers are encouraged to go to
www.MissionPointPress.com to contact the
author or to find information on how to buy
this book in bulk at a discounted rate.

MISSION POINT PRESS

ISBN: 978-1-943995-16-5

Library of Congress Control Number:
2016913341

Printed in the United States of America.

*Ten percent of the proceeds from the sale
of this book will be donated to wounded
service member programs.*

Coming Home to Yesterday

S.G. TOLLEY

Mission Point Press

Dedicated to service members, their families, and the difficult road they may travel to heal the physical and emotional scars of war.

Part One

The Beginning of Forever

Love is something eternal;
the aspect may change, but not the essence.
— Vincent Van Gogh

Chapter One

"GEEZ! WATCH WHERE YOU'RE GOING!" ANN CALLED out as she spun around and just missed ricocheting into Lindsey, who walked beside her.

The two young ladies' somewhat random pathway from the parking lot to the field bleachers had steered them too close to one of several yellow school buses used to bring visiting baseball teams to Summersville. Ann's leading step had just reached the area immediately adjacent to the bus door when it abruptly folded inward and the first player came barreling out.

"Me! Why don't *you* look where you are going!" Bill could not believe that this errant, diminutive attacker was accusing him of running into her. In a split second, he'd gone from excitedly exiting the bus to colliding with an obviously out-of-place pedestrian. Now feeling embarrassed and surprised, he snapped back as he regained footing and turned to fully face her. "You had the whole parking lot! Why would you walk two inches from the bus? Smart move, *Shorty*."

In the same instant, she began to equally dress him down. "Hey No. 12," came her immediate response in a sharp tone as she looked him up and down, taking in his uniform and ball cap. "Maybe you should look before you come charging off the bus! It would be nice if you had some manners — like saying excuse me — but I doubt you are taught any manners where you come from — *farm boy!*" Ann emphasized "farm boy" after recognizing

9

the name of the school district on the bus: a small, farming community downstate.

Bill found himself speechless. A few seconds earlier he was feeling excited about being in Summersville and having the chance to play in the baseball senior league semifinals then *she* got in his way. Bill couldn't believe this errant, wayward, intrusive stranger was now attacking him, his actions, and his hometown. But just as he started to reply, she cut him off.

"Nice, real nice! What a jerk! Your apology is accepted!" Ann used her most sarcastic tone of voice, then turned away to storm off in exaggerated disgust, looking back to add, "I hope your team gets creamed!"

"Wait up," Lindsey called out in an effort to catch up with Ann. She had been left behind, standing flat-footed at the scene of the confrontation, watching it unfold and giggling as Ann put the clumsy ballplayer in his place. "No one messes with Ann," Lindsey thought as she made it to Ann's side, then asked. "Are you OK?"

Ann had reluctantly stopped but continued to rub her left shoulder, which she had been holding since the collision. "I suppose, but my shoulder hurts. What a jerk," Ann repeated. "He never did apologize."

"But he is sort of a cute jerk," Lindsey added.

"I didn't notice," Ann replied, but her ever-so-slight smile seemed to indicate otherwise.

Bill watched in disbelief as this errant spitfire stormed off. Besides being surprised and somewhat embarrassed by the unexpected collision, the only other casualty of the encounter was that his baseball glove had been knocked from his hand and onto the ground. Bud, the team's hulk of a catcher and forever-clown, picked up the dropped mitt and handed it to Bill.

"Hey *O-T*, I think she likes you!"

Bill grabbed the mitt and used it to smack Bud on the back. "Don't call me *O-T*! And, no, that crazy girl doesn't like me!" Bill did not like being called *O-T* and was in no mood to be teased with it now. The nickname had been bestowed upon him a few years earlier and, unfortunately, it had stuck like glue. More than once his face had turned red when someone called out *O-T*, with whispered comments and nervous giggles coming from the girls as they spread the word of its meaning.

"What are you ladies waiting for?" Coach Smith barked. "Grab the gear and head to the visitor's dugout! We don't have much time to warm up and, in case you forgot, we have a game to play. Get moving!"

The players' collective thoughts were immediately brought back to reality with the coach's commands and, like a bevy of alarmed geese, they hurried off in the direction of the baseball diamond. As they made their way toward the ball field, an uneasy silence fell over the Henderson Tigers. The paved parking lot, the crisp, well-groomed field and the picturesque setting adjacent to the bay were intimidating for these first-time visitors, and a far cry from the bare-bones facilities that they called home field in their small town of Henderson.

"Playing third base for the Henderson Tigers and batting third, No. 12, *Bobby* Weber!" came the broadcaster's booming introduction from the speakers strategically mounted on four of the light poles surrounding the manicured field. With just a slight pause and a big grin, Bill sprung from the dugout and onto the baseball diamond to take his rightful place at third base. "Where in the world did 'Bobby' come from?" he thought to himself as he grinned. It was William Harold Weber – aka *O-T* — who now stood on the Summersville baseball diamond, but the announcer's error did little to faze him. The excitement of the moment embraced Bill. Even at age 17, he just knew that playing on Henderson's first-place, senior league team and now being in the semifinals would surely be recorded in his personal annals of triumphant days.

Spence, the shortstop and second batter in the lineup, had immediately preceded Bill onto the field. As the broadcaster's next introduction brought Bud on the field to the catcher's position, Spence made his way over to third base. "Hey Bill, isn't that the girl who tried to run you over?" Spence smacked his glove and flicked his head upward, using both gestures to point to the bleachers down the third base line.

Bill tried to take a subtle look in the direction Spence had indicated. "Crap! That is her! Why couldn't she sit someplace else?"

"Maybe Bud was right; maybe the *Shorty* from Summersville does like you," Spence teased and laughed.

Bill said nothing in return, just glared to let Spence know that he didn't think his comment was very funny.

Phil Marlow, Henderson's best pitcher, had no problem striking out the leadoff batter for Summersville. After the batter swung and missed for the third strike, Bud threw the ball down the third base line for once around the horn. His throw was fast and slightly off its intended course, causing Bill to turn and reach far to his right in order to catch the throw. Reaching as he did also resulted in another glance at the fans in the bleachers. There *Shorty* sat, looking right back at him with what Bill saw as a mocking smile. She seemed to stand out among those in the bleachers.

As the inning progressed, Bill found himself taking a couple of quick, peripheral glances at the stands, trying to determine if *she* was still there, still displaying that mocking smile. One of the glances had lingered a few extra seconds longer, and he was pretty sure she was looking at him. But she was wearing dark sunglasses, so he couldn't be positive. "Why does it matter anyway?" he thought.

Summersville's first inning at bat ended with a fly ball to deep center field and now it was Henderson's turn; Bill would bat third.

From the dugout and now in the batter's circle, Bill watched Summersville's pitcher throw bullets past the first two batters. "Man he is fast," Bill thought as he took one last practice swing, doing so in unison with Spence, who was at the plate and whose swing was way behind the pitch. He hadn't come close to connecting, and that made the third strike. Now it was Bill's turn.

"He's bringing the heat, just be ready," Spence advised as the two passed one another: Spence to the dugout and Bill to the batter's box. Bill nodded to Spence and was confident he would be ready. There was a reason he batted third: a .342 batting average and 17 homers in the regular season. He would be the hitter to tame the pitcher, and show the Summersville hometown crowd what the Henderson Tigers were all about. As he made the final adjustments to his stance, holding up his hand to signal the pitcher that he was not yet ready, Bill imagined himself rounding the bases after smashing the ball over the left field fence. Maybe it would even make it to the bay, which now shimmered from the sun sinking lower in the sky. As he would approach third base, he would stare straight at *Miss Shorty;* his look would tell her just what these downstate *farmers* were all about — home runs! She could just take her smug comments and go home.

"Strike!" The umpire called out after the pitch popped into the catcher's glove, and Bill was caught looking.

"No problem," Bill thought. "I've seen his speed now; just throw another fast one and it is out of here." The ball left the pitcher's hand, and Bill set into motion a powerful swing. But rather than another fastball, it was a slider that handcuffed his swing as the ball moved inside. Bill's bat made only slight contact with the ball, sending it in a gentle roll down the first baseline. His meager effort made for a quick play and easy out by the first baseman. Bill had taken only a few strides when the first baseman stepped on the base to complete the play and the third out for the Tigers.

"Damn," Bill said under his breath and started to return to the dugout for his glove. Bud emerged wearing his catcher's gear and tossed Bill his glove, saving him the effort of retrieving it. He also offered encouragement: "You'll get a better piece of it next time." Bill hustled to his spot on the field, trying not to look into the stands, when he heard her again.

"Nice hit *Bobby*," came the loud, irritating proclamation of a singular voice from the third base bleachers. Bill did not have to look to see who made the insulting remark. He knew it was *Shorty*. Bill smacked the pocket of his glove and then once again a little harder. He would ignore her. He would not look her way. He would show her the next time.

But the next time and then one final time at bat proved to be not much different. Making it to first on an error, courtesy of the second baseman, and a strikeout — the big K — were the sum total of Bill's trips to the plate. His teammates had not fared much better with the final score 5-0 in favor of the home team, the Summersville Eagles.

Chapter Two

"ANYONE ELSE HEADED TO THE CONCESSION STAND?" Bill asked as he and Spence broke off from the rest of their team-mates. The Henderson Tigers had exited the dugout and were slowly making their way to the bus, feeling the sting of defeat and ready to leave.

"Might as well, Coach won't be ready to go for another half hour," Bud replied.

Bill saw Coach Smith still standing near home plate talking to one of the other coaches and knew it would take him quite awhile to reach the bus. Coach was a real talker. After he finished talking to the one coach, he would then make his rounds with the umpires, and the next two coaches taking the field. No player dared to suggest to Coach Smith that he might hurry a bit.

Just one other player, Mark, the right fielder, joined the concession-bound trio of Bill, Bud, and Spence. He was the only one on the team to make it to third base during the game and now walked with them in silence. The loss was a big disappointment and fresh on all of their minds. When the four reached the concession stand area, their silence was broken by the sound of cleats clacking on the concrete. Around them fans and ballplayers were coming and going, but all of this commotion was rather muted for the four. They were thinking about their defeat at the hands of Summersville, the season now ended, and the three-hour bus ride home.

As a means to reserve one of the weathered picnic tables, Spence tossed his glove on one to the far left of the concession stand. The other three Henderson players followed suit before making their way to the back of the line of waiting customers. The line wasn't too long, but the attendant didn't seem to be working very fast; it would take a little while to get their orders and make it back to their table. But, with Coach Smith still talking away, there would be plenty of time. The four remained quiet, still consumed by thoughts of the game. There would be no celebration; they had their butts beat and were now headed home, not in victory but as the rather soundly defeated ones. Then the absence of conversation was broken not by one of them but by an outsider.

"Nice game, *Bobby*."

The way she said it, the way she mockingly pronounced his errant name was like fingernails on a chalkboard to Bill. He knew immediately who said it. "Yeah, thanks, *Shorty*," he responded, as he fought not to look her way and be drawn into another unpleasant encounter with her. He was in no mood to do so.

"That's not my name!" Ann retorted sharply, "Don't ever call me that again!"

Bill turned to face his tormentor and each now stood looking at the other. As he again sized her up, he noticed a few things that he did not recall from their brief encounter at the bus: a smell of lotion or perfume that was different but nice, and a sparkle in her eyes that drew him in.

"OK, so what is your name?"

16

"Like I would tell you," came her immediate reply. Then she walked off, disappearing into the crowd as quickly as she had suddenly appeared.

Bill was fed up with it all; he just wanted to go home. He couldn't take any more of this no-name gnat that kept pestering him, or any more of Summersville, for that matter. Despite the initial excitement of being in the semifinals, of the manicured beauty of the field and the sparking water in the bay, all of its allure had been lost. When the four finally had their drinks and food, they navigated their way through the growing crowd back to the picnic table reserved by their ball gloves. But as they started to sit down, Bill noticed that there were only three gloves on the table, not four, and it was his glove that was missing. Although it was a good glove, it was not the best one of four.

"What the?! What happened to my glove? Man, I can't believe this! Someone stole it! Great, just great!" Bill looked around to see if, by chance, he might spot it being carried off by someone, but no such luck. He had no luck today, for anything. Bud, Spence, and Mark looked around as well, but the glove was not to be found. Bill ate and fumed in silence.

"Let's go ladies!" Coach Smith's bark was heard well before he reached Bill and the other three. Now that he was ready to go, he was rounding up the players who had not made it to the bus. Bill jumped up, as did the others, but then he moved closer to the coach.

"Coach, I lost my glove, or I mean someone took it," Bill stated in a manner that seemed to both seek sympathy and assistance.

"What do you want me to do about it? Did you leave it lying around? Shouldn't have done it!" Coach Smith almost bellowed in response. Though the coach seemed to summarily dismiss Bill's plight, he also surveyed the crowd, looking around as if in search of the missing glove. After a minute or so, he did manage to say in a slightly milder tone, "Sorry, but we got to go."

Bud had saved Bill a seat on the bus — third row, right side, by the window. The inside of the bus was still warm from the heat of the day even though dusk was starting to set in and the air outside had begun to cool. Bill opened the window to let the cool air in and as a resting place for his elbow. "Man, this place is the pits," Bill muttered to sum up the time in Summersville.

"Hey *Bobby*, did you lose something?"

Bill looked out the bus window and could not believe what he saw! There *she* stood, holding his glove and now taunting him with it. "Give it to me!" Bill demanded. As he did, the driver shifted the transmission into first, the bus lurched slightly forward, and the grinding gears nearly drowned out his command to her.

"Sure. Here you go, catch." Ann lowered her arm then started an upward swing to toss the glove but, midway she made a slight pause to add, "Oh yeah, you wanted to know my name and now you do." With that, she completed her toss, which was just sufficient enough to reach Bill's outstretched arm.

He made the catch, stabbing the closed glove out of its trajectory and pulling it inside the bus. Bill slammed the mitt against his lap, huffed a time or two, and stared straight ahead. He did not want to look at his antagonist one more time! "Just get me out of here," he thought.

"Man, that girl is into you," Bud commented in response to this latest exchange between Bill and *Shorty* from Summersville. Then he added, "Too bad that she lives here and not Henderson."

"Man, I don't ever plan on coming back to Summersville," Bill summarily responded, choosing to ignore Bud's comments about *Shorty*.

As the school bus pulled out of its parking space in an effort to merge into a line of traffic exiting the ballpark, Bill heard her voice once again, "Oh Bobby, don't forget my name."

Bill had said nothing back to her, but thought, "How would I know her name? She didn't tell me." He didn't know if her comment was meant to be sarcastic or not, but felt pretty sure that it was. It didn't matter.

With the bus now rumbling down the highway and many more miles to go, Bill and Bud began wiggling about, trying to find a comfortable position on an uncomfortable seat. As Bill maneuvered around, he shifted his weight and his baseball glove fell from his lap. When he bent to pick it up, he saw it! *Ann Marie O'Connell. Shorty* had written her name in large, bold, flowing cursive letters on the inside of his glove, along the whole left side, just above the stitching. Bill quickly closed the glove. He was furious! "How could she do that?" raced through his mind. He wasn't sure which was worse, losing the glove or having it defiled by this girl writing her name on it. There was no way he could use this glove again. Once his friends and other players found out about it, the relentless, unmerciful teasing would start. "Damn," Bill muttered under his breath, but it turned out to be loud enough to prompt a comment from Bud.

"What's up with you?" By now, Bud had pulled his cap down over his eyes in an effort to go to sleep and did not see what was now indelibly written on Bill's glove.

"Nothing, I just want to get home."

"I hear that," Bud endorsed Bill's sentiment then pulled his hat further down over his face and found sleep in a matter of minutes. Not Bill; he sat upright and stewed — at the loss of the ballgame, at his poor performance at the plate, and at his defaced baseball glove. In an initial repetitive cycle of thoughts, he would think of the magic marker signature on the leather of the glove then take a quick glance, as if in hopes that he had just imagined it and that her name wasn't written on it. But, every time he looked, he read *Ann Marie O'Connell*. Without being fully aware of the change, his thoughts of anger toward Ann seemed to slip away and were replaced with thoughts of what she looked like, her spitfire spirit, and her voice. A pleasant voice filled with emotion and zest.

Transitioning thoughts of his glove and of Ann were interrupted by Coach's booming voice.

"First and only stop coming up, ladies. If you need to go, do it now." The bus began to slow then exited the highway, pulling into the gas station.

Bill sat motionless for a moment as he watched a few of his teammates step off the bus. Then, with a sudden impulse, he jumped up, worked his way past Bud, and made his way out the door and headed in a different direction. The rest of the players were all going toward the right side of the building to the bathroom entrance; Bill made his way to the other side of the station — to the phone booth.

Finally, luck was with him. Hanging beside the pay phone was a local phone book. Opening the black, hard plastic cover that contained the directory, held secure to the booth by a sturdy silver wire, Bill flipped through the white pages until he reached the O's, grabbed the next 10 pages, ripped them out, and quickly tucked them under his shirt. He raced back to the bus, hoping the lone station attendant had not seen what he'd done. Coach Smith was standing by the bus door and gave Bill a *What the hell?* kind of look but said nothing. Bill vaulted past Bud to take his seat. Figuring his teammate hadn't seen what he did, Bill relaxed. He wanted to look through the concealed directory pages, but kept his shirt closed over them for now. The two sat in silence as the bus pulled away.

By the time the bus was again rolling down the highway, all but the last of the sunset had disappeared and the interior of the bus was dark save the few dim lights at the front of the bus and the fleeting light provided by passing cars or illuminated signs. With Bud sound asleep, Bill pulled the pages out of his shirt. He could barely make out the last names on each page and needed to use the brief lighting interludes to narrow his search. Finally, he was able to zero in on the O'Connells and saw there were nine listed. With only the use of first and middle initials, except two names — Mark and Steven — Bill had no idea if Ann was a family member of one of these listings or not.

It was a crazy idea that had flashed before him and led him to make a dash for the phone booth, but even in its craziness a strand of determination ran through Bill's mind; he wanted to know Ann. In a perfect world, there would be a single O'Connell in the directory to which he would write. Now, it would take nine letters, all potentially ending in failure or embarrassment. He didn't even know for sure if she lived in a home where O'Connell was the last name or, if she did, maybe they did not have a phone. Neither of these discouraging thoughts was beyond the realm of possibility. Bill's spirit sank a little as the magnitude of his ill-conceived idea played out in his mind. He wasn't even sure what he was going to say in the one letter, which he had imagined would be directed at her. Now, he would have to write nine if he was to have any chance of reaching Ann.

The bus ride home seemed to take forever, but finally it pulled into the Henderson High School parking lot, where parents and others were waiting to provide transportation the rest of the way home. Having thought about it more and more as the bus rolled along, Bill had decided his hastily derived idea was really lame, and no way would he write the nine letters. Standing under the light in the parking lot, waiting for his sister to pick him up — she was always a few minutes late for everything — he reached into his pocket to retrieve the crumpled directory pages. Just to his right was a half-full trashcan. Bill first dropped the waded-up pages into the can, hesitated for just a second, then retrieved one page; the one with the O'Connells listed. That one he folded and placed in his uniform's back pocket.

As he did so, Bill's ride home arrived. He opened the door and Sarah, his sister, immediately asked, "Win or lose?"

"Lost, 5-0."

"Did you get any hits?"

"Nope, went 0 for 3."

"Anything exciting happen?"

"Nope, nothing."

The rest of the ride home was in silence except for the radio. Sarah knew her brother was upset with the outcome and decided not to push for conversation. As Bill looked out the car window at the darkness, he let out a soft chuckle. His thoughts were no longer about the game or the music on the radio; they were about meeting *Ann Marie O'Connell.*

Chapter Three

"TIME TO RISE AND SHINE, BILL. IT'S 6:15; YOU DON'T want to miss the bus on your first day as a senior!"

"Thanks, Mom. I'm awake." Bill had been awake for some time, but his mother's soft knock on his bedroom door and wake-up call interrupted the early morning thoughts that had begun to stir in his mind — some were new, like starting his senior year of high school, and some not quite so new. He thought of Ann, this time wondering if she too was starting school today. Bill heard the sound of his mom's footsteps fade down the hallway as he stretched one more time before swinging his feet onto the floor. With little forethought, Bill grabbed a pair of jeans and a new plaid shirt out of the closet to dress. Then he paused to repeat a pattern established in recent days.

Bill extended his right arm upward to the far corner of the top closet shelf and retrieved his baseball glove. Three weeks had passed since the team's trip to Summersville, the baseball season closing with a disappointing finish and his glove being autographed by Ann. Any ill feelings over her signing his glove had long since disappeared. Bill examined her signature on the glove and smiled as he thought of Ann tossing it to him and the way she looked — her bouncing ponytail and the mischievousness in her voice. With one final glide of his finger across Ann's signature, he returned the glove to the shelf, safely out of sight.

William Harold Weber was experiencing a first: He had become quite smitten with Ann Marie O'Connell. This seemed so very odd to him since they had shared nothing but brief, sharp exchanges and his sideward glances at her sitting in the bleachers, all of which had been limited to a singular brief encounter on a day that Bill would otherwise choose to forget. Bill's feelings — what he thought to be very special feelings — were all new to him. He had not shared these feelings with anyone and doubted he ever would. Well, maybe Spence at some point, but never Bud and never his own sister. Bill didn't fully understand what these new feelings were all about and why he was feeling this way. Why was it that the thought of Ann made him feel both warm inside and almost sick in his stomach? Why her? Why now? Bill had had only one previous girlfriend, Carol, but his feelings about her were different. None of these butterfly feelings or however they might be described had really surfaced throughout the three months they were known around school as boyfriend and girlfriend. It was definitely different with Ann, a difference that kept her on his mind and fueled a desire to see her again, both which ran counter to the facts that he really did not know her and had been unsuccessful in doing anything about it. Regardless of any rational logic he tried to apply to the situation, these crazy, exciting, mixed-up feelings inside prevailed.

Bill looked at himself in the mirror over the dresser and decided he was ready to take on the day.

"Just look at my boy; so handsome and grown-up! I just can't believe my baby is a senior! Now, tuck your shirt in and give that messy hair of yours another swipe with the comb," Sylvia said to her son as he entered the kitchen for breakfast.

"Ahh, Mom." Even though Bill managed to express a passing resistance, he did as told and then plopped down at the table. Bill knew he needed to display a level of coolness when he showed up at school for the first day of senior classes, but any further loosening of the shirt or restyling of his hair would have to wait until he was on the bus. With his mom, there would be no negotiating on these two matters.

"So, how does it feel to be a senior?" Sylvia asked as she set the cereal and milk on the table.

"About the same, I guess."

"Well, I think you better know, not guess." His mother was teasing but making a point. She wanted Bill to both enjoy his senior year but also to use it to begin setting a course for his future, whatever that might be. Bill had set his sights on college, and she was going to make sure of that.

With his breakfast consumed in hasty, gulping bites, Bill grabbed his lunch, packaged in a brown paper bag, and headed for the door.

"William Harold Weber!" Sylvia said, punctuating each part of his name for emphasis.

Bill halted in his tracks and, without another word spoken, did an about-face, moved back across the kitchen, and kissed his mom on the cheek.

"Just because you're a high school senior doesn't mean you are too big to kiss your mother."

Yes ma'am," came Bill's rather sheepish response. Then it was out the door and down the street to the school bus stop where Bud and Spence stood waiting.

"Hey, Bill."

"Hey, Bud."

"Hey, Spence." Each had responded to the other with a level of detachment that belied the excitement of starting their senior year. No further words were spoken and, within a couple of minutes, the school bus arrived. Their senior year was now officially set into motion.

In just under 30 minutes, the bus came to a rather squeaky and jerking halt as the new driver attempted to maneuver it to stop precisely at the student drop-off point. Bill, Bud, and Spence exited the bus, took a look around the gathering underclassmen, and walked through the double doors of Henderson High School for the first time as seniors. Heads were held high, swaggers slightly exaggerated, and their rightful degree of prominence accepted. Their senior year was under way: orienting to the class schedule, bemoaning the amount of homework given so soon, undergoing grueling football practice after school each day, and contemplating the upcoming season opener consumed their thoughts and time.

The three friends had endured nearly a week of two-a-day football practices, which left little energy or time for anything else: part of Bill's procrastination with writing Ann. Based on his size, Bud anchored the left side offense; with his speed, Spence would see duty as a safety, and Bill's role fluctuated between defensive end and special teams. Henderson High's team, led by Coach Williams, had been a football powerhouse, and early indications were that this year would be no different.

Coach Williams had become a permanent fixture at Henderson High, leaving only long enough for college then returning as an assistant coach. His dream of going professional was not to be, denied by a devastating injury the second game of his senior year in college. Coach Williams had been a high school teammate and close friend of Bill's dad, Walter. The senior high school year of Coach Williams and Walter, or Walt to his friends, produced a dream team that logged a perfect record and included state champs at the double-A level: 12 wins and no losses that year.

Every fall Henderson fans would recall that perfect season and the incredible running ability of Walt Weber. Similarly, Bill's older brother, Walt Junior, had been a standout player, and just five years ago was an all-state selectee. Walt had played a couple of years in college before an injury sidelined him as well. Bill's prowess on the gridiron did not match that of his brother or dad. He knew he was just an average player — no all-state or college football for him. Bill simply did not possess the football gene shared by his dad and brother.

The first football game of the year was played the following Saturday afternoon, an away game. Henderson racked up a lopsided defeat of Templeton with the final score 37-6. The 90-minute bus ride home after the game, with the sun disappearing over the horizon and darkness overcoming them, brought vivid reminders of the ride from Summersville, but mostly about Ann — seeing her through the bus window, her tossing the glove, the look in her eyes and her beautiful, mischievous smile. By the time the bus made it back to the school parking lot, Bill knew he had to write the letter to Ann that very evening. It could not wait any longer.

"Hey Bill, let's head down to Smitty's for a burger!" Bud called out as he grabbed his equipment from the bus's storage area. But, when Bud stood up and turned, he saw that Bill had already started walking away. Bill responded without looking back, "Bud, I gotta take a pass. I need to get home and take care of something that has been on my mind for a long time."

"Ah come on, it's the weekend and *Kimberly* may be there. I think she likes you," Bud said with a grin. Bud was always telling Bill that some girl might like him, when in reality he didn't have the faintest idea if what he was saying was true or not.

"Can't do it; maybe next time," Bill emphasized in an effort to end the conversation and to catch up with Spence, whose parents were waiting on them and would give him a ride home.

Chapter Four

"ANYBODY HOME?" BILL CALLED OUT AS HE FIRST opened the front door then paused briefly to listen for a response. There was none. He was almost sure no one else was there; his mom was working the evening shift, which she did not like, and Sarah most likely was out with her friends. Bill was glad he did not have to face either at the moment. Hanging his coat on the hall tree and then moving through the living room and down the hallway to his bedroom, he was on a mission.

Without hesitation or distraction, Bill sat down in the desk chair that had been his dad's, pulled a folder from the middle drawer, and opened it once again to stare at the contents: several blank sheets of lined paper and a single page from a telephone directory, which had begun to show signs of wear from repeated handling. Taking the page into his hands, he focused on the nine O'Connells listed. Did one of the addresses belong to Ann? He had no idea, but the time to find out could wait no longer.

Bill had been at this point before — staring at the folder and blank pages — but tonight's effort and outcome had to be different. A half-dozen or so tries had all barely made it past the *hello*. Now prepared to write, he held the pen upright and motionless. At first, no thoughts or words propelled it to move across the paper, and Bill started to feel a slight sinking feeling set in. Then he smiled and began to write. He knew the way; he would write to Ann just as if having a conversation with her.

If he couldn't have a conversation with her in person, then he would do it through his written words.

Ann,

Hi. Are you wondering who is writing this letter to you? Even when you read my name, you won't know because the broadcaster at the baseball game this summer was wrong when he called me Bobby. Actually, my name is William Harold Weber, and I go by Bill.

Sorry that I ran into you when I got off the bus. I should have been looking. Is your shoulder OK?

I do appreciate you telling me your name, even if it did take writing on my glove to do so. I was sure surprised to see your autograph there! It will be there forever.

School started two weeks ago, and I am a senior at Henderson. We had our first football game tonight and won. I play but prefer baseball, even though I didn't do so well in Summersville.

I bet you are wondering how I got your address. It probably sounds a little crazy, but on the way out of Summersville, I grabbed the phone directory page that had your last name. Since there are nine O'Connells, I am hoping that one of them will be the right address to reach you. Maybe you are related to the other O'Connells, and they will give you the letters they receive. Hope none of them give you a hard time about the letters.

Yes, I wrote nine identical letters trying to make sure one made it to you. Since I wrote nine, will you at least write one back to me? I would like to write to you more in the future. Even though we have just barely met, it feels like I have lots to tell you and hope that you will do the same.

Now that we know one another's names, I would like very much to know a little more about you. What you like, what you are thinking about doing after high school, what you think about what's going on in this crazy world. For some reason, I keep thinking that maybe we met some- place before, but I have never been to Summersville before last summer. Have you been to Henderson? I hope to visit Summersville again next summer.

Your (Maybe) Long-Distance Friend,

Bill

P.S. There sure are a lot of "T's" in this letter, which is bad, but "I" wrote this letter just like we were having a conversation. Hope you send me lots of "T's."

With the letter to Ann now composed, Bill read it over and over again with his thoughts on both the content of the letter and that first chance meeting. Had they connected, besides the collision? Had there been a spark of something? Had he lost his mind thinking that she had even given him a second thought? Bill couldn't label it, but he knew she was someone very special, someone he had to know more about.

In his best penmanship, Bill copied the letter nine times, each using a single sheet of lined notebook paper. The envelopes were addressed to Miss Ann Marie O'Connell, followed by one of the nine addresses copied from the phone directory page. He thought of writing *To Be Opened Only By* after her name, but decided against it. Bill placed the nine letters, bundled in a rubber band, into his school notebook. The 10th letter was his copy; he wanted it as a reminder of what he had written and of time spent with Ann — not of the summer's day, but this moment in his room when the first letter was crafted and his thoughts placed her nearby, as if in a conversation. Bill liked this feeling, that Ann was close by as he spoke to her through his written words.

As Bill prepared for bed, he began to have nagging thoughts that his efforts would be nothing but a wild goose chase and doubted if any of the letters would ever reach her. Even if one did, would she write back? He turned off the light for the night and made his way into bed. Lying there, his eyes slowly adjusted to the room's darkness. A sliver of moonlight squeezed in past the curtain that fluttered with the breeze flowing through the open window. The stream of light made its way across the room to partially illuminate the stack of schoolbooks and spiral notebook sitting on his desk. He could see the envelopes extending from the notebook and knew that they were destined for the corner mailbox Monday morning. Despite his earlier doubts, seeing them stacked and ready to go momentarily restored his belief that an answer from Ann would come.

Monday morning rolled around too soon. Bill left the house just a little early, hoping to make it to the street corner to drop the letters into the mailbox before Bud and Spence arrived, but Bud — ever wondering, ever inquisitive — was already there.

"Hey, Bud," Bill spoke as he maneuvered slightly past him and to the mailbox.

"Hey *O-T*, whatcha mailing? It's too soon to be sending out Valentine's Day cards to all your girlfriends." Bud spoke then chuckled.

"Yeah, that's it, you got me. I decided I better get an early start." Bill played into Bud's joking, while thinking there was no way he was ready to tell his friends, certainly not Bud, about the letters. He then turned to Spence, who had just arrived and had been greeted by Bud's announcement of, "Bill is sending out his Valentine's cards."

Spence looked at Bud as if to say, "Have you lost your mind?" then looked at Bill, who shrugged his shoulders, indicating he had no idea what Bud was talking about. Spence chose to ignore Bud and then asked Bill about their algebra homework. Any further questions about the letters evaporated; that is, except within Bill. His lot had been cast and now the uncertainty began, whether or not he would ever receive a response from Ann was the question that lingered in his mind.

With the passing of one week, Bill began paying more attention to the mail delivered to his house: 933 Grover St. Bill rarely received mail at all; normally just a single magazine each month, but when anything did arrive for him, his mom always placed it on the hallway table. Ten days after mailing the nine letters, Bill came through the front door and, while hanging his jacket on one of the wooden knobs, looked at the table to see a letter-size envelope lying there along with his magazine. Bill froze in place as he stared at it. While he was anxious and excited about the possibility of actually receiving a response from Ann, he hadn't really prepared himself for this moment. What would she say? Would she want to know more about him? But, before Bill took the first step toward the table, his mom called out from the kitchen.

"Who is Ann Marie O'Connell?"

Terror suddenly struck Bill. How did his mom know? What was he going to say? Why did he write the stupid letters anyway?

Sylvia came from the kitchen and now stood adjacent to Bill, with arms crossed, and leaned against the dining room doorframe. She had a mischievous grin on her face, and Bill could tell that he was in for some good-natured teasing. She reached over to the hallway table, picked up the envelope, and held it against her folded arm. She waited for an answer, smiling.

"She's just a girl," was all Bill could come up with on his first try.

"I figured that much out, given the name and all," replied his mom, still smiling.

"I sort of met her when I went to Summersville." Bill paused, hoping that was a sufficient amount of information.

"I'm listening," his mom replied, barely able to contain the fun she was having teasing her son.

"Oh, come on, Mom," Bill exclaimed in exasperation. "You know. Ann's a girl; I got her address out of the phone book, and finally decided to write her. Maybe we will be pen pals or something."

Bill's mom decided she had teased her son enough, tapped the letter a few times against her arm, and then handed it to him. As she walked away, Bill heard her say, "Maybe I should have gone to Summersville with you and met her." He did not see his mom's big smile as she said it.

During the uneasy conversation, the envelope had been turned face down as Sylvia tapped it against her arm. Flipping it over, his heart sank. It was not a letter from Ann; rather it was one of the letters he had mailed. Across the envelope, written in large letters, was "No Such Person. Return to Sender."

Two days later, another envelope for Bill lay on the hallway table. Before Bill picked it up, he could see that it was also one he had mailed. Like the previous letter, it read "Return to Sender." As he studied the penmanship of the three scrawled words, Bill wondered if it was Ann who wrote on this one. The envelope was not marked "no such person," so maybe this was Ann's way of saying that she did not want anything to do with one William Harold Weber. Bill took the letter to his room, opened his desk drawer, and placed the returned letter in the folder.

At the dinner table that evening, there was no mention of the returned letter. Bill was quiet as the three members of the Weber family ate their meal. Bill's dad had passed away nearly five years earlier, and Walt, the oldest of the siblings, was now through college, living on his own in Madison. So, it was just Bill, his mom, and Sarah at the table. Sarah possessed the ability to always carry the conversation at dinnertime and never seemed to be at a loss for words. His mom sensed that her baby boy was feeling down. Bill had never shown a lot of interest in girls, but this one in Summersville, Ann, must be something very special for him to be acting as he was. She offered no teasing. It was Bill's turn to clear the table, and Sarah had already left the dining room. Sylvia studied her son a little more then asked, "Are you OK?"

Bill knew what she was referring to, but tried to deflect the potentially uncomfortable conversation. "Sure, just thinking about homework."

"You wouldn't be thinking about a young lady from Summersville?"

"No ... well, maybe. I thought she would write."

"Give her a little more time. Sometimes things just don't happen as quick as we would like. If she is thinking of you, like you seem to be thinking of her, then you will hear from her." Sylvia added, "Besides, you are so smart and handsome, any girl would be crazy to not have a crush on you!"

Bill just smiled and thought, "I hope Mom's right." But Bill wasn't interested in *any* girl; it was only Ann.

Disappointment set in; passing days turned into weeks and no more letters arrived for Bill. In resignation, his first glance upon entering his house after school was no longer at the hallway table. In fact, he tried not to look, because to do so meant disappointment. Sometimes he would take a quick, reluctant glance, as if to sneak up on the table in hopes of finding a surprise, but each time he did not. Each time he looked, whether first thing upon entering the house or sneaking a glance as he walked by the hallway table, the result was always the same — no letter from Ann.

In makeshift retaliation, Bill examined his baseball glove and Ann's signature less frequently. His morning ritual of pulling the glove from the top shelf of his closet and running his finger across the letters of her signed name halted for a few days. Then something would happen to cause another glance. Once, as he reached for a box on the closet shelf, the glove tumbled down. He caught it, and there was her signature starring at him. When he saw it, Bill smiled while feeling both the closeness of a welcomed reunion and the emptiness of something lost.

It had been at least a week since the mitt fell from the shelf, but the absence of seeing it did not stop Ann from crossing his mind. Sometimes he thought of their first meeting and the fire in her eyes, sometimes he felt both anger and sadness that she had not written, but most of the time he just thought of her. Thoughts of what she looked like — her bouncing ponytail and sparkling blue-green eyes, her spoken words that despite their taunting nature drew him closer to her, and her flowing signature on his glove.

Then it happened. Four days before Halloween, Bill walked through his front door, hung up his coat, and started toward his bedroom. He stopped. There on the hall table a single letter, facing up, lay waiting for him. As he picked up the letter, Bill saw that his name and address were written in a flowing style that he immediately recognized. Bill smiled. He knew it was Ann's handwriting.

Chapter Five

"NO! HE DIDN'T! I CAN'T BELIEVE HE WROTE YOU!" Lindsey abruptly stopped in mid-stride and yelled in response when Ann leaned in toward her to quietly share the news about the unexpected arrival of the letter. The two were walking down Summersville High's hallway when, in an almost nonchalant manner, Ann told her best friend that she had received a letter from "the baseball guy." Despite Lindsey's initial outward vocal expression of disbelief and tacit disapproval, the look on her faced sparkled with eager anticipation of learning more about the surprise Ann had just revealed to her.

"Shhh! Not so loud. I'm telling you, not the entire school," Ann cautioned her friend as she grabbed and continued to squeeze her arm until Lindsey let out an "Ouch!" Ann kept her firm grip in order to pull Lindsey to the side of the hallway and out of the way of the other students, who were all moving in herd-like fashion from one classroom to their next.

"OK, OK! But what did he write? How did he get your address? Are you going to write him back? Of course, you won't." Lindsey's rapid questions and self-derived conclusion were all rattled off before Ann could even begin to answer. Just as she opened her mouth to reply, the loud, obnoxious, one-minute bell rang. It was the warning to let meandering students know they had just 60 seconds to be seated for their next class. Failing to do so guaranteed a trip to the vice-principal's office.

With the bell clanging in the background, Ann first smiled then teased, "I'll tell you after school or ... maybe I won't." She then turned quickly to make it into her next classroom, just one more doorway down the hall. Lindsey couldn't believe she had to wait until much later in the day to hear all the details. She watched in disbelief as Ann disappeared into her classroom.

With the schoolday finally over, Ann exited the school's double doors to the outside, where she was met by crisp autumn air and beautiful blue skies. She waited for Lindsey at the corner, just past the line of school buses.

A few minutes later, Lindsey came out the same doors, spotted Ann, and rushed in her direction. Rather than a "Hello" or, "Can you believe we have so much science homework?" or, "What time is Jim picking you up for the game?" Lindsey dove right in, "I can't believe baseball guy wrote you! What a dweeb!" Lindsey liked the word "dweeb" and used it often, but really didn't know its precise meaning.

Ann began. "It is so embarrassing what Bill did! Not only did he send a letter to my house, he sent letters to at least two of my relatives. Aunt Phyllis called last night to let me know a letter for me came to their house. Mom saw Dad's Uncle Charlie in the grocery and he mentioned receiving a letter addressed to me!"

"I'm confused," came Lindsey's response, matched by the expression on her face. "I thought the guy's name is Bobby."

"His name isn't Bobby, it's Bill. Guess the baseball announcer had it wrong. He lives in Henderson — definitely in farm country — and is a senior. After his team left Summersville, the bus stopped for gas on the way out of town — probably at Speedy's — and Bill grabbed pages out of the phone book there, or at least he took the O'Connell pages. He wrote every O'Connell in the directory! I guess all the letters were addressed to me, just sent to different addresses."

"Did you tell Jim?" Lindsey interrupted to ask.

"No! ... not yet, but I'm going to or I think I'm going to," Ann replied, without looking at Lindsey.

The "no" had been emphatic, but Ann's voice trailed off after that, as if undecided. Jim was Ann's first real, serious boyfriend, or so everyone thought. They had known one another since grade school. Jim's mom — Ilene — and Ann's Aunt Phyllis were life-long best friends. Ilene let everyone know that she thought Ann was just right for Jim, hinting what a perfect daughter-in-law she would be one day. Once Lindsey tried to start a conversation about being the maid of honor at Jim and Ann's wedding, but Ann would have none of that. "I seriously doubt that Jim will one day want to marry me, and I am certainly not thinking about marrying him — now or ever!"

Lindsey was sure Ann would change her mind; Jim and Ann made the "perfect couple," at least Lindsey thought. It just made sense to her that their relationship evolving into a marriage was the obvious life path to travel. Lindsey had reached a point in her life that marriage was a topic of considerable thought. She evaluated every couple in terms of potential matrimony and day-dreamed of one day being a glamorous bride. But at the moment Lindsey lacked a boyfriend.

"You don't need to tell Jim," Lindsey offered. "Since you won't be writing baseball guy back, he will get the message to bug off." Lindsey waited a moment for Ann to affirm her assumption then, when met with Ann's continued silence, added in frustration, "Why would you even think of writing him?"

"He said he has lots to tell me, and besides he just wants to be friends," Ann answered.

"Well, I have plenty to tell you and you have plenty of friends, so you don't need to add him to the list," Lindsey emphatically stated, seeking to build her case that Ann have nothing to do with some guy so far away, especially one from Henderson, especially since she had Jim.

Ann did not comment further and the two walked for nearly a block in silence with slight, undefined tension. Then Lindsey snickered and asked," Did *baseball guy* mention your autograph on his glove?"

Ann stopped, and looked directly at Lindsey. "His name is Bill. He said he would have the glove forever."

Lindsey first rolled her eyes and then noticed Ann's expression. In the years that Lindsey had known Ann and in all the late-night conversations the two of them had about boys, Lindsey didn't recall ever seeing that look on Ann's face or hearing that exact tone in her voice. In unspoken words of sisterhood, Lindsey sensed what Ann had not yet said. For whatever reason, Ann felt an undefinable connection to Bill. And, though she did not know Bill, Lindsey had a sinking feeling that he felt connected to Ann in much the same way.

The pair continued their walk home, mostly in silence. Nothing more was said about Bill. Lindsey's home came first, but only six houses and one intersection separated them. "You want to come in for awhile?" Lindsey asked.

"I better get home. It's my day to start supper."

"OK, see you tonight at the game," Lindsey responded, as she made her way up the three steps to her front porch.

Ann was deep in thought as she walked away from Lindsey's house. Ann knew that she felt irritated by Lindsey's comments and attitude toward Bill and his letter. But she didn't know exactly why she felt that way or at least wasn't willing to fully acknowledge it just yet. She also wasn't sure why she had lied to Lindsey; it was not Ann's turn to start dinner. She just didn't want to be with Lindsey now, a very rare and unfamiliar feeling, since the two were almost inseparable.

Ann stopped at the corner, but not because of any traffic; the intersection of Elm and Ohio streets was silent and at peace, with no moving cars in any direction. At first, she paused in an effort to shake the annoyance she was feeling toward Lindsey, but then she began to take notice of her surroundings. The intersection offered an image, nearly Norman Rockwell-worthy, of tree-lined streets in every direction. The sky displayed a brilliant blue and an intensely shining sun, yet the air offered a degree of crispness that foretold of cooler days to come.

The beauty of the moment seemed to overtake Ann. It was as if the world had somehow been expanded to offer another dimension or another sense. While holding her notebook and two textbooks cradled in her arms against her chest, Ann felt along the edge of her science book until she found the envelope tucked between the pages. She removed it in order to examine it once again. His writing, his return address, and his letter were now part of the experience. For a moment, Ann thought of her original intent to show the letter to Lindsey, but then she became lost in thoughts of Bill, thoughts that took her back to that summer's day.

"Are you going to stand here all day?" Bob's voiced startled her and his question brought her back to the reality of the moment. Bob, her older brother by just 14 months, had approached unnoticed as she stood there looking at the envelope. "What are you doing carrying that stupid letter with you?"

"Get lost!" Ann snapped at him before she bolted across the street while simultaneously trying to tuck the letter back in her science book. Bob caught up with her and continued playfully needling his sister. "Did he mention in the letter what a great pitcher I am? I think I struck out that loser two or three times when we beat them in the regionals. What's his name again, Bob or Bill or Betty?" Bob smiled at his words, but stopped when he saw the anger on his sister's face, "Oh come on; I'm just kidding," he said.

"Of course he didn't mention you in the letter! Why would he? Everything is not about you!" Ann replied.

"Why don't you lighten up a bit there, little sister?"

"Because you are a, a ..." Ann couldn't think of just the right word to put her brother in his place, and not finding the right word was rare. Quick with her tongue and ever-ready wit, Ann could always put her peers in their place when need be. But this was her brother, and calling him a name in anger wasn't her intent. However, she did want him to back off and wondered if maybe she had made a mistake telling Bob about the letter.

Bob and Ann were the closest of siblings and able to talk about most everything, at times even boyfriends and girlfriends. Bob and Jim had been best friends since grade school, which is how Jim came to know and have a crush on Ann. In their earlier years, Lindsey had had a crush on Jim, before she knew that he liked Ann. Then she had a crush on Bob, which Bob wanted nothing to do with. Lindsey seemed to have fleeting crushes and often returned to one for Bob, although he never reciprocated.

Ann loved her brother, considered Lindsey her very best friend, and had feelings for Jim, but sometimes all of this small-town closeness was too much for her. She sometimes wondered what it would be like to get away. Bob would graduate in the spring and had received a partial baseball scholarship to Central, so he was headed out of town in the fall. Central was only 100 miles away from Summersville, but that sounded like a great distance to Ann. She would miss Bob when he left for college and had thought that maybe she would go to Central after she graduated the following year.

As they turned to walk up the sidewalk to their front door, Ann — without warning — smacked Bob in the arm. "Yeah, you're a jerk, that's what I meant to say!" But, as she hit him and Bob let out an exaggerated "That hurt!" she also smiled a big smile, and Bob knew that all was forgiven for his treading on sensitive territory.

"Takes one to know one," was Bob's response. Unlike Ann, Bob was not quick with tongue or wit. One in the family was enough, he thought.

Bob and Ann walked through the front door then went their separate ways. Bob headed to the kitchen and Ann to her bedroom. She casually tossed her books and notebook onto the small, painted desk in the corner. The jarring of the books striking the desk's surface caused them to bounce slightly and, when they did, Bill's letter broke free from the pages of the science book. It caught flight, sailed off the desk, and landed on the wooden floor, gliding under Ann's bed before coming to rest out of sight, wedged between two stowed boxes.

After changing into jeans and her favorite pink sweater, Ann thought she would read Bill's letter one more time and maybe start composing her response. She wasn't sure how many times she had read the letter since its arrival four days ago, but every time she did so had been a mixture of thoughts and emotions — both repeats and originals — that played out across her mind. Ann always giggled or smiled at the image of Bill ripping the pages from the phone directory, which would dissipate when she recalled that look on his face when he realized she had his glove. When Bill's letter showed up — at Ann's house as well as at several of the relatives' addresses — she was both surprised and thrilled that he had written, yet embarrassed as well. At her adamant insistence, all errant letters delivered to relatives were to be discarded.

She picked up the textbook and flipped through the pages, but no letter was to be found. She repeated the action and still nothing. A rush of questions and panic started to build in her mind: Had she lost the letter? Had she dropped it at the street corner when Bob surprised her? What if someone else found it? What's Bill's address? She hadn't written it down any place! The rapid succession of questions and panic were soon replaced by a sinking feeling as she again flipped through her other school books and notebook. Bill's letter was gone.

Feeling dejected, Ann flopped down on her bed, lying diagonally across it on her back, first staring at her ceiling and then looking downward to take into view her photographic collage of life. It did not take long for her thoughts and eyes to focus on the pictures taken at Bob's first regional tournament game. Though she had taken a couple of him on the mound as he delivered pitches, more were of the other team — the Henderson Tigers — and specifically photos including their third baseman. Ann had snapped several photos of Bill when she was sure he wasn't looking her way, able to capture his profile or while fielding a play. Ann had never before felt quite the pull or attraction she had experienced that summer's day, but she knew it was somehow special.

"How could I have lost his letter?" she thought in disgust. "I can't believe I blew the chance to write Bill back." Ann began to mentally retrace her steps and actions once again, trying to figure out what happened to it.

Her internal struggle up to this point had not been whether to write Bill or not, she knew that she would, but rather *what* to write. Each time she had read Bill's letter, her thoughts regarding a response took a somewhat different direction or slant. She imagined herself telling him about her life in Summersville, and she had lots of questions to ask of him. Ann knew that she wanted to know more about Bill and could imagine herself telling him about her life, which seemed odd given the brevity of their interactions. Now, she had blown the chance to do so.

Chapter Six

"DID YOU HEAR ANYMORE FROM BILL?" LINDSEY ASKED in a nonchalant manner as Ann and she hurried home at the end of the school day. Unlike the beautiful fall day two weeks earlier, when Ann had first shared with Lindsey the story behind receiving Bill's letter, today's sky was an ominous gray, chilling winds swept around them, and the light rain that fell seemed destined to turn to snow.

"No," was all Ann offered in reply, then immediately sought to change the subject. "Glad I'm not going out tonight; this weather is the pits. I can't believe it's going to snow before we even make it to Halloween."

"I thought you and Jim were going to the movie." Lindsey said.

"Not tonight. Jim needs to study. His test grades haven't been so hot, and unless he hits the books harder, he'll be in real trouble by the end of the semester. I told him he needs to get serious with studying, but he didn't listen. He never does." What Ann spoke to Lindsey was intentional and successful. She wanted to deflect any further questioning about Bill. She had not told Lindsey or anyone else — not even Bob — that she had lost the letter.

"Call me," Lindsey requested as the two parted when reaching her home.

"I will," Ann replied and quickened her pace, eager to reach the warmth of her home. Bounding up the steps, she opened the storm door just as a gust of wind struck. As she struggled to keep it from flying wide open, she dropped her books onto the porch. Before Ann could react, two of her school papers slipped out of the notebook and sailed off the porch then across the yard. There was no chance of catching up with them.

"Damn! This is a great way to start the weekend!" Ann muttered to herself as she bent to pick up the books and notebook. She was pretty sure that one paper was the English homework assignment, which she could borrow from Lindsey, and the other her last biology exam, a B+. While the loss of either really did not matter, dropping her books and seeing the papers blow away mirrored the way the entire week had gone: fighting with Jim, homework every night and more for the weekend, a tear in her favorite jacket courtesy of the school locker and what appeared to be a losing battle with a cold.

As she stepped into the living room and closed the front door behind her, she heard no greeting or activity and realized she had the house to herself. Bob was at football practice and her parents were still at work. Stopping only long enough to hang her jacket in the hall closet, Ann headed to her room. Before changing her clothes, she decided to first stretch out across her bed for just a minute. It was nearly two hours later when her mom woke her for dinner. Ann wanted to say, "I'm not hungry," much preferring to stay in bed, but being present at the dinner table and participating in *family time* was a cardinal rule in the O'Connell household. After the evening meal, family time was when everyone shared a little about their day and discussed world events.

"Hey sleepyhead, what's up with you?" Tom asked his daughter as he stood at the stove and saw Ann sleepily shuffle into the kitchen.

"Nothing, just tired," was all Ann could muster in response before falling into her chair at the table, still wishing she were in her bed sleeping.

"We're having your favorite — fried fish!" Tom responded with mock enthusiasm, knowing Ann did not care for his fried fish, and choosing to ignore the shade of grumpiness that was in her sleepy voice.

After the meal was consumed, it was family time, and the conversation soon took a serious tone. The president had announced the beginning of a large buildup of troops for deployment.

Bob was all for it. "Better to stop the Communists over there than have to fight them here one day."

"I can't believe you could be so stupid, wanting us to go to war!" Ann said.

"Now, Ann, don't call your brother stupid," Barbara corrected her daughter.

"Sorry, but I wasn't. I am just saying that going to war is so stupid. I could never support our country sending soldiers to Vietnam."

"Jim thinks it's a good idea, too," Bob added to bolster his position.

"He better not!" Ann said.

"OK, that's enough for now," Barbara said, then to change the subject, asked "Ann, do you know where the boxes are with the Halloween decorations? I thought they were in the hall closet but couldn't find them."

"No," was Ann's first response, given more in haste than thought. She was still fuming about Bob's strong support for sending troops. "Well, maybe. I think we tried to fit them in the closet last year but there wasn't enough room, so then I think I

47

stuck them under my bed. I'll go look." Ann dried her hands and headed to her room.

Turning on the overhead light, Ann made a mental note that it was time to do a little straightening up. On all fours, she looked under her bed, saw the boxes, then reached for one, stretching to grab a corner of the closer box. Ann pulled it out along with with a thin layer of dust — and an envelope. The envelope! Bill's letter! It had not been lost outside but had somehow fallen under her bed. It had been there all along. Ann held up the letter and gazed at the return address. She could finally write — tonight!

Now seated at her desk, Ann read Bill's letter once again and smiled. She felt as if she had reconnected with a lost friend. But when she counted up the weeks that had passed since Bill's letter had arrived, a sinking thought came over her. With so much time passing, had Bill written her off, completely forgotten about her? Ann decided all she could do at this point was write. How she felt about Bill was an anomaly: a stranger, on one hand, yet close in thought and somehow touching her heart, on the other. It took little time for Ann to complete her first letter to Bill.

> *Hi Bobby, (Oops – Bill),*
>
> *I am so sorry that it has taken me this long to write this note to you. Hope you haven't forgotten about me. Your letter was lost or actually misplaced for several weeks but I just found it tonight.*
>
> *It was a real surprise to receive your note but pretty special of you to go to all that trouble. My relatives still tease me about the letters that ended up at their houses but that is OK.*

Thanks for being a good sport about the glove. Sometimes I get a little carried away. When you get to know me, you will see that I can be "rather feisty" (as my Dad says!) and "autographing" your glove was a pretty tame example.

As for me, school (a junior), babysitting, and family keep me busy. My shoulder is fine; I am pretty tough! Never been to Henderson and don't think I want to (just kidding). You know, I also thought maybe we had met before but guess not.

I am not very good at writing letters. Why don't you call me? My number is 640-1879. If you do, I have lots to tell you as well.

Ann

Ann held the completed letter in her hands. First, she wondered if Bill would write again and then she reviewed one final time what she had written, or more honestly, what she had not — no mention of Jim. It wasn't like Ann to be less than completely straightforward, yet she was holding back. Ann had a feeling of excitement as she wrote to Bill, a feeling that drew her closer to him, and ever so slightly narrowed the distance between the daily world that surrounded her and this new, exciting uncharted world with Bill.

Ann mailed the letter the next morning. As she dropped it into the mailbox, Ann wondered what might happen next. She said nothing to her mom or Bob about her letter to Bill as she passed by them and out the door to "run an errand." Equally so, there was no mention of it to Jim or Lindsey that evening at the game.

Chapter Seven

"ANN, IT'S FOR YOU!" HER DAD CALLED OUT IN AN irritated manner. Having just sat down in his favorite chair, a brown leather recliner that was the worse for wear, Tom had tried to answer the phone with his left hand while holding his unlit pipe in the other, and, at the same time, gripping a cup of coffee between his knees. The result was the source of his irritation — spills of both coffee and tobacco in his lap. As he began efforts to recover from the mess, he laid the phone receiver on the arm of his chair and headed down the hallway.

Ann picked up the phone, just sure it was Jim, and said in a cheery voice, "Hi Babes." They were headed out on another date soon, and before each one he routinely called to see if she was ready. Instead, her greeting to the caller was met with an uneasy silence that led Ann to sense she had erred. She then offered another greeting in a questioning, uncertain tone, "Hello?"

A terrible sinking feeling had instantly overcome his nervousness when Bill heard the "Hi Babes." He slumped further down into the chair next to the phone in his living room and thought how dumb it was for him to phone her. At least no one else was at home to witness his blunder. After quickly debating whether to hang up or not, he reluctantly offered in a dejected voice, "Ann, this is Bill."

For an instant Ann thought, "Who is Bill?" but equally as fast it registered. "Oh, hi Bill!" she replied in a voice that expressed enthusiasm equal to the *Hi Babes*. "Just a second, I'm going to go to the phone in my room. I'll be right back, don't hang up."

In the few seconds it took to reach her bedroom, Ann's thoughts grimaced at the unfortunate fact that she had answered with "Babes." Bill used that same amount of time to conclude that Ann had a boyfriend and that he should hang up before she had the chance to make it to her room to continue the conversation. But stronger forces within him overrode these thoughts, and he held onto the receiver until she spoke again.

"Hello!" Ann said again; this time in her cheeriest voice.

Bill let out a slow, audible exhale then said, "I think maybe I called at a bad time." His tone was unsure and rather defeated.

"No, now is fine, but I only have about 15 minutes," Ann replied as encouraging as she could be.

Bill remained focused on ending the call. "OK. How about if I call tomorrow or maybe next week?" he asked, more than ready to hang up the phone.

Ann responded to Bill's reluctance in the direct manner for which she was known. "Look, you called, let's talk. I want to talk to you and am not one to play games." As she stretched out across her bed, she asked in a softer voice, "Now, how are you?"

Bill was taken aback by Ann's directness, but clearly realized she meant business, and it would be in his best interest that this conversation not end now. "Well, I guess I'm fine, but nervous about calling you and wondering about *Babes*," Bill answered in a stronger voice as he now paced the full length of the telephone cord that stretched across the living room.

Ann choose to circumnavigate the *Babes* issue with her quick wit. "Oh, I always answer calls from *strangers* with 'Babes.' It helps make you feel more relaxed. Right?"

"Can't say that I feel too relaxed right now. Maybe next time."

"So, you plan on calling again?" Ann teased.

"Sure, that is if it's OK, but for now, I want to tell you what pretty hand-writing you have, especially on leather."

Ann giggled. She knew what Bill was referring to but chose to ignore the unspoken reference. "Why, thank you." Then asked, "so, how does it feel to be a *senior?*"

"Rather lofty; something perhaps you'll achieve one day," Bill responded with a lightness and comfort that surprised him. "What classes are you taking?" he asked.

As the minutes passed, Bill and Ann effortlessly exchanged information, thoughts, ideas, and laughter. Never so quickly had Bill opened up as he was doing now, and Ann was amazed at the flow and ease of the conversation. In their efforts to know and understand more about one another, they had become engrossed in the conversation; all reference to time passing by was lost.

Only when Ann heard the horn of Jim's car sound did she realize that it was time for her to leave. Ann hated that Jim blew the car horn rather than coming to the door for her, and they had fought about it a few times. Ann's parents didn't like it either and had expressed their displeasure to Ann but decided to let the two of them work it out. Jim's rationale was that she knew he was coming; it was just quicker and easier for him to honk and Ann could then grab her coat and come out to the car.

Ann interrupted Bill as he responded to her last question about family. "Sorry. I hate to cut you off like this, but I've got to go," then quickly added, "Please call again. Soon."

"I will, I'll call soon." Bill answered then heard Ann hang up. He gripped the receiver in both hand without hanging it up. Their conversation played back in his mind: Yes, it had an awkward start and an abrupt ending, but between — wow! Never had he connected so quickly and desired to know so much more about someone as he had with Ann. But beyond the thoughts was a feeling, something deep within and something that he had never felt before. It was both exciting and scary. Bill finally hung up the phone, smiled, and returned to his bedroom with a hopeful feeling that this had been the first of many conversations to come with Ann.

Ann hung up the phone, grabbed her coat, and took a quick look in the mirror. But rather than determining how her hair looked, her eyes were drawn to the mirror's reflection of the photo collage on the wall behind her. She turned to examine the photo of Bill smiling and in motion to throw the baseball after snagging a line drive hit toward third base. Ann smiled at the photo and for her happiness: happy that they had met on such a beautiful day, that he had called to make the connection complete, and for the warm feeling she now felt within.

Just as each had felt that summer's day and had now been confirmed, they were drawn to one another in a very special way that neither fully understood for now.

Ann headed out the front door to Jim's car, where he was impatiently waiting. He thought it had taken Ann too long to come out once he blew the horn. Seated in his car, she slammed the door with all the force her petite frame could muster. Jim hated it when Ann did so.

"What's your problem?" Jim barked in a gruff manner.

"You and your damn horn, that's my problem," Ann snapped back at him.

"I tried to call but your phone was busy," Jim countered in response.

"Let's go," was all Ann offered and sat in silence the rest of the way to the theater. But, more than the irritation with Jim, more than the horn, Ann's thoughts were on Bill. Their brief conversation had left its mark, a feeling that could not be described but one she did not want to ignore.

The frequency, intensity, and duration of the phone calls between Ann and Bill increased in rapid fashion. Before long, Ann found herself making excuses about not going out or taking extra babysitting jobs. She loved the kids — especially the Adam family's twin boys — and after they were in bed for the night, she and Bill could talk, sometimes for hours. Finally, with both reluctance and relief, Ann told Jim about Bill, the phone calls, and how she was beginning to feel about him. In his typical fashion, Jim both bullied and begged, but Ann knew it was over between them and held her ground.

As Christmas grew closer, Bill struggled with what would be an appropriate gift for Ann. At first indirectly and then more directly, Bill would ask what she might like. "I know you're tired of me asking, but is their something special you would like for Christmas?"

In previous tries, Ann had always answered with, "Nothing really," or, "Why do you want to get me anything?"

Bill had a pat response for the latter, "So I can give you something really nice with MY autograph on it." They would laugh, both knowing exactly what he was referring to, but Ann's answer to Bill's persistent question never came.

Christmas decorations were up and time growing short for Bill to find a special gift for Ann. As they talked Friday evening, just two weeks before Christmas Day, Bill asked again. This time, Ann responded differently, "I want you to come to Summersville and be my date for the Winter Formal in February."

Bill was shocked by the invitation, but a huge smile came across his face as he immediately asked, "When in February?" The two had previously shared thoughts about him coming to Summersville, her going to Henderson, or trying to meet half-way, but never had either been so direct in seeking to make it happen.

"The 22nd," Ann answered.

Despite the resistance and obstacles he would face, Bill knew there was only one answer. "Merry Christmas, I'll be there."

After the call ended, Bill sat on the edge of his bed — filled with excitement that he would finally see Ann again, under very different circumstance and fully acknowledging to himself that he had just agreed to a huge undertaking that would not be easy to do. At this point, he did not know how he was going to pull it off, but he knew he would. The phrase *to move heaven and earth* crossed his mind. He had never undertaken such a task, but making it to Ann's winter dance would be the first.

At times, Bill did think he was trying to move heaven and earth. There were answers of "No," and points of resistance just about every step of the way. His mother did not like the idea that her son was missing out on his own school's winter dance, rather choosing to go to one at a high school a long distance away and with a girl he had just met once. All of this seemed very strange to her, but she could see the resolve her son displayed in response to each question, each concern, and each doubt she expressed. Bud couldn't believe Bill was going out with *Shorty* and knew that Becky was just dying to go to Henderson's winter dance with Bill, even though Bill had never been out with her. It was another one of Bud's conjectures. Spence did not say too much but was disappointed, since he had planned on the two of them double-dating when it came time.

Ann encountered her share of strong resistance as well. Bob and Lindsey both argued with Ann, repeatedly pointing out why she should cancel the date with Bill and give Jim another chance. Ann's parents expressed concern that "she hardly knew the boy, and where would he stay?" but they also saw the determination their daughter displayed, and it was a prevailing force through every point of resistance.

With Christmas now in the past and a new year underway, Feb. 22nd finally arrived. Bill had marked off each passing day on the calendar tacked on the wall above his desk, and with each new mark his anticipation and excitement had grown. He finished packing the family car for the trip by hanging his rented tux on the hook by the rear door. As he shut that door and began to open the driver's door, he saw his mom standing on the porch.

"Be careful," Sylvia called out. "Take it slow."

Bill gave her a wave, stopped for a second, and then ran back up on the porch to give her a kiss on the cheek. "I will. I'll call you when I get there and when I get ready to leave tomorrow. And Mom, thanks for letting me do this." Sylvia smiled at her son. She was sure Bill had never been so happy and excited.

As Bill pulled from their driveway onto the street, he again thought about his mother's caution, wondering why she had said it as she did. She knew that he was a good driver and never speeded. Sylvia watched her son drive away; she too thought of her advice to her son. She knew Bill was a good driver. It wasn't so much about his driving that she offered the advice; it was about his heart and not having it broken. Though Bill had been reluctant to share much about Ann, Sylvia knew Ann was very special to him.

Several weeks earlier and purely by accident, Sylvia had discovered Bill's autographed baseball glove. She was reaching for a blanket in the top of his closet when the glove fell and struck her on the shoulder. As she bent to pick it up, she saw Ann's signature. It took just a minute or two to sort it all out in her mind, but then she knew. Sylvia never told her son that she knew about his glove, but she thought of it often and worried. What if Bill were going to be really hurt by all of this?

Despite the cold temperatures and the trace of snow blanketing the ground, Ann suggested that they meet at the ballpark when Bill first made it into town. She figured that he knew how to find his way there and could then follow her back to meet her parents. After those introductions, he was to drive to the house of a friend of a friend where he would spend the night after the dance. All the parents had been adamant that Bill would not stay at Ann's house, which was about the only concession Ann and Bill made in their determined efforts to be together for the Summersville High Winter Formal.

Bill pulled into the deserted parking lot at 2 o'clock, 15 minutes early for their scheduled meeting time. He parked his car and began an anxious wait for Ann's arrival. He could see the ball field and the bay. Both looked so very different than it did during his first visit to Summersville. No sunlight shimmered off the bay, no warm breezes blew, no smell of fresh-cut grass permeated the air, but all of that was eclipsed by his excitement of seeing Ann again. With great fondness and detail, Bill recalled the events of that summer day. As the minutes ticked away and approached 2:15, Bill grew even more excited with the reality that he would soon see Ann. He smiled broadly at that thought and how it would be so very different than their very first meeting at the ballpark. Bill laughed to himself and shivered slightly — both from the cold and from the excitement of seeing Ann once again.

2:15, 2:20, and then 2:25 arrived but not Ann. With each passing minute, Bill glanced at his watch while his thoughts bounced between concern and doubt. What if Ann had changed her mind? What if she didn't show up? Bill started to play out the difficult scenarios in his mind and with each successive round the results became worse. He had reached the point of imagining himself being the laughingstock of Henderson when he noticed an approaching car in his rearview mirror. He smiled, and all doubts immediately evaporated. Bill knew it was Ann from the description of the family car she had given him.

In just seconds more Ann was parked adjacent to Bill's car. Each looked toward the other through car windows; views distorted by the melting snowflakes leaving water streaks on the glass, but each with a smile that made a sunny day seem pale.

"Hi!" they each mouthed in unison just before car doors opened and each quickly moved in the direction of the other. When just a few feet separated them, they stopped and looked at one another, as if taking in the moment when desire became reality. Beyond the huge smiles that each had for the other, their gazes echoed relief, amazement, and validation of the fact that they were now actually standing in front of one another. The remaining distance closed, open arms closed to an embrace and each held the other tight. Any awkwardness in doing so had melted faster than a snowflake on a warm windowpane and was immediately replaced with a feeling that neither one wanted to let go — ever.

"Finally," Bill spoke first.

"I can't believe you're here," Ann replied and then nothing more was said with words, but feelings and emotions flowed between them as neither had ever experienced before. After minutes passed while the two stood motionless holding onto one another, Ann suggested they sit in her car for a minute, all the while not letting go of Bill. Bill said, "OK," yet made no move to release Ann.

"Ann, before I let go, I would like to ask you something." Bill said softly and with nervousness in his voice; his knees quivered slightly.

"Sure," Ann replied with her head buried against his chest.

"May I kiss you?"

"You know," Ann began her reply as she leaned slightly back so she could look him in the eyes. With a smile on her lips and a sparkle in her eyes, she continued, "I think we have waited long enough, so it's about time you did!" Lips met — softly at first and then with the intensity that their desires summoned. After the long-moment of that kiss, each pulled back just enough to gaze into the other's eyes and smile: warm, welcoming smiles that beamed the happiness felt.

The Winter Formal was just OK for Ann and Bill; at least for the 30 minutes or so that they were there. Jim had tried to make an ugly scene, stating several times to all those within earshot that he was going to "kick that farmer's ass!" But Bob backed him down. Jim thought he was tough but knew Bob was a lot tougher. It wasn't that Bob didn't want Jim to put a hurt on Bill, but trumping all was his commitment to his sister's evening not being ruined by a fight.

Ann made the rounds to greet her friends and introduce Bill, introductions that were often met with cool reception. The two next headed to the dance floor, and for a couple of songs, tried to dance as well as talk over the music. Before the next song started, Bill and Ann looked at one another — each seeming to know what the other thought without exchanging a single word. They made their way around the perimeter of the room and slipped out through the exit door. Hardly anyone noticed them depart.

Bill and Ann drove to the ballpark by the bay, drawn to it by its natural beauty and the fact that it marked the place where it had all begun for them. The air was cold and crisp and the sky was ablaze with stars. Bill parked so they could see the moon shimmering off the water.

The rest of the evening was perfect. Ann and Bill shared their stories: their past, their present, and their dreams for the future. They talked, laughed, and occasionally drew quiet to listen to a favorite song on the radio as one's hand squeezed the other to emphasize that the lyrics of the song now belonged to them. Once Ann opened her car door, grabbed a handful of snow off the ground, and tossed it at Bill. He laughed and was sort of surprised, but then not really. He was starting to understand more and more about Ann, and every tidbit he absorbed, he cared for her more.

"Are you still planning on going to Fullerton?" Ann asked Bill. She was sitting as close to him as possible, and he had his arm around her, holding her tight. It was a warm, wonderful, comfortable feeling for both.

"I'm sure I will. It's close to home, so I can help out Mom when she needs it, and I'm pretty sure I want to try their ROTC program," Bill answered.

Ann pulled away and turned quickly to face Bill. "Let me assure you. You are not interested in their ROTC program!" And then she leaned back into his chest again, desiring the closeness and warmth that it offered.

"What's wrong with ROTC?" Bill asked, confused by Ann's strong response to his idea.

With rapid succession, Ann responded. "Oh, just about everything, including you end up in the Army. Have you been watching the news lately? By the time you finish college, who knows where this stupid war will be or how many soldiers will be fighting in Vietnam."

"But, if I do well the first couple of years in college, I may be eligible for an ROTC scholarship for the last two years. Besides, I want to fly, and this could open the door for that."

In a flash, Ann was right back at him with, "How about taking another part-time job or taking an extra year to graduate and, believe it or not, you can learn to fly at the airport. See, problem solved; no need to go into the Army."

"But, I want to fly helicopters, and I don't want to take five years to graduate."

Before Ann offered her rebuttal she noticed the time displayed on the dashboard clock and realized that their time together was nearly gone. She decided to refrain — for now — from any further persuasion efforts. There were still several months before Bill would head off to college, and she would work hard to change his mind about ROTC and flying. As she wrapped her arm tighter around his waist, she spoke again. "I have a better idea," Ann said as she rose up slightly and turned to face Bill again. "Shut up and kiss me." Bill responded by pulling Ann closer. Lips met, and their worlds melted away — one into the other.

With great reluctance, Bill drove Ann to her home; their incredible time together was coming to a close.

"When will I see you again?" Ann asked as she looked at her watch and saw it was two minutes until midnight.

"Maybe you can come to Henderson or maybe I will come back in a few weeks. We'll work it out," Bill answered with conviction but also with a degree of sorrow; he could not believe their evening was over.

Ann smiled, grabbed the door handle and at the same time leaned back toward Bill for one last kiss. She said, "Don't get out; I can get my door, and yes, we will, William Harold Weber. We will work it out!"

Just as she opened her door for a last-second dash to her front door, Bill spoke. "Annie, I love you."

Ann turned back toward him and smiled at Bill. "That is the first time you called me Annie. I like it coming from you." She reached across the front seat, squeezed his hand, and kissed him one more time then added, "I know. I love you too."

Chapter Eight

"YOUR DAD WOULD BE SO PROUD OF YOU," SAID SYLVIA, a quiver in her voice and bursting with pride as she entered the room and saw Bill. He was standing in front of the mirror on the back of the door, making the slightest adjustments to his tie and jacket uniform. Bill had done so countless times during his years in ROTC, but this was a special day, and he wanted to look his very best.

"Thanks, Mom. This day wouldn't be happening without all the sacrifices you made, and Dad too." After just a slight pause, Bill added, "You know, part of Dad is here with us."

Sylvia knew that Bill was referring to his tie. Though black and plain, the tie he had placed around his neck to wear with his uniform was indeed special. It had belonged to his dad, and Bill had asked her if he could have it soon after starting ROTC and realizing he would be wearing a black tie, just like his dad's. It had been almost 10 years since Bill's father had passed away after battling cancer. He was missed every day and even more so on special days like this one. She watched him for just a moment longer and then turned slightly away, as if to examine the fabric of the window dressing adjacent to her.

This was a doubly special day: Bill's graduation from college and his commissioning. William Harold Weber was soon to be a second lieutenant in the U.S. Army. Now, just an hour from the commissioning ceremony, the Weber family — Sylvia, Walt

63

Jr., Sarah, and Bill — had come together in celebration. College graduation had taken place earlier in the day, and at 3 p.m. the Weber family would walk the short distance from the hotel to the Reserve Officer Training Corps (ROTC) building on campus for the swearing-in ceremony. Bill and 11 fellow cadets were soon to raise their right hands as they swore allegiance to their country and, with that oath, move forever beyond the days of cadets to become commissioned officers.

As the Weber family relaxed in the sitting area of the hotel suite, Walt Jr. searched the TV channels for the latest sports scores, Bill paced slowly about the room, and Sarah joined her mom sitting on the couch by the window. She leaned closer to her mom and attempted to whisper, but what came out was an easily discernable exasperated tone, "I thought Ann was coming!"

"Shhh!" Sylvia sternly hushed back, but to no avail. All in the room — including Bill — heard Sarah's ill-timed question. He did not respond nor did he stop his pacing to face her.

"Ann had to change her plans at the last minute, but she wanted to be here," Sylvia responded in a low, calm voice, all the while giving Sarah a look as if to say, "We'll talk about it later.' Sylvia sat back on the couch; her thoughts were now on how disappointed she knew Bill felt, but she also understood the reason why Ann wasn't able to be there. In many ways, today's situation reminded Sylvia of the turbulence and absences surrounding the on-again, off-again relationship that Bill and Ann had shared over the past five years.

What started off with a baseball outing to Summersville and then a single letter had, at times, blossomed to its fullest; but distances, challenges, outlooks, and life in general seemed repeatedly to deny the two of them a greater future shared. There had been periods of time when the roads were kept hot between the two colleges they attended or between Summersville and Henderson in the summers, with the two of them trying to spend every possible moment together. Then there were times when their relationship cooled much more than Sylvia could ever understand or Bill would share with her.

When Sylvia saw the two of them together, Bill beamed, and his love for Ann was so very apparent. Likewise, Ann glowed in her love for Bill. Sure, Ann gave him a hard time with her quick wit and opposing politics, but when the two of them were together, the world knew that a very deep love and respect were present. Sylvia was sure that each would do anything in love and sacrifice for the other.

As Sylvia tried to recall, it was about six months earlier when the relationship winds had once again shifted, with Ann and Bill suddenly more distant from one another. She didn't know why; Bill had not shed any light on the reason and avoided all discussions about Ann. Sylvia did know that this latest twist with Ann weighed heavily on her son's heart and mind. Bill had become unusually quiet and had distanced himself from friends and even family. If Ann's name were mentioned in conversation, Bill would either change the subject or leave the room. Even though something had taken place to drive this current wedge between the two, Ann had accepted the invitation to attend today's ceremonies, and everyone was looking forward to seeing her again — especially Bill.

After a few additional minutes of silence, with only the TV emitting sounds in the room, the phone rang. Bill grabbed for it before the second ring. As he pulled the receiver to his ear, he came alive with a big smile and said, "*Soon to be* Lt. Weber speaking, sir or ma'am as the case may be." Bill knew it was Ann calling; she said she would, and as soon as the phone rang, Bill knew it was her.

Ann laughed at Bill's greeting and replied in witty fashion, "Well, I see you are practicing that *military stuff* even before you take the real plunge. You still have time to tell them no thanks."

"Not practicing *ma'am*, I am the *real* thing or will be in about 45 minutes," Bill kept the banter up with Ann as he turned away from the family and made his way into the adjoining bedroom that was his.

"Are you excited?" Ann asked, knowing the answer already.

"Of course, I am! My car is just about packed and I will be on the road at 6:00 tomorrow morning, or in the military vernacular *zero six hundred*," Bill responded, even though Ann already knew the details of the day and what Bill had planned.

Ann sighed and then said in a soft and heartfelt tone, "You know I would be there if I could."

"Sure, I know that," Bill tried to reassure her even though it was difficult to hide his disappointment. "How is your dad feeling?" he asked. Ann's dad had been in and out of the hospital over the past four months; he had routine surgery at the start, but it was followed by one complication after another. Two days earlier he'd taken a significant turn for the worse, and Ann knew she needed to be with her mother rather than attend Bill's graduation and swearing-in ceremony.

"He's about the same. His fever spiked again last night and the doctors are running more tests this morning."

"Is your mom at the hospital?" Bill asked.

"Yes. She hardly ever leaves his side; can't get her to eat much, and she looks terrible — just so exhausted." Bill could sense in Ann's voice just how worried she was about both of her parents.

Changing the subject, Ann asked, "When do you think you will get the chance to visit Summersville again?" They had seen each other only once since January, since their last breakup, which took place one miserable, cold winter's day in Summersville. While he welcomed Ann's inquiry, her question also struck hard at Bill; he believed she now asked more so as a friend, a very close and special friend but not as someone so special who would find her way back into his arms.

"It could be awhile," Bill spoke in a disappointed tone and then continued, "The officers' basic course will last three months. After that it's sort of up in the air for now." While his orders directed a follow-on assignment to Fort Lewis, he had been told that initial commissioning orders were often changed while attending basic — all based on the needs of the Army. If he ended up at Lewis, then he would be over 2,000 miles from Summersville. Bill also had his sights on being selected for flight school just as soon as he possibly could.

Without asking, Bill knew that there was very little chance of Ann traveling to see him. She had one more year of college, and any plans beyond that were put aside for now. She was very close to both her parents, so always being nearby or even moving back to Summersville after college remained at the forefront of her thinking. Unbeknown to Bill, occasionally Ann had shared with Lindsey her thoughts of leaving Summersville or even the state. One time, fueled by a second margarita, Ann had pro-claimed she was going to join the Peace Corps and go as far away from Summersville and Bill Weber as was possible. Lindsey was never quite sure if the catalyst for Ann's desire to get away was growing tired of Summersville or anger at Bill. Lindsey had wit-nessed or heard about all the ups and downs of Ann and Bill.

After just a few more minutes of light conversation, Bill reluc-tantly said to Ann, "I really need to go; it's time for us to pay a visit to Col. Luck." Graduates and family members would soon assemble in Snyder Auditorium, where the swearing-in of the cadets would take place.

Ann's voiced cracked as she said, "You know I love you. It may be different now, but there is and always will be a love in my heart for you."

"I do know, and I love you. Loved you from day one and always will," Bill spoke softly and then their call was over.

They had loved each other from the start and still did. Both felt as if the love would somehow, some way, always be there, despite the distance and the darkest of moments between the brightest ones.

Bill made his way back into the suite's living room and all eyes turned toward him. "Ann said to tell you all hello, and wishes she could be here," he stated to his family but with his eyes cast downward. "We need to go, time for me to become an *officer*," Bill announced in a highly exaggerated manner, seeking to draw a funny response from one or both of his siblings as well as turn the attention away from Ann's absence.

The walk to campus, the swearing-in ceremony, the reception afterward, and saying good-bye to his family became a blur by the next morning. His thoughts bounced between the excitement of finally being on active duty and trepidation of the unknown that he now faced, both as an officer and with Ann. He had not heard from her again after the ceremony, which seemed a little unusual, but these were difficult days for her and her family.

It was the second week of the Officer Basic Course, with reality and fatigue settling squarely into Bill's cortex. The days were long and demanding, with young captains and seasoned non-commissioned officers taking great delight in both bringing chaos and imposing unattainable standards on the daily requirements of the mostly bewildered lieutenants.

Bill had just made it back to his room after a very long and fatiguing day. He collapsed into the worn, faded, semi-comfortable chair that was one of three pieces of furniture that decorated his Army *furnished* room. When the phone rang, it startled him; immediately sensing that he had dozed off, he tried to shake off the fog of confusion.

"Lieutenant Weber speaking," Bill announced into the receiver as his mother began immediately speaking in a tone that alerted Bill to trouble before she ever got to the matter compelling her to call.

"Bill, Ann called a few minutes ago — well, actually it was her friend Lindsey. Son, Ann's dad passed away this afternoon. She has been trying to reach you, but when she couldn't they called here. The funeral will probably be Friday, but nothing definite just yet." With that, she paused and was met with silence. "Are you there?" she asked.

"Yes, Mom, I am," Bill answered but didn't say the two thoughts that had raced through his mind so quickly: how much Ann must be hurting now and that he was almost certain he would not be able to leave OBC to attend the funeral. "I'll call her now," Bill said to end the conversation with his mother.

When Bill phoned Ann's house, he did not recognize the male voice that answered the phone in a firm and solemn tone. "May I speak to Ann; this is Bill Weber calling."

His request was met with "Just a minute," and then, with just the sound of a crying gasp for air and a nearly inaudible "Bill," he knew Ann was holding the phone.

"Annie, I am so sorry," Bill said and then he heard the sound of her sobbing, which stopped his speech and brought tears to his eyes. The next thing Bill heard was Lindsey's voice.

"Bill, this is Lindsey. Ann can't talk to you now. Please call her tomorrow; she wants to know when you will be arriving. Gotta go."

The conversation ended too abruptly for Bill. He wanted to ask more about Ann and somehow broach the subject of the funeral. As he sat on the edge of his bed, still holding the phone, he thought of his dad's passing and that now Ann had lost her dad as well. Bill knew the pain that Ann was feeling, and he knew he could not be there for her.

Early the next morning — before the first formation on the day — Bill went to Capt. Young's office. Bill had only spoken with Young, his tactical officer, once before and knew very little about him other than that he was an academy graduate and really did not like the job he had, preferring to be with a combat unit rather than responsible for a bunch of new lieutenants.

"Sir,..." Bill began, but before he spoke another word, Capt. Young blurted out as he shuffled through a stack of papers, "I've just got a couple of minutes before I need to head out, so make it quick."

"Sir," Bill began again, "there has been a death, and I need to see if it is possible for me to take emergency leave to attend the funeral on Friday."

Capt. Young stopped what he was doing, and, for the first time since Bill had walked into his office, looked at Bill directly. "Lt. Weber, I am sorry for your loss. It was a family member that passed away?" the captain asked.

" No, sir, not a family member." Bill paused as thoughts of Ann's grief and needing him there raced through his mind, then blurted out to add, "Not yet anyway but will be. It was my fiancee's father." He couldn't believe that he had just *stretched the truth* to his commanding officer.

"I am sorry lieutenant, but the policy is no leave granted during OBC unless it involves the death or serious injury of an immediate family member. The battalion commander has not granted any exceptions to this policy in the past, and I am sure he will not for you either. My condolences to your fiancee."

Bill didn't know what to say and momentarily stood in front of Capt. Young's desk before starting to leave. He then stopped, faced the captain — who was now standing and reaching for his hat — and rendered a salute before doing an about-face and exiting the office. As he did, all Bill could say was "Thank you, sir." Then he thought, *What am I thanking him for?* Captain Young's response was what he had expected. Bill felt disappointed, yet even more so he felt terrible that he was letting Ann down by not being there for her.

It was lunchtime before Bill could get away to phone Ann's house. This time, Ann answered.

"Hi Ann, I am so sorry ..." was all Bill could say before she started to talk.

Ann interrupted with a broken voice to say "Thanks," and, "When do you think you will get here?"

Bill swallowed hard. How he hated to tell her that he would not be there, "Ann, I won't be able to get away. I asked this..." Before Bill could describe the reason why, Ann hung up on him.

Bill's mom and sister drove to Summersville to attend the funeral that Friday. The funeral home was overflowing with mourners and the procession to the cemetery long. Tom was well-liked by so many, a lifelong resident of Summersville, and involved in numerous community projects.

After the service, many of those in attendance returned to the O'Connell's home, where the dining room table was piled high with food. Sylvia could not help but notice a young man who seemed to be paying a great deal of attention to Ann. As those who had gathered began to leave, Sylvia and Sarah finally had a little time to speak with Barbara and Ann. Both looked drained. The four hugged and cried together, each knowing they shared the bond and heartache of losing a dad, a husband.

When Sarah and Sylvia began to say their good-byes, Barbara finally asked, "How's Bill doing?"

Sylvia responded, "Oh fine, just busy and very sorry that he could not be here."

Ann said nothing but turned and walked away, straight to the young man Sylvia had noticed before.

Chapter Nine

"SIR, LT. WEBER REPORTING," BILL SPOKE AS HE knocked on the frame of Capt. Young's office door. The directive to see Capt. Young came in the form of a note he found on his desk in the OBC classroom. It gave no indication as to why he needed to see his tac officer, just to be there at 11:45. He had not spoken with the captain since the day he had inquired about taking leave for Tom O'Connell's funeral. Bill was hungry and hoping that whatever business he had with Capt. Young would not take very long.

Capt. Young looked up from his desk at the sound of the knock and motioned for Bill to enter. With five quick steps, Bill stood in front of the officer's desk, rendered his salute, and waited as he stood at attention. Capt. Young returned the salute, stated "At ease," and then picked up a document that was lying on his desk, turned print side down so Bill had no idea of its contents.

"Lt. Weber, do you consider yourself to be a *lucky* or *unlucky* individual?" Capt. Young asked with a degree of seriousness.

"Sir, to be honest, no, not very lucky," Bill answered, still without a clue as to where this conversation was headed.

"Lt. Weber, I have in my hand your new orders. There has been a change; you are not going to Fort Lewis." With that stated, Capt. Young paused.

As soon as Bill heard that Fort Lewis was not to be, he began to prepare himself for the worse. At OBC, word got around as to the best and worst locations to be stationed. Fort Lewis was considered a real paradise compared to some of the hellholes he could end up at. Bill mentally braced to hear Bliss or Polk — both in contention for the very worst the Army had to offer: hot and remote.

"Lt. Weber, you are only the third lieutenant I know of that this has happened to out of OBC, and one of the two remaining is your classmate, Lt. Bill Estep." Capt. Young paused, as if to hold into suspense a little longer. "You're headed to Fort Rucker. You are going to flight school."

Hearing that announcement, Bill was stunned at first and didn't seem to notice the officer rise to his feet and extend his right hand to offer his congratulations, as well as hand Bill his new orders.

Bill managed to say, "Thank you, sir," as he saluted again, and did an about-face to exit the office. As soon as he made it past the door, Bill stopped in the hallway to look at the orders and try to take in all that had just happened. He read the orders a couple of times — Permanent Change of Station: Fort Rucker, Alabama. Reporting Date: 20 September, Assigned to: 401st Aviation Company, Rotary Wing Entry Class 01-09.

Since arriving at OBC, all Bill had heard was that no one went directly to flight school out of OBC and that everyone spent at least 18 months in a ground assignment before even being considered for flight school. Yet, here he was, two weeks from graduation and just three weeks from the first day of flight school. Still in shock and still looking at his orders as if to ensure that they would not change before his eyes, Bill began walking down the hallway, turned the corner, and nearly collided with an on-coming officer. Each shifted slightly to their side, said, "Excuse me," and started to continue their respective ways when Bill realized who it was—Lt. Estep.

Bill knew who he was but had never really had a conversation with him. There were 85 lieutenants in the OBC class. "Lt. Estep, it's me — Lt. Weber," Bill called out to stop him in a manner that indicated much more than just a greeting. Lt. Estep stopped and turned to see who was calling out his name but did not make the connection until Bill held up his orders, smiled, and said, "Flight school!"

Just as soon as the two lieutenants completed their brief conversation about their good fortunes, Bill headed to the phone to call Ann. Since the funeral, phone calls between Ann and Bill had been limited and strained. Every time Bill thought of calling her, he also thought of the hurt, the sadness, the disappointment, and the abandonment that Ann must have felt toward him when her dad died. Bill missed the connection that the two of them had shared so often. He began to have hope that letting her know that he was headed to flight school — a dream Ann knew he held high — would be the conversation that helped ease the tension and maybe even start them on a new path.

"Guess who's going to flight school?" Bill blurted in quick response to Ann's "Hello."

Instead of the anticipated *congratulations* and an immediate flood of questions from Ann, she replied in a cool, detached fashion, "Oh, hi Bill. That's good news. Listen, you have caught me at a bad time. Maybe we can talk later."

"Sure, no problem. Just give me a call when you have the time. Talk to you later." Bill heard the click of Ann's phone and the dial tone but held onto the phone, trying to comprehend what had just happened. It was obvious that something was up.

Ann placed the phone back on the table, took a breath, and turned to face Ken — her fiancé. Ken had proposed to Ann just two days before. His proposal came quickly and as quite a shock to Ann. Equally shocking was her response of "Yes." Ann had planned to call Bill to let him know but continually found one excuse after another to not do so.

"Who was that?" Ken asked.

"Bill Weber, calling to let me know he was selected to go to flight school." As she spoke, Ann avoided making eye contact with Ken.

"I didn't think you heard from him much." Ken said in both a casual and probing manner.

"I don't really; we just touch base from time-to-time."

"Does he know you are engaged?" Ken's voice tightened as he asked the question with several more forming in his mind.

"Back off," Ann snapped. "We are not going down that road. I am engaged to you and he is an old friend. Got it?"

Ken had never seen Ann react as she just did, but could see the look in her eyes and knew he would not cross that boundary. "Let's go; we don't want to be late for dinner with my folks," was his way of backing down and changing the subject.

Ann said nothing as she grabbed her sweater and headed to the door.

During the last weeks of OBC, Bill and Lt. Estep spent a great deal of time talking with one another about flight school and beyond. Lt. Estep, his wife, and 1-year-old son lived in a tiny apartment off-post. Bill was invited over a couple of times for pizza and beer. He enjoyed their company; Lt. Estep's wife reminded him of Ann, and seeing them with their son led Bill to think about his future children.

Bill and Ann had, at times, talked about marriage and family but mostly in general terms. Bill knew Ann loved kids and they loved her. She had a way with them that Bill admired, and because of this had always been in great demand for babysitting. When she talked of having a family one day, it was always in terms of five or six children. Bill never had strong feelings one way or the other about the number of children, just as long as Ann was the mother.

Graduation from OBC was not such a big deal; Bill's thoughts and focus had fully shifted to flight school. More than ever, Bill wanted to see Ann, to let her know how sorry he was for not being there for her at her Dad's funeral and perhaps take the first step in drawing closer once again. But no matter how much he ached to see her, to make things right, the lack of time would deny him from doing so now. Over and over again, Bill calculated the options against the available time, and there just wasn't enough of it. His car was loaded with all his possessions, and the drive to Fort Rucker would take the better part of three days. Even if flights were available, the shortest possible trip to Summersville and back to pick up his car would still require two days because of limited airline connections. His reporting date to flight school was in exactly five days, and he knew he had to be ready — mentally and physically — from day one. He could not risk reporting late to flight school, no matter how much he wanted to see Ann.

According to Bill's orders and further instructions from the unit's orderly room, flight school began the following Monday morning at 0700 in room 201, Willington Hall. The hall turned out to be a rather decrepit World War II building in need of paint, and Room 201 was nothing more than a large, unadorned briefing room filled with small tables. Three chairs surrounded each table: one for the Instructor Pilot (IP) and two for the student pilots — referred to as stick buddies. Bill was the third student to arrive and, after being told to sit anywhere by the NCO standing near the podium, he moved to the center of the room and pulled out a chair to sit. As he did, Lt. Estep arrived, and Bill motioned for him; they had decided early on that they wanted to be stick buddies. What they did not know was who their IP would be.

By the time 0700 arrived, the two student-pilot seats per table were filled. Forty anxious students now sat at 20 tables awaiting the arrival of the brave souls who would risk their lives in an effort to make actual helicopter pilots out of the nervous and excited wannabe's. As they looked around at one another and awaited the arrival of the IPs and cadre, many wondered what faces would not be there come graduation time. The attrition rate for each flight class was about 30 percent, not so much from the academics but from the flying proficiency evaluations — check-rides — that were given at the end of each phase of training.

The door opened and the students jumped to their feet to stand at attention until told to "Take your seats." In marched a procession of assorted individuals. It was led by Col. Barron, the school commandant, followed by his staff officers, Maj. Smith — the flight leader for this class, and finally 20 IPs: a mixture of civilians, warrant officers and commissioned officers. As Col. Barron moved to the podium, the IPs broke off from the procession and began taking their seats at each table. A tall, thin, weathered civilian sat down at Bill's table without saying a word. The two Bills looked at one another, and each raised his eyebrows to signal disbelief. Through their 24-year-old eyes, the IP — Mr. Vernon as his name tag read — appeared ancient. Long wisps of gray hair protruded from underneath the dirty baseball cap he wore. His fingers bore tobacco stains, and his brown bomber jacket looked as if it would soon just fall apart. Their thoughts ran from *How could this guy still be instructing, let alone flying?* to *Why did we get stuck with him?*

After the introductory marks by the colonel and Maj. Smith, it was time for the IPs to take over. Mr. Vernon turned to the two lieutenants and in a gruff, direct manner asked, "What's your names?" His breath was heavy with tobacco. Both lieutenants answered *Bill* simultaneously.

"Oh hell no! There is no way in hell that I will have two Bills in the cockpit! Had a real bad experience once when the two students had the same name. Besides, when I am yelling at one of you, I damn sure want you to know which one it is." Mr. Vernon then looked at Bill Weber and barked, "Odd or even?"

Bill didn't have a clue as to what he was up to, but responded "Even."

"You lose; you change your name."

Bill had no idea what he meant; he couldn't even think of how to respond. Finally, in a disgusted manner, Mr. Vernon continued, "It isn't that hard. What is your middle name?"

"Harold. William Harold Weber," Bill replied, still without knowing what was up with the inquiry.

"OK. From now on, you go by *Harry* when you are on the flight line with me or any of the other civilian instructors. Don't expect me to refer to you as *sir* or *lieutenant*. I'm not in the Army now — did that a long time ago — and said all the *sirs* I'm going to."

Still stunned, all Bill could manage to ask was, "Why Harry? Why not Harold?"

"Because I like Harry and don't like Harold. It's too damn formal-sounding," Mr. Vernon stated in no uncertain terms. The manner in which Mr. Vernon declared the name change as fact let Bill know there was no further room for discussion. Bill figured it was a minor, temporary inconvenience and did not want to start out on the wrong side of his IP.

Four days after flight school started, Bill phoned Ann. It had been six days since he had received an unexpected note from her that just said, "Call me," and —unbeknown to Bill — two weeks since Ann had broken off her brief engagement with Ken. Bill smiled when he heard Ann answer the phone.

"Hello," It was the sweet voice of Ann that Bill heard.

"Hey you, it's me — aspiring helicopter pilot to be."

"Oh my gosh, do I ask for your autograph now or wait until you graduate?" Ann asked and giggled.

Bill loved to hear her laughter. "Since you're special, I'll give you both."

"So, how is it? How does it feel to be flying in something that doesn't look like it should be flying?"

"Now, for that question, I will have to get back with you. As close as we have come to flying is sitting in the cockpit, as part of the orientation to the aircraft. But, tomorrow is the big day! We take our first flight."

"What's your instructor like? Ann asked.

"Well, that's an interesting topic. It is a Mr. Vernon, and he is quite a crotchety character. Less than five minutes after we met, he changed my name; everyone is starting to call me Harry now." Bill continued to explain how the name change had come about.

"Well, I don't like it; you won't ever catch me calling you *Harry*." Then Ann changed the subject by asking, "So, what are your plans?"

"Well, graduation is next July and after that I am not sure where I'll be assigned. I plan on asking for Fort Carson, which is in Colorado, but not sure I'll get it."

"Will you get a chance to come home anytime before graduation?" Ann inquired.

"It'll be tough to get away during flight school, but I really want to see you as soon as possible." Bill then added, "Maybe you can come for graduation?"

"Yeah, maybe. I would like to see all those handsome men in flight suits. I hope the good-looking ones wear their flight suits real tight," Ann teased.

Bill laughed and realized, again, that it was impossible for him to match Ann's wit.

During the months of flight training, Bill's name change to Harry stuck. There were a total of five Bills in his class, which did cause some confusion. Lt. Harry Weber was the first in his class to solo, which helped to permanently solidify his new name among his classmates. The solo by Harry was celebrated later that evening at the Officer's Club with a couple of rounds for the house courtesy of Harry, a rather inebriated one.

Flight school was tough, and twice Bill did wonder if he was going to make it. But Mr. Vernon was an incredible instructor and always able to push his students to perform at their very best. As it turned out, Mr. Vernon was a combat veteran, could fly just about anything with fixed or rotary-wings, and twice had been recognized as the best instructor at Fort Rucker. It had indeed been Bill's good fortune that Mr. Vernon had chosen to sit at his table that first day of class.

Finally, the last checkride was out of the way and time for graduation had arrived. Sylvia was the only one able to attend the ceremony and was quite confused when Bill crossed the stage to receive his wings as the speaker announced Lt. Harry Weber.

Later, she also heard several of Bill's classmates refer to him as "Harry" when they gathered after the ceremony. Sylvia let Bill know she was not happy with his renaming, especially at the direction of some instructor. Bill acknowledged her protest, but figured his new name of Harry was here to stay, at least while he was in the Army.

For a brief time, it looked as if Ann would attend Bill's graduation, but the date of the ceremony ended up being during the week of her final exams. However, luck did show its rare appearance in Bill's life. He would be on leave immediately after flight school and able to attend Ann's college graduation, which would take place the following week. After that, he had almost two more weeks of leave before heading to his next assignment, one that he had not yet shared with Ann.

Having said good-bye to his mom and most of his classmates, Bill headed to the Orderly Room to sign out. Lt. Estep was there, and the two had a brief conversation about leave plans and their next assignments; both were being assigned to the same aviation battalion. Then Bill drove away with Fort Rucker in his rearview mirror, aviator wings on his uniform, and headed to Central for Ann's graduation. After that, he would go to Summersville to spend his remaining leave time with her. Life was good.

Chapter Ten

"WHERE ARE YOU HEADED, LT. WEBER?" AN UNKNOWN voice called out.

The question startled Bill and brought him back to the moment. He had stopped to fill up his gas tank and was daydreaming. It was a beautiful summer's day. The cloudless sky was blue and a gentle breeze blew; he was headed to see Ann. In addition to being surprised by the question, Bill had no idea how this person was able to address him by his name and rank, since he wasn't wearing his uniform.

Bill turned to face the man who had spoken to him. He was standing next to his vehicle on the other side of the concrete island housing the gas pumps. Without asking first, Bill knew that the question had come from a veteran. Though he wore no distinguishing identification as such, he had the look that Bill was coming to know — a stature, an appearance, a sparkle from his eyes that reflected respect and kinship.

"Oh, I am headed to Summersville for a week or so. Actually, I am headed to Central State College first, for a friend's graduation, and then to Summersville."

"If you don't mind me asking, where are you stationed?" inquired the questioner. Bill hesitated for just a second and then responded, "Well, I just graduated from flight school at Fort Rucker. I'm headed overseas for my next duty assignment."

"Congratulations on flight school; I always thought it would be great to fly those birds. Say, you're not headed to Vietnam are you?" Now, the questioner showed concern in his voice.

"Yes sir, I am."

"I got a nephew in Nam, and he says it's pretty damn rough," offered the stranger as he placed the fuel nozzle back onto the pump. Just as he was about to get back into his car, the man stopped, and turned toward Bill. "Good luck, son; stay safe."

"Yes sir; I plan on it. Thank you," Bill answered, returning his nozzle. As he turned toward his car, Bill knew the answer to his question. His uniform jacket was hanging in the back seat, pressed up against the car window. The stranger could see the nametag, rank, and brand new wings. Bill smiled, and then a very good feeling came across him; he was quickly coming to appreciate his chosen career.

Back on the highway, with over two hours still to go, Bill felt impatient with the flow of the traffic. It seemed too slow, but he'd already seen two cars pulled over on the shoulder of the road, state police lights flashing. Rather than take a chance, he kept to the speed limit as the remaining miles slowly slipped away. As time and miles passed, his thoughts remained consistant — bouncing between the excitement of seeing Ann and the dread of telling her about his assignment.

Bill wasn't exactly sure how either would play out with Ann. Their closeness had been strained after her dad died, but over the past few months it had begun to change for the better — more phone calls and more notes. She was again more like the Ann that Bill had loved since the first day they'd met. Sure there had been ups and downs, but through it all Bill had always known there would never be anyone but Ann. As far as his next assignment, he was certain Ann would not be happy — at all — but would she be so unhappy that she would again pull away, or worse yet, have nothing to do with him? Bill knew how strong Ann felt against the war in Vietnam. She was certain to ask a hundred questions about it. The best Bill had to offer was that the assignment was just for a year and that he would be stationed with Lt. Estep.

Finally, he reached the interstate exit for Central. Graduation was not until the following afternoon, and he wasn't supposed to meet Ann until dinner that night. He knew she was busy with last-minute graduation details and decided not to phone her until later to confirm what time to meet at the restaurant. Bill first thought he would head to the hotel, but then decided to drive through the campus area to look around. He had visited Central quite a few times when things were going well with Ann and thought the campus was actually prettier than his alma mater, Fullerton. As he slowly made his way down the main campus drag, students were moving about — some getting ready to graduate and others just starting out. Bill thought of the fact that only a year earlier he was graduating and now he was an Army aviator soon to head overseas.

Bill had just stopped at a four-way intersection when he spotted her. Ann and two other young women were standing on a grassy knoll about 50 yards straight ahead and just to the right. He smiled, remained motionless, and watched her until the driver behind him grew impatient and honked his horn. Bill pulled through the intersection and into a parking spot. He continued to watch Ann and, as he did, a flood of emotions rushed in, resurfacing after having been suppressed for too long.

Ann looked so beautiful to Bill. Her sparkling blond hair was pulled back in a ponytail, her complexion tan and glowing, her smile radiant. Though he had no clue what they were talking about, all three were animated and happy. He watched as they shared laughter. He loved Ann's laugh: Childlike in its innocence, she would giggle more than laugh, but it was her eyes that made it so very special. When she laughed, Ann's eyes sparkled as Bill had never seen in anyone else. The sparkle danced about as if sharing in the laughter and made her blue eyes appear even more beautiful.

After starting to debate whether he should he get out of his car to say hello or leave Ann alone to finish what she needed to accomplish before their dinner, Bill quickly decided there was only one answer. He got out of his car and started walking with a quickening pace toward the three. When Bill was just about 10 yards short of reaching them, Ann turned just enough that she could see him approaching.

Bill's unexpected presence took a second or two to register, but just as quickly the confusion was gone. Ann shouted in excitement, "It's you!" then dropped the books and papers she was holding and ran toward him. She did not stop before reaching Bill, but jumped into his open arms, with legs wrapped around his waist and arms tightly embracing his neck. Bill was able to hold his stance for just a brief moment before the force of Ann's jump took over and both went tumbling to the ground. They rolled a couple of times down the knoll before both came to a stop, face up and side by side laughing.

"You were supposed to catch me," Ann said as she giggled.

"I didn't know you were going to tackle me," Bill responded with equal parts word and laughter.

Ann raised herself up on one elbow, looked at Bill and said, "I am so very glad that you're here." Then she rolled on top and kissed him — a kiss that said much more than the words she had just spoken, a kiss that contained hints of passion and untold feelings, a kiss that melted Bill from within. When the kiss ended, Ann looked deeply and longingly into Bill's eyes, then in a flash rolled off him, smacked him lightly on the chest, and said, "OK, Army man, I have got to make it to the Registrar's office now or you won't see me walk across the stage tomorrow. How about 7:00 at Willie's?"

In an instant, Ann was on her feet and walking back to the two young women who were still standing where she had abruptly left them, wondering what had just happened. Ann scooped up her books and with a brisk pace headed in the direction of the Administration Building. All Bill could do was smile, watch her walk away, and think about the kiss they had just shared.

As Ann made her way through the restaurant, she scanned the large, crowded room until she spotted Bill, then smiled and waved. He returned her smile and chuckled a little as he took a quick glance at his watch — 7:15. Ann was just 15 minutes late. He had made the reservation for 7:00 and arrived precisely at 6:55. Always the organized one, always the punctual one, Bill had come to accept and admire Ann's free spirit and — with the exception of her usual tardiness — her unpredictability.

Not yet one-third of the way to where Bill sat, Ann paused to greet two couples sitting at one of the tables. Bill didn't mind. Watching her interact with the couples, he was able to observe her and feel all that she brought to his world. When Ann laughed at something one of the four must have said, her head tilted slightly upward, her blond ponytail flipped across her shoulders, and her smile lit up the room. It had been too long since Bill had last seen Ann laugh as she did, too long since he had held her close.

Ann broke away from the couples and rushed toward Bill. As he stood to greet her, she wrapped her arms around his neck, kissed his cheek, and in a rapid flow of words, said, "I am so sorry I am late. I thought I had plenty of time to finish up on campus then I ran into Wendy — do your remember her? — then I had to go all the way across campus to say good-bye to Dr. Willington — he has been such a great adviser —and when I made it back to my car, I had a ticket! I grabbed it and raced to Security to pay the fine and ..."

Bill smiled and interrupted Ann with "Slow down, it's OK. Just great to see you and now you're here." Ann kissed him on the cheek again and sat down in the chair he pulled back for her.

"So, how are you?" Ann asked with the enthusiasm and a smile only she could muster.

"I'm fine. I ..." Before Bill could go further in his answer, Ann broke in to say, "It is so good to see you! I'm so happy that you're here for graduation. I really appreciate you making the trip."

"You are most welcome," Bill's words answered but on the inside he was feeling so much more. He was filled with excitement — seeing Ann, her open, welcoming gestures toward him, and having almost two weeks of leave that he could spend with her. All seemed right in his world.

Ann reached across the table to give Bill's hand a loving squeeze, smiled her beautiful smile, and said, "OK, I want to hear all about you. No more interruptions from me. Tell me more about flight school and the graduation ceremony. When do you report to Fort Carson? Isn't that the name of the place you said you were requesting?"

Bill looked away for just a second — a sinking feeling rose from the pit of his stomach — and then returned his eyes to Ann's to answer. "I'm great, now that I'm here with you! Flight school was real tough at times but also a blast." Then he stopped.

Ann drew a bit of a quizzical look on her face from Bill's brief response then asked, "OK, well what about graduation?"

"It was good. Mom was there, and she heard folks call me Harry. She doesn't like it either."

"Always a man of few words," Ann kidded Bill about his second succinct response, then continued. "So what about Fort Carson?"

When Bill heard Ann say Fort Carson, he looked away in an outward stare. "There's been a change in my orders," he answered, while slowly returning his gaze to look into her eyes. In a hesitant, flat tone, Bill responded. "I'm not going to Carson." He paused then added, "I'm headed overseas ... Vietnam."

"No! Hell no, you are not going there!" Ann said with fire in her eyes and steel determination in her voice. "Why are you going there? Why do you want to go? Just tell them no!"

"I don't have a choice, Ann. It's all based on the needs of the Army; the buildup over there."

Ann's face was flushed. "What do you mean you don't have a choice? Everyone has a choice in what they do with their lives."

"You don't understand," Bill said, then wished he hadn't used those words. "There's just a need now; I didn't fully realize it at the time, but that's probably why I got to go to flight school right out of OBC. Besides, what I do is not that dangerous. I won't be near the fighting that much. I'll just be shuttling soldiers and supplies back and forth, all from the comfort of my helicopter." Bill added the last part in a futile effort to change the tone of the conversation, but the look Ann gave him in response let him know that she was not buying it.

Ann stared in anger at Bill. Her lower lip trembled and tears started to form in her eyes. "When did you find out?"

"Just a couple of weeks ago," Bill replied.

"A couple of weeks ago and you are just now telling me?"

"I wanted to tell you in person ..." Bill started to answer but was stopped by Ann's action.

She stood, a look of hurt and agitation on her face. "Thanks. Thanks a hell of a lot!" Ann spewed. "Bill, I am so pissed at you now! I'm leaving, but this conversation is not over — not by a long shot! Then, she tossed her cloth napkin on the table, turned, and walked away.

Bill sat motionless and said nothing as he watched Ann walk away. He sensed neither sounds from the crowded restaurant nor enticing smells from the kitchen. He was numb. Ann was gone and his dreams of their time together shattered.

"Is everything OK?" The waiter asked, his voice bringing Bill back to the moment.

"No, not really," was all Bill could say.

"Would you like to order dinner now?" the waiter asked, but with an inflection in his voice that was hopeful Bill would not.

"No, not tonight." Bill rose from the table and began making his way out of the restaurant. He thought he could still smell the perfume Ann was wearing.

Early the next morning, Bill's phone rang in his hotel room. Not fully awake, he reached for the phone with hopeful thoughts that *Ann is calling; we can smooth over the ending to their dinner* ... As soon as he heard his mother's voice rather than Ann's, those thoughts evaporated. His mom rarely phoned him; almost always Bill would call her, but when she did it usually meant there was a problem, sometimes big and sometimes small.

"Son, Bud's mother called me last night," Sylvia said.

Bill broke in with, "How's he doing? I've been meaning to catch up with him; I think it's been almost two years since I last heard from that big guy." By now, Bill had found the light switch and was seated on the side of the bed.

There was a pause, a long difficult pause, and then Sylvia said, "Bill ...Bud's dead. He was killed in action. His mom said he had only been in Vietnam for about three months, the Army less than a year."

"What? Oh my God! Not Bud! I can't believe it!" Bill was stunned; he didn't even know Bud had joined the Army, and now he was dead. "Oh, I am so sorry. When did it happen?" Bill asked.

"He was killed three days ago; his body arrived home yesterday evening. Bud's mom asked where you are and if there is any chance you could come home to be a pallbearer. I told her you were planning on coming home soon for a few days, and could probably adjust your schedule to be home for the funeral. Visitation will be tomorrow evening and the funeral the next day."

"Sure, I'll be there; I'll head home right after Ann's graduation."

"That's good you're coming home for Bud, " Sylvia replied then asked, "Have you seen Ann yet?"

"We had dinner last night," was all Bill shared, except "I think I will see her again after graduation this afternoon."

Sylvia could sense from the tone of his response that dinner had not gone well and that Bill had no intention of telling her more. So she refrained from asking, and then ended their conversation with, "I'll see you this evening; drive careful coming home."

After he hung up the phone, Bill continued to sit on the edge of the bed, thinking about Bud, about him being dead. Across Bill's mind came flashes of times with Bud, including that he had been there when Bill ran into Ann getting off the bus. Other images and thoughts came to Bill's mind but all kept returning to a single one: Bud is dead.

Ann's baccalaureate service was held outside on a picture-perfect day — not a cloud in the sky and just enough air stirring to create an ideal temperature for those in attendance. Bill did not know the commencement speaker, but she spoke of the graduates' future and the future of the nation, now at war. Ann's mother and brother were present for the graduation, but he could not find them before the ceremony. As he searched afterward, Bill finally spotted the three of them standing together and among all the celebrants.

"Congratulations, Miss O'Connell. How does it feel to be a distinguished college graduate?" Bill spoke just as he reached them.

Barbara and Bob both turned toward Bill to say hello. Ann looked at Bill, then responded, "It feels great. How does it feel to be going off to a terrible, useless war?" The look in her eyes said much more than her words. Barbara and Bob felt uneasy at Ann's answer, and both looked at her, not sure why she had answered as she did.

Bill knew that Ann had much more to say to him but was holding back — for now. He did not respond to her question but rather asked Bob about the high school baseball team that he had helped coach. With that question, Bob talked for 10 solid minutes until Barbara cut him off, saying, "Son, we need to get on the road. Bill, will we see you again?" she asked.

"I believe so. I'm planning on being in Summersville for several days, but I do need to make a little change to when I arrive." As he spoke, he turned slightly toward Ann, giving her a questioning look as if to say, "*You didn't tell your mother I'm visiting?*" while Ann seemed to be saying back with her look, "*What do you mean your plans are changing when you arrive?*"

As Barbara and Bob walked away, Ann and Bill stood for a moment in uneasy silence. Then Bill sought to break that silence with, "Ann, I really am proud of you; you worked so hard these last four years and *summa cum laude* to boot." Ann looked down, looked away, and then looked at Bill. He noticed tears starting to form in her eyes.

"Thanks. I wish Dad was here, and I wish you weren't going *over there.*" Bill put his arms around Ann. She first resisted but then relaxed and allowed Bill to draw her close, each holding the other tighter and tighter as the seconds ticked away. Though surrounded by noise, laughter, and hundreds of people, in moments like these Ann and Bill were aware of only one another. They created their own world.

Finally, Ann spoke as she reluctantly loosened her embrace of Bill but held onto his hand, "I need to start for Summersville now myself." As they began walking hand-in-hand toward her car, Ann added, "And why are your plans for arriving in Summersville now changing?"

Bill had dreaded this question ever since he'd spoken with his mother. "Mom called this morning." Bill stopped; he couldn't get the other words to come out.

"And?" Ann asked, with slight impatience and concern.

He let out a deep sigh and then continued, "I need to go home for a funeral. But, just as soon as I can, I will be in Summersville." Ann knew Bill, knew there was more to the story, and just looked at him the way she had done so many times in the past, the way that always led him to open up to her.

"It's Bud; he died a few days ago. He was in the Army and — and was killed fighting in Vietnam." Bill said nothing more and waited for Ann to speak.

She looked at him at first almost in disbelief, then she leaned back against her car, as if to help keep her upright, and started to cry. He reached out to pull her close to him, to hug her and say comforting words, but this time Ann jerked away.

"Don't touch me!" she demanded as she moved to the front of the car and turned her back toward Bill.

Bill moved a little closer to where Ann stood, hesitated for a moment, then spoke. "I'm headed home now. The funeral is the day after tomorrow, and I will drive to Summersville that evening."

After several minutes of silence, Ann wiped her eyes then turned toward Bill but without making eye contact. As she brushed by him to open her car door, she spat out the words, "I'll see you in Summersville." Then she was gone. Bill watched her car grow smaller in the distance.

Chapter Eleven

"ARE YOU SURE YOU DON'T WANT TO STAY FOR DINNER?"

"No, Mom; I want to make it to Summersville before dark. But I'll be back in four days. Maybe I can talk you into fixing my favorite meal then."

Sylvia smiled and said, "Sure, now drive safe, and tell Ann to come visit me sometime soon now that she's finished with school." It was 3:00 when Bill headed to Summersville, but the strain of the past 24 hours had worn on him and he felt drained.

With a backdrop of low, gray clouds, the mournful sound of "Taps" being played by the lone bugler had slowly brought Bud's funeral to its close. Each note had seemed to hang and echo across the rolling hills of the cemetery. The graveside service had begun at 11, with a military funeral detachment present to render a final salute to Bud. Bill, Spence, Phil, and three of Bud's cousins served as pallbearers. When the funeral detachment commander presented the American flag that had covered Bud's casket to his mom, she hugged it tight against her chest; her body shook as she sobbed.

There had also been visitation at the funeral home the evening before, and many of Bud's high school friends had come to say good-bye. Bill had the chance to reminisce with Spence and Phil. The three of them had scarcely seen each other since high school graduation, and knew what little that they had been doing mostly through their parents exchanging information on a few occasions. Both Spence and Phil were now married, had kids, and lived in Henderson; each had asked Bill when he was going to settle down and marry. They talked mostly about Bud and the clown that he was — big as a giant and a heart to match. Bud would do anything for his friends. Only once in this sad reunion did Spence refer to Bill as *O-T*, and it was related to something that Bud had said. Spence said that he had seen Bud about four months earlier; he was getting ready to ship out and had been home on leave. According to Spence, Bud was the same ol' Bud — joking, laughing, and in constant search of companionship and food. Bud's plans were to return to Henderson after his enlistment. When Spence had told Bud about Bill being an officer and pilot in the Army, Bud was excited about the possibility that they might be stationed together one day.

Bill had debated whether or not to wear his uniform at the visitation and funeral and finally decided he should. When Bud's mom saw Bill, she hugged him and through her tears said, "Bud would be so proud of you; you were always his best friend. You look handsome in your uniform." She swallowed back a sob and added, "So did Bud."

Bill thanked her and said, "Bud was like a brother to me."

It was hard to believe that Bud was gone.

For his stay in Summersville, Bill had rented a small, summer cottage. On his many trips to Summersville to see Ann, his accommodations had varied. Most of the time he had stayed at a friend of a friend's house or a hotel. Once or twice he slept in his car, and a couple of times at Ann's parents' house, but this time, he was fortunate to have this cottage right on the bay, no less. It belonged to the parents of one of the friends he had stayed with previously and — thanks to a last-minute cancellation by the intended occupant — the owners offered it to Bill. The cottage was rustic, but comfortably furnished. A wooden dock extended out into the bay and was a perfect spot for Ann and him to spend their days together. Bill phoned Ann to let her know that he had arrived but only managed to leave the message with her mom.

The next morning, Bill heard a car arrive and headed for the door. He was sure it was Ann, even though she had not returned his call. Bill stepped off the back porch, just as Ann shut her car door. When she saw Bill, she stopped, stared, and crossed her arms over her chest. Though less than 20 feet separated them, there was a distressed, emotional distance that was abundantly present.

"Good morning," Bill offered with some lightness and still at a considerable distance from Ann.

"Is it?" Ann responded, arms still folded.

"It is for me, now that you're here."

"Well, it's not for me. What the hell are you doing Bill?" Ann snapped, her voice raised and tight.

"I'm not sure what you're asking."

"Oh, let's see. You start my graduation celebration off by *informing* me you're going to Vietnam, which — by the way — you had kept silent about for two weeks. Then, at graduation, you *tell* me your plans have changed. Why? Because you are going home to bury a friend; a friend that *just happened* to get himself killed in Vietnam! The place you are headed to. Now, you show up in Summersville and *tell* me your day is good because I'm here! Let me tell you; your day must be a hell of lot better than mine, because my day is not good — not by a long shot."

Bill reeled from the wave of Ann's anger that had rushed over him. At first, he didn't know what to say but knew he better say something fast or she might leave, so in a flat, dejected tone he asked, "Can we go inside and talk about it?"

Ann did not answer with words, but after a few minutes of standoff, she walked toward the cabin, past Bill, and through the back door; Bill followed. Inside the cottage, Ann stood by the sliding doors leading to the dock and the bay.

Following a moment of uneasy silence, Bill spoke. "First, I am sorry that I didn't tell you about the change in my assignment. I ..."

Before Bill could continue, Ann interrupted with, "You *mean* Vietnam, right?"

"Yes, Vietnam. I'll be there for one year, and then I will be back; I promise." Bill's response was firm, spoken not in anger or defense but with conviction.

"Do you think Bud made that promise?" Ann's voice had softened slightly, expressing more concern than anger. Bill could sense this and felt some relief.

"Ann, I don't know but probably. I'm so sorry that he didn't make it home, but every day there are hundreds who do come home to their families, safe and ready to continue their lives. That is what I want more than anything, to come home and have the chance for you and me to have a future together."

"Bill, for us to have a future together you have got to always be straight-up with me — no more avoiding, no more trying to soften whatever it is that needs to be shared, no more trying to protect me from whatever the truth is."

"I understand, and I will. I will try my best."

The two talked for another hour, and then it was time for Ann to leave. She had planned to spend as much time with Bill as possible during his stay in Summersville, but most of the day had been previously committed.

Bill watched her drive away, disappointed that she could not stay longer but looking forward to seeing her tomorrow. Throughout the rest of the day, he lounged around the cottage, but did take a few dips in the bay — cool and refreshing. After each swim, he would lie on the dock and feel the warmth of the sun against the coolness of his wet skin. A few times, thoughts of flying in Vietnam and what it was going to be like crept in, as did images and memories of Bud, but most of his thoughts were of Ann. Bill wondered what the future might hold for them, but knew what he wanted it to be.

It was 10:30 when Ann arrived the next morning; 30 minutes later than planned, but Bill was just glad to see her and grateful to have this time together. Bill called out to Ann as he walked to her car to greet her, "Good morning. You ready for a day of fun and sun?"

"Sure, let's give it a whirl." Ann tried to sound cheerful, but her voice was subdued and her smile faint.

After a brief hug, but no kiss, Bill asked, "Do you want to head out to the dock?"

"OK," was Ann's only reply and with that brief exchange, the two passed through the cottage and made their way out onto the dock. They sat with their feet dangling in the water and without saying much. Bill asked about Ann's mom. Ann said that she was OK but working too much and that she needed to pick her up after her evening shift. Ann asked about Bill's mom and how he spent the previous day.

After another period of awkward silence, Ann made a strong kick in the water and said, "So, you really are headed overseas, to Vietnam no less. How nice, since you just buried your best friend because he ended up there — fighting for God, country, and the American way!" Ann turned her head away.

Bill thought tears were now in her eyes and, if so, she did not want him to see her cry. He was, at first, caught off-guard by her words, but just as quickly realized that it was naïve of him to think the conversation was over after the previous day's discussion. Ann was still processing it all.

"Annie, what is it that you want or what is it that I can do?" She did not answer. He continued, "God only knows how much I wish the war hadn't taken Bud or any soldier for that matter, but it happens. It happened in the past, it's happening now, and, unless this crazy world changes, it will happen again in the future."

Ann wiped her face, then turned to look at Bill while at the same time rising to her feet. "Spoken like a true military man," was all she said before turning to walk away.

Bill continued to just sit there; he didn't have the energy or the answers to try to convince her otherwise. He listened; fully expecting to hear Ann's car start and her drive away, but no such sounds came. The longer he waited, the more he wondered what she was doing; she must have gone into the cottage and stopped. After Bill sat there just a little longer, raindrops began to fall; they quickly turned into a downpour. It was time for him to go inside.

Ann was sitting on the couch and wiped her eyes as Bill entered the cottage to escape the pouring rain. "Did you get wet?" she asked.

"Some but not too bad," Bill answered.

"That's a shame; I was hoping you would drown," Ann responded but in a tone that let Bill know she was joking and her way of dialing back the tension that had surrounded them.

"Sorry to disappoint you," Bill joked back then asked, "Do you want something to drink?"

"Just water, thanks."

Bill retrieved water and a soda from the refrigerator then joined Ann on the couch — sitting close, but not touching her. After several minutes of silence and sipping their drinks, Ann reached out to take Bill's hand, then leaned in so her head was against his shoulder. "I have missed you so much and needed you. Just when I thought things might start to settle down in our lives, you are headed farther away and risking your life — for what?"

Bill answered, "I have missed you so much too and ..." but before he finished Ann interrupted with, "I would really be pissed off if you got killed, you know." She sort of laughed and cried at the same time as she moved herself closer to Bill and wrapped her arm around his waist.

"I'll be fine. Being in the air really is safer than being on the ground, and I'll be careful. It's just for a year, but I'll have a 30-day R&R in the middle. I'll be back before you know it."

"Do you know where you'll be stationed when you come back?" Ann asked.

"Not really. I would like to go to Fort Carson, but so do lots of other officers."

Ann popped up a bit and with a mischievous look in her eyes asked, "When will you be a captain? I think I would rather marry a captain."

Bill fell for it. "So, you are going to marry me, are you?"

"What gave you that idea? I just said I would rather marry a captain. I didn't say anything about that captain being you. I'm sure you could introduce me to some good-looking captains stationed at Fort Carson." Ann laughed, gave Bill the look of *gotcha again*, and snuggled back into his arms. She loved to tease Bill, loved to feel his arms wrapped around her. Ann sighed and gave Bill a gentle squeeze.

Bill didn't answer Ann's question about other captains; his thoughts were on marrying Ann.

The two remained close on the couch until the room began to grow dark as evening arrived. Throughout their afternoon, there had been moments of silence, moments of thunder and storming, moments of kissing and touching that aroused greater desire in each, moments of holding one another tight, as if they were fighting against an invisible force trying to tear them apart, and moments of laughter — many moments of laughter. When Bill was with Ann, he laughed more than at any other time.

"Are you hungry?" Bill asked.

"A little. What do you have in mind?"

Bill stood, pulled Ann up by her hand, and said, "Let's go get a bite to eat."

Their dinner at Pete's Place — a great hamburger joint in town — consisted of burgers, fries, and beer. With their conversation pretty much nonstop, Ann and Bill did not notice the restaurant begin to clear out and the waiter repeatedly pass by their table. It was almost 10 by the time they left.

The clouds had cleared as the evening progressed; twinkling stars and a sliver of silver moon over the bay created a beautiful nighttime sky. Bill had put the top down on his car and drove slowly through town. The radio was tuned to their favorite station and, by chance, played *their* song, the one from the Winter Formal. Ann squeezed Bill's hand when the melody started.

When they arrived at the cottage darkness surrounded them. There were no city lights, and the tall oak and maple trees encircling the cottage blocked out any light from the night sky. Bill kissed Ann before he opened his door and then walked around the car to open hers. Normally, Ann was out of the car before Bill could get to her door, but this time she waited.

Now out of the car, Bill and Ann kissed again, pressing tightly against each other. Each knew what the other desired, what they desired, and passionate kisses and embraces consumed the moments that followed. Finally, Bill asked, "Do you want to go inside?"

"Yes, but I can't. If I don't leave now, I'll be late picking up mom."

Bill was disappointed but tried not to let it come through in his response, "Sure. What's the plan for our tomorrow?"

"I'll be back at the same time —10:00 or maybe 10:30 — then spend the day with you, the entire day."

"That'll be great," Bill replied as he drew Ann closer and kissed her good-bye for the night.

It was a restless night for Bill. As he tossed and turned, his thoughts were of Ann, kisses shared, her teasing — what was the marriage comment all about? — her perfume, and that he had only one more day with her. After their good-byes, it would be at least six months. Bill wasn't sure what time it was when he finally dozed off, but the ringing phone woke him at 8:00. He only managed a groggy "Hello," and then Ann was off and running with the conversation.

"Good morning! How did you sleep? It's going to be a beautiful day. Have you been outside yet? Listen, it will be closer to 11:00 before I get there, but I will be there, then I am yours for the rest of the day. Do you want me to bring anything?"

Bill was having a hard time taking in all of Ann's rapid-fire, one-way conversation, but then he said, "Good morning to you too! Are you bringing your bathing suit today?" Bill asked in reference to Ann forgetting it the day before.

"Maybe. OK, gotta run. See you soon." Ann paused and then asked, as if in a rhetorical fashion, "Bill, you know I love you, right?"

Her saying that made Bill smile and respond, "Yes, I know, and I love you even more."

"That would be impossible, but nice try," came Ann's quick response, then she added, "See you soon!"

Bill stretched out on the bed again and thought of Ann. Her saying that she loved him made him smile and think about just how much he loved her. Ann seemed back to her old self — warm and loving, even when she was teasing. Bill loved the way Ann could tease just as much as he loved her quick wit.

Ann's car pulled up outside the cottage at 11:05. Bill was standing at the kitchen window, drying the last of the breakfast dishes, and had just looked at his watch, wondering what time Ann would arrive. When he saw her car, he smiled; Bill always smiled when the moment included Ann. He wiped his hands dry then walked outside to meet her. As Ann approached the cottage porch, she waved, smiled, and then said, "Good morning! Let's get this day started!"

"OK! I'm ready."

"But not before a kiss! Pucker up, Baby!"

"Wow! What a great way to start the day," Bill said after Ann had slowly pulled away from the kiss and turned toward the cottage door.

The two of them spent most of the day sunning on the dock or kayaking along the shoreline. By 3:00, clouds covered the sky, with some dark ominous ones that foreshadowed the rain that was sure to come. Their earlier shared mood of happiness and laughter had quieted, their conversation, now filled with long silences, slowed. Each realized that with the passing of a few more precious hours, their time together would be gone.

Ann stood and said, "I'm going to jump in one more time. Want to join me?" Before Bill could answer, Ann was in the water. The cool, fresh feeling of the water surrounded her, and for just a moment took her thoughts away from Bill's leaving. Ann swam a short distance from the dock, then turned to head back. As she pulled herself up the first of three steps of the dock's ladder, she saw and felt the raindrops begin to fall. Ann looked up from the ladder to see Bill facing her with his camera poised, ready to take a picture. Ann was not a fan of having her picture taken, but before she could protest, Bill insisted, "Smile!" and the shutter snapped to record the moment.

"Thanks. Now that'll be a lovely picture — me all wet and looking so *beautiful* in this bathing suit," Ann protested as she picked up her towel and headed toward Bill.

"It will be a great picture, and you *are* beautiful," Bill responded.

"Right," was all Ann offered as she rolled her eyes at Bill's last comment. When she walked past him, Ann made an effort to push him into the bay, but he was having none of that. After they wrestled around a bit and each threatened the other with going back into the water, they made their way to the cottage. The raindrops had begun to fall harder and thunder sounded in the distance.

After a brief discussion about dinner, it was back to Pete's for a repeat of the night before. This time, though, the conversation was quite subdued and neither spoke of Bill's departure. After only an hour at the restaurant, they headed back to the cottage.

Bill had just parked the car beside the cottage when Ann spoke. It was her first words since leaving the restaurant. "I don't want you to go," she said in a soft, pleading voice that was filled with sadness and hurt. Her lower lip quivered.

Bill felt himself choke. Fighting back his own tears, he cleared his throat and, trying to sound confident and caring, responded, "I know you don't. Do you believe me when I say I will be back?"

"I want to, but I'm scared," Ann answered then opened her car door and began walking toward the cottage.

Bill followed then opened the wooden screen door to the cottage as his hand searched for the light switch. The only light visible in the cottage came from a single moonbeam passing through the sliding doors facing the bay.

"Don't turn on the lights," Ann said as she placed her hand upon Bill's back. "Let's go sit on the dock." Ann took Bill's hand and led the way. Once at the dock, each again sat on its edge, with their feet dangling in the water. The stars sparkled above and a gentle breeze flowed around them.

"What a beautiful night," Bill said to break the silence that had again overtaken them.

"I love this bay, this town," Ann responded. "Sometimes I wonder if I will ever leave."

"Do you want to leave?" Bill asked, really not sure what Ann would say in response.

"Guess it depends on what would take me away."

"Do you know what might take you away?"

"I don't think anything would, except you." Ann turned to look at Bill.

"I'd like that. I mean not that I want to take you away from something you love like Summersville. Annie, I think we will always be together. Not just our lifetime but beyond — for an eternity."

"Eternity? What makes you think so?

"Well, you remember me taking an American Lit class my sophomore year at Fullerton?"

"Yeah, the *easy* elective that almost put a dent in your GPA?"

"OK, so it wasn't my best decision to take the class, but we read Emerson, and a couple of things he wrote really got me to thinking. It was right after spring break, and I had been in Sumersville to see you. We were doing really well; it was a great visit. Emerson wrote something about *a day being a miniature eternity*. As we studied him, I thought about what he said and about the wonderful days we had just shared. If there really is an eternity that takes us beyond the life we live, then it must be possible to share it with the love of your life and that love, my dear, is you.

At first Ann remained silent, contemplating what Bill had shared. Then she spoke, "I don't like *eternity*." Bill was surprised at Ann's comment and started to ask why, but she stopped him with, "Let me finish. To me, *eternity* sounds cold and dark, an emptiness of sorts. When I look at the sky at night and there are no stars or moon, it's dark, so empty, and that emptiness extends into eternity." Ann paused, smiled as she looked at Bill, and then added. "But, I do like the sound of *forever*."

Bill gave her a quizzical look.

"Forever is warmer and sounds like what you would share with the person you love. Like what I want to share with you."

"I think I follow you. But, how about this. I will have my *eternity* and you can have your *forever*, just as long as we are together ... *eternally forever*." Then with a slight chuckle, Bill added, "I doubt Emerson would appreciate us using those two words together, but if it works for us then that's all that matters."

Ann nodded, as if in agreement, as she spoke. "So, what we have is *eternally forever*. Then her voice softened when she continued. "Bill, I never want to be without you and your love. When you are not around ..." Ann began to choke on her words and her lip trembled as she fought back the tears to finish, "I will feel your love with me." When a moment had passed without either saying anything more, Ann squeezed Bill's hand tightly, then rose to her feet. Following her lead, Bill stood, stretched, and took Ann's hand as they walked back to the cottage.

Bill couldn't believe that the evening was coming to an end. It was getting late. He wasn't exactly sure of the time, and thought that Ann needed to leave to pick up her mother again. But when they entered the cottage, Ann paused momentarily in the living room and then, rather than proceeding to the door where her car was parked, she turned toward the bedroom, still holding Bill's hand.

Through all their time together, they had always refrained from — often with great difficulty — consummating the relationship. There had been torrid moments of passion shared and touching that explored all, but never the ultimate act of love. They had talked about it at length; it was Ann's deep desire to wait, and Bill had accepted this without pressuring her. He wanted Ann to know how much he loved her, and felt that this was another way, an important way, to demonstrate the depth of his love.

Ann turned toward Bill, smiled, and extended both arms upward as she looked deep within him. He hesitated briefly then lifted her top to slide it over her head. Bill removed his shirt, and they stood beside the bed, holding each other tight and feeling the warmth of each other's skin, the heat of the sun still there, intensified by the passion growing within both of them. As they kissed and their hands explored, Ann reached behind to unhook the clasp holding her bra. They fell onto the bed without releasing their embrace or their kiss.

With urgency and passion, they stripped away the rest of their clothing, and for the first time they were mere moments and movements away from loving further than they ever had. Lying side by side, legs and arms intertwined, they spoke words of love, their desire flowing freely.

Bill kissed Ann's neck and shoulder as he whispered, "Annie, are you sure?"

Ann did not answer with words; she rolled onto her back, and in doing so, pulled Bill onto her. As their bodies united, Ann and Bill crossed into another world, one without sound except the words of passion spoken, moans of desire, and beating hearts. Love and desire freely flowed between them. When exhaustion and fulfillment finally overtook them, each found sleep, bodies intertwined and lips touching, each breath shared.

The sunlight of the new day making its way into the room woke Bill. It took him a second or two to clear his head, figure out where he was, what had happened the evening before and well into the night, and to realize that Ann was not in bed. Bill looked at the empty space where she had been and then saw the note pinned to the pillow that just hours before had cradled her head.

> *Bill,*
> *I needed to leave early and decided not to wake you.*
> *It's better this way. I didn't want to say good-bye, rather I will look forward to the day when I see you walk toward me again, back into my life.*
> *Until then, I will keep you and your love in my heart, grateful that we will have our tomorrows and our forever to share.*
> *I love you, Bill.*
> *Forever,*
> *Ann*

Chapter Twelve

"AS WE NOW BEGIN OUR DESCENT, PLEASE REFRAIN from moving about and make preparations for landing," announced the flight attendant.

The bell-like sound, indicating an announcement was forthcoming, startled Bill from his restless, fatigue-induced sleep. *Finally*, he thought. After leaving home, he had first reported to Charleston and spent four restless days waiting to be manifested on a flight. Then he flew to California, only to spend another two days waiting on a flight into country — Vietnam. Flying into a combat zone via chartered aircraft had at first seemed odd to him, but there was a great deal yet to learn about the ways of his chosen career. Eleven hours had passed since the plane left the West Coast and over three weeks since he last saw Ann. Bill and the other 246 souls on board were more than ready to depart the cramped seats and confinement of the aircraft. He stretched as much as he could and looked out the window, trying to see Vietnam — his home for the next 12 months. Most of what he saw appeared as a sea of green, a dark, rich canopy of vegetation concealing everything below it.

During the descent, Bill's mind played over and over again memories from his last few days at home. His mom cried when he said good-bye, as had Ann when he called her the final time from the airport just before boarding the aircraft. He was so glad he had made it home to Henderson and was able to spend time with his family, but even then he had had guilty feelings about really wanting to be in Summersville with Ann. Bill also had thoughts of Bud, a few from growing up together, trying to remember the last time he had seen Bud, and of the funeral.

Finally, it was time to exit the plane. Bill made his way — along with the rest of the military passengers — to the door, and as they stepped onto the platform to descend the stairs, a blast of hot air hit them with a ferocity that most had never felt before in their lives. He could not believe that it was this hot, this windy, and this humid; he wondered if this was what Fort Polk was like.

"What unit are you being assigned to, L-T?" The question came from behind as they stood in line to process through the reception station. Bill turned to see if the question was addressed to him. It was, and the one asking was a major.

"Sir, my orders are for the 237th Aviation Battalion but not sure what position they'll assign me to. But it really doesn't matter, just as long as I get to spend a lot of time in the air; no desk job for me."

"You do need to get lots of hours under your belt, and the 237th is flying a lot of support missions right now. I'm headed there myself, getting ready to take over as the battalion XO." As the in-processing line slowly progressed, Bill and the major — Major Tom Howe — talked aviation, assignments, and what it would be like to fly in this environment — with the heat and the hostile threats. Bill mostly listened; it was the major's second tour. Talking to Maj. Howe made the time pass more quickly, and then they were finished — ready to be picked up by the battalion.

The next two days were a blur. Jet lag, as well as a difficult and demanding environment, drained his energy. There was an endless array of in-processing requirements with the company and the battalion. At times, his head ached as it never had before. Among the endless requirements for settling into life for the next year was obtaining his local flight clearance from the flight surgeon, which took the better part of the second morning.

At the end of the duty day, Bill made his way to the chow hall for dinner. It would be his third of a few hundred meals he figured he would consume there. Just as he was about to take his first bite of food, he heard a familiar voice.

"Hey, Rookie, is this seat taken?" It was Lt. Estep.

Bill smiled at the sound of the voice, jumped to his feet, and shook his hand. "When the hell did you get in?" Before he could answer, Bill added, "Man, It's great to see you! I thought maybe you ended up being assigned someplace else."

"Nope, I'm here and ready to fly. Made it in yesterday evening," Lt. Estep answered as he sat his tray on the tabletop then swung his leg over the rough, wooden bench to take his seat. "What about you?"

"It was two, no, three days ago. Everything still seems like I'm in a fog; this jet lag is kicking my ass," Bill answered as he used his fork to dab at his food; he had no appetite.

"I hear you. Say, what assignment did you end up with?"

"Second Platoon Leader, Charlie Company. How about you?"

"I don't know for sure yet, but think I will end up as a platoon leader in Bravo Company."

Bill thought for a moment that spoke. "We should still be able to fly together some. I understand that when it comes to flying the missions, the battalion is so short of pilots that they will put whoever is available in the cockpit together, doesn't matter about the company."

"Yeah, I heard there is a real shortage too."

When they finished, Bill suggested they head over to the club for a drink and to finish catching up. It was their first time in this club for both lieutenants, and they were a bit shocked by its appearance. Unlike the clubs at OBC and Flight School, this one was nothing more than a Quonset hut, filled with smoke, loud music, and a heavy smell of booze. The two of them hung in for one drink then decided to take their conversation outside.

Bill asked about Lt. Estep's family.

"They're great, pretty much settled in back home with her folks and looking forward to life after this tour," he answered then asked, "And you, my friend, how is Ann? I want to hear all about your time in Summersville." As the lieutenants' friendship had grown during flight school, Bill had shared more and more about Ann. What started out as bits and pieces of information had grown until Lt. Estep knew pretty much everything about their relationship, even Ann autographing the baseball glove.

"Man, I'm crazy about her!" Bill answered.

"Well no shit, tell me something that I don't know."

Bill laughed and then began to describe his time with Ann. "There were definitely some rough spots, but we worked through it. We always do; well, almost always. But this time was really different. I know Ann wants to marry me, and that's what I want more than anything else in this world. I'm going to ask her to marry me — probably on mid-tour R&R."

"That's great! I better get an invitation to the wedding."

"Are you kidding me?" Bill playfully grabbed Lt. Estep's shoulder as he added, "You'll be standing there beside me. I want you to be the best man."

"You bet, my friend. I'm honored and will be there for sure." After another hour of nonstop conversation that bounced from family to flying in-country, Bill said, "Think I'm ready to call it a night."

The two made their way back to the officers' billeting area, which consisted of seemingly endless rows of plywood structures. Each housed four with living areas separated by three-quarter-inch plywood walls and makeshift curtains. A cot, a footlocker, a folding chair, and a wardrobe closet as well as a small desk

— both made out of plywood — were the furnishings for each cubicle.

"I think I'll write Ann a quick note before heading to bed," Bill said as he stopped in front of his assigned quarters.

"Tell her I'm looking forward to meeting her."

"I will. See you in the morning."

Bill was exhausted but wanted to write, even if it would be just a few lines.

> *Hi Annie,*
>
> *I sure do miss you!! How I miss our conversations, our time together, and all that we share!*
>
> *All is well here, still in-processing and still wondering when I will take my first flight – can't wait!*
>
> *I ran into Lt. Estep this evening. He said to tell you hello, and he is looking forward to meeting you one day.*
>
> *Between my schedule and the uncertainty of mail delivery, the arrival of my letters may be sporadic, at least starting out — sorry. I am writing this one on the 28th, and will write as often as I possibly can.*
>
> *I miss you more than words can describe, and you are constantly on my mind. Ann, there is so much to tell you, so much I want to ask you. I think about the future we will share.*
>
> *It is late, and I am beat, so I will close for now. Take good care and know my love is with you always.*
>
> *Eternally,*
>
> *Bill*

Another morning of in-processing and orientations kept Bill on the go and moving forward with settling in. It was at the in-country safety orientation that he saw Lt. Estep again. Afterward, the two walked back to the battalion area.

"When do you think we'll get a chance to fly?" Lt. Estep asked as they walked.

"Do you have your medical flight clearance yet?" Bill asked.

"Not yet."

"Man, you have got to get to the clinic to get that squared away. That's step No. 1 in getting you cleared to fly."

"I think I'll try to do that now. Didn't we just pass the clinic?" Lt. Estep asked, turning to look over his shoulder.

"Good idea. I'm going to stop by OPS to see if there's a chance of flying tomorrow, and then I am meeting with my platoon sergeant."

"OK, I'll find you when I make it back from the clinic," said Lt. Estep, as he walked away.

Bill stood by himself inside the battalion's Flight Operations Center and looked out the window at the flightline with all the aircraft coming and going. His thoughts drifted between flying and missing Ann. She was never far away from his thoughts.

"You Lt. Weber?" came the question from behind. Bill turned and responded, "Yes sir."

It was Capt. Jackson, the Charlie Company commander and an Instructor Pilot, or IP, to boot. The combination of the two did not occur often.

"Grab your gear. You're going with me. We have a supply run, and I can use this flight as part of your orientation and in-country checkride. Meet me at the bird in about 20 minutes." Then

Capt. Jackson was gone, filing a flight plan and attending to all the other details required to launch the bird. For this flight, the *bird* would be November 0545 — the aircraft's tail number and call sign.

Bill was thrilled; he was actually going to fly! He couldn't wait to get in the air, his first flight time in a combat zone! He could tell Lt. Estep all about it at dinner.

"Clear," Capt. Jackson called out after he keyed his mic then pulled the trigger to start the engine popping and the blades turning. Bill's limited duties included reading the checklist and monitoring the gages, which was all Capt. Jackson wanted him to do for now. The third member of the flight crew, the crew chief — Sgt. Kinsley — was outside the aircraft for the startup but then climbed aboard. Within minutes, they were cleared for takeoff. Bill felt the aircraft lift and tilt forward as it accelerated. Soon they were above the trees, seeing the airbase from a helicopter pilot's perspective. Bill could not stop grinning.

Once clear of the airfield control zone, their helicopter descended to no more than a hundred feet off the ground. They were headed north on a resupply mission. Bill's head rotated as if it were on a swivel. He tried to take it all in as well as listen to Capt. Jackson talk nonstop, flooding him with information.

"We are now on Route Tango; you'll learn these routes over time, but always keep the map handy. There's a turning point near the end of the route that can be a little difficult to spot. Normally, the weather is not an issue until we hit the rainy season. What's the normal engine temperature range for this aircraft?" Capt. Jackson asked, wearing his IP hat. "Don't look down at the gage," he cautioned as Bill started to answer.

The question brought back memories of flight school and the constant quizzing from Mr. Vernon, but all for good reason. Bill answered the engine temperature question and then offered a couple other operating ranges as well. Capt. Jackson did not comment, but moved onto the next topic.

Flying the left seat, the one reserved for the PIC (pilot-in-command), Capt. Jackson began holding the cyclic control stick between his legs with his left hand and pointing to various landmarks and checkpoints with his right. It was a clear day, so visibility was good, and details could be made out in the distance. In the barrage of information being delivered by Capt. Jackson, he announced to Bill that they were about 20 minutes from their destination — Out Post (OP) Apache. Perhaps five more minutes passed, maybe six, when Capt. Jackson moved the cyclic and began a roll to the right and descended further. The entry portion of the route to the OP required that they head down the valley and then pop up at the last minute. OP Apache was on the high ground and critical to controlling the area.

Capt. Jackson, still flying with his left hand on the cyclic — a feat Bill had not fully mastered — was pointing up the valley with his right, all the while maneuvering the aircraft as a highly skilled pilot while he talked. "I'll let you fly us back to base after we drop off the supplies. Think you can find your way back? Usually it takes ..."

And then all hell broke.

The next few seconds became surreal. On one level Bill's mind could not process what was happening and on another level — a level of survival — it instinctively took over. He knew that Capt. Jackson was starting to say something about the number of times it takes to fly the routes until you are familiar with them, but his words were brought to a halt by a hail of bullets striking the aircraft, shattering the cockpit bubble at their feet.

Capt. Jackson's right hand, the one he had been using to point out all the checkpoints, was hit; his arm went flying upward and his hand evaporated in a burst of red. Bill saw the captain's head snap back. Even though his face was hidden by the helmet's visor, he knew that the captain had caught a round in his throat or upper chest area — just above the flak vest each wore. Capt. Jackson was mortally wounded, and his limp body no longer flew the aircraft, which had started violently pitching right and upward.

Bill grabbed the cyclic and keyed the mic as his feet found the pedals. "Mayday, mayday, November 0545, enemy fire, going down short of Apache. We are ..." He started the mayday call, intending to tell whoever might hear the distress call that they were about 10 clicks (kilometers) short of the landing zone for OP Apache. But the next hail of bullets caught Bill and stopped his efforts to communicate further. He felt a burning pain in his left thigh and a lesser one near his right forearm. Bill tried to ignore the pain and fought to control the aircraft. The sounds from the engine and turning rotor blades let him know that they were losing power fast.

He instinctively did what he had been trained to do at flight school — flair the aircraft to reduce the forward speed in a way that the aircraft would descend or fall through the trees, trying to save the last of the power to soften the impact just before the bird hit the ground. Bill knew they were going to hit hard. In another few seconds it was over. The rotor blades struck a treetop and then the aircraft began to shake violently just as Bill pulled the collective, using up the last of the lift from the damaged blades. The aircraft struck the ground and began to roll.

Chapter Thirteen

"HARRY. COME ON, BUD, TIME TO WAKE UP AND TELL me something good." Lt. Estep stood by Bill's hospital bed throughout the day and spoke these words to him over and over again, just as he had done yesterday and the day before. It had been four days since enemy fire had downed Bill's chopper and up to now he had shown no responsiveness to anyone's voice.

"What?" Bill's muttered word came out barely audible as he tried for the first time to respond to Lt. Estep's voice. He tried to speak again, to return to the land of the conscious, but couldn't. No words could get past his disorientation, past the fog enshrouding his thoughts, past the drugs and the wounds that tore at his body. Bill tried to move, but pain shot through him; tubes, lines, and large bandages all restricted his movements as well.

"Hey Bud, take it easy. Glad to see that you decided to rejoin us." Lt. Estep spoke to Bill as he touched his uninjured shoulder and sought to calm him down.

"What?" was all Bill could manage once again before slipping back into his land of unconsciousness and the dreams and nightmares that filled those moments. Nearly two more hours passed before he made another sound. This time it was a gasp from the pain, followed by an *ooh*.

Over the next few hours, Bill rallied some but still struggled with every word or phrase he tried to say. By the time evening rolled around, he spoke short, fragmented sentences to ask for something or in response to questions from either a nurse or Lt. Estep. Bill had not asked about the crash or his injuries. After another period of silence, Lt. Estep thought Bill had dozed off and decided he would leave for the night, then Bill spoke again.

"Ann ... send a note."

"You want me to write a note to Ann for you? Is that what you are asking?"

"Yes ...Ann."

"Sure, I can do that. What would you like me to tell her?" Lt. Estep asked, encouraged that Bill was again awake and focused on Ann.

In response, Bill mumbled something low and undistinguishable.

"Say that again, please."

Now seemingly irritated, Bill answered in a stronger voice. "Fine! Just fine. Not hurt much. Write later."

"Do you want to talk to her? I can place the call and hold the phone for you." Lt. Estep thought it would be good for Bill to hear Ann's voice.

"No ... No." Even in his exhausted state, Bill's voice sounded adamant in his answer.

"OK, I'll write Ann just as soon as I make it back to my hooch." Lt. Estep started to ask Bill another question and then realized that he had drifted off to sleep again. He watched his friend sleep for several minutes, thinking he might rally again, then picked up his hat and headed to the door. He was sure Harry was out for the night.

Lt. Estep wrote to Ann, just as Bill had asked. He added a few extra details, trying to give her a little more information but without sounding too alarming. He could not say that Bill had been severely injured, that he was lucky to be alive, and that it would take months if not years for him to heal. All of that, he thought, Harry could share with Ann over time.

Bill had been in the field hospital's intensive care unit for five days, with signs of significant improvement over the last two. When he was transferred to the surgical ward, Bill began trying to ask the doctors about his injuries and recovery but had little success. They seemed to either ignore his questions or suggest he hold them for now. When the time was right, the surgeons and other specialists involved in his care would all talk to him. Finally, that time arrived.

The chief surgeon, Ltc. Walters, entered Bill's room on the sixth day, and again Bill began to ask his questions. This time, the doctor responded, "Hold that until this afternoon; your team will be in to answer all your questions. Later today will be a good time. Your thinking is pretty clear, and the plan is for you to be evacuated, probably within the next two or three days."

"Evacuated? Sir, I don't want to be evacuated! Why can't I stay here?" Bill seemed to plead. This was the first time he had either heard or understood that he was to be evacuated.

All Ltc. Walters offered was, "We don't have the rehabilitation services you'll need or the bed space. See you this afternoon." As he left the room, the surgeon almost collided with Lt. Estep, who was just coming in. He stepped to the side and asked, "What did the friendly doc have to say?"

"Shit! They want to evacuate me out of country. I don't want to go. I want to stay right here. I want to fly again," Bill answered, though not looking at Lt. Estep.

"Harry, you got to get well. You've got to get ready for your big day with Ann, and if that takes leaving country, then that's what you need to do."

Bill remained silent for several minutes before he asked, "Is Capt. Jackson dead?" This was the first time he had mentioned the captain or anything about the crash.

Lt. Estep hesitated, cleared his throat, and then answered, "Yes. I'm sorry. They think he was killed with one of the very first rounds to hit the aircraft. It probably happened real quick."

After a little more silence, Bill asked, "What about Sgt. Kingsley?"

"Barely a scratch. He has a broken ankle and lots of bruises, but is doing great. He was only in the hospital a couple of days." Lt. Estep paused then added, "They say the way you handled the aircraft as it went down was like a pro, which is why you and Sgt. Kingsley are both alive. You are his hero."

Bill did not react to either statement. After an uneasy period of silence between the two, Lt. Estep asked, "Anything I can get for you?"

"Yeah! How about my damn life back before I was shot all to hell, before Capt. Jackson died, before all this!" Bill lashed out as he tried to gesture to the massive bandages and casts that enshrouded his wounds.

Surprised by Bill's tone and anger, Lt. Estep wasn't sure what to say, only to offer, "Hang in there, buddy. You're going to get well. It will get better."

Bill said nothing more, just closed his eyes and remained motionless. Lt. Estep wasn't sure if Harry had gone to sleep or was just acting that way as a means to avoid talking. After a few more minutes, Lt. Estep left.

Bill was not asleep. The same recurring thoughts and questions churned over and over again and again in his mind: swirling fears of uncertainty about his future, about the future Ann and he were to share. Would he fly again? Would he be able to stay in the Army? Those were uncertain, but time and rehabilitation efforts would determine the answers. But what about life with Ann, a life as a family with Ann as a mother to the children she so wanted to bring into this world? Would the doctors confirm what he feared, what he dreaded to hear, what would forever change the life and family he was to share with Ann?

Lost in thought, Bill stared blankly out his window, unaware of the changing shadows and the passing of the afternoon sun. He was surprised when the door swung open and four doctors — or he assumed doctors — now stood at the foot of his bed. The only one that Bill recognized was Ltc. Walters, although one other doctor looked familiar.

Ltc. Walters spoke first. "Lt. Weber, we are here to discuss your injuries and answer questions you might have. This is Maj. Robbins, urologist; Capt. Livingston, orthopedic surgeon, and Ltc. Griffin, general surgeon." Ltc. Walters' introductions and his pronouncement of why they were gathered was all very matter-of-fact — as if he had done the same thing many times before.

Capt. Livingston led off. "Your left leg was severely damaged by two projectiles. The first struck your calf and traveled up your leg before exiting. The second entered your adductor magnus – a part of your hamstring then tumbled upward, which did most of the damage to your groin and abdominal regions. The leg will require additional surgeries, but you should regain full use of it. Your left arm is broken in two places as a result of the crash and should heal without issues. A third projectile damaged your right arm and clavicle. Your shoulder area will require an additional surgery and extensive rehabilitation. Only then will you know the full range of motion and limitations." He ended with, "Any questions of me?" Bill shook his head no and then Capt. Livingston was gone, hurrying out the door to see his next patient.

Maj. Robbins spoke next. "I assisted during your surgery. Congenitally, you suffer from monorchidism. Correct?"

It had been quite awhile since Bill last heard that medical term and it caused him to give a confused look to the doctor, who restated what he had surmised. "I believe you were born with just one testicle."

Bill laughed and then said, "Yes sir, growing up a couple of my friends gave me the nickname of *O-T.*"

Maj. Robbins did not respond to Bill's comment, but continued. "Your urinary function is returning, but the catheter will remain in place for a few more days." Maj. Robbins seemed to pause, as if he was finished.

"Dr. Robbins," Bill started to ask, "what about my testicle?"

"The scrotum is now intact, but your testicle sustained significant damage."

Bill asked with a single word, "Kids?"

Maj. Robbins paused. "I am afraid not. Circulation to the prostate was damaged as well. However, if your recovery goes as I believe it will, you should be able to achieve an erection, but no delivery of sperm will occur."

Bill just nodded in response. In part he was stunned and yet he had also been trying to prepare for what the doctor had now confirmed. For a second or two, his thoughts returned to earlier recurring ones that had begun to form in his mind. But then he was brought back to the moment as the doctors continued explaining their assessments.

Ltc. Griffin was next and described his efforts at resectioning the bowel and repairing the damage to his stomach. Bill tried to listen, but echoing in the background was Maj. Robbins' death sentence: "No children."

When Bill had no additional questions for Maj. Robbins or Ltc. Griffin, Ltc. Walters asked, "Anything else?"

It was difficult to ask, but Bill needed to know. "Will I be able to stay in the Army? What about flying again?"

Ltc. Walters offered a single, succinct response to both, "Too early to tell." With that uncertainty conveyed, the three doctors turned to leave his room. But Maj. Robbins paused, looked at Bill, and asked, "Do you have children?"

Bill shook his head *no* as tears began to roll down his cheeks.

"I know this is tough news, but try not to be discouraged. Life has plenty to offer you. It may not be kids, but still plenty, and there is always adoption."

Bill did not respond to the doctor.

"How you doing today, my friend?" Lt. Estep asked as chipper as possible when he entered Bill's room.

At first, Bill offered no reply, just stared at the floor and allowed an uncomfortable silence to build. Finally he spoke. "Not so good. Spent some time with my doctors yesterday evening, and they were just full of *good news.*"

Lt. Estep waited for Bill to say more, but when he did not, hesitated and then asked, "What did they have to say?"

Bill didn't answer the question. Instead, he said, "I need to send a couple of letters to Ann. Will you write them?"

"Sure thing. Do I get to write your proposal?" Lt. Estep asked, trying to kid Harry.

Without acknowledging his friend's question, Bill started dictating the words for his letters to Ann, and, in turn, Lt. Estep began to write. As he recorded Bill's words, they seemed a little strange, but he didn't stop writing to question. He did give Bill a quizzical look a time or two then read it back to him

Dear Ann,

I am writing (actually Lt. Estep is writing for me) to let you know that I am doing well, just sort of stiff and sore. From the sound of things, I will probably be in the hospital a few more days than what I had expected.

I start physical therapy soon and they say it is exhausting. If so, I may not be up to sending many notes, but I will be thinking of you and all that you mean to me.

You know that I would do anything for you and anything to make your life complete.

Eternally,

Bill

Lt. Estep looked at Bill and asked, "Why are you lying to Ann?"

"I'm not lying, what did I say that is a lie?! I am sore — sore as hell. I will be in the hospital a few more days — probably the rest of my damn life! And I will start therapy one day." Bill had a tone of anger in his voice that Lt. Estep had never heard before.

"Harry, come on, don't do this, don't pull away from Ann now. You guys are meant to be together."

Bill offered nothing in response but an uneasy silence, which was finally broken when he said, "She needs a whole man. Next letter. This one I want you to mail after I am evacuated. "

Before Lt. Estep could ask why, Bill began to dictate the second letter. As he wrote Harry's words, he could not believe what was coming out of his friend's mouth. Finally he stopped Bill with, "Wait! Why are you doing this? Why are you telling Ann some made-up, bullshit story? She doesn't deserve this; she deserves the truth and for the two of you to work out your future together."

"Just keep writing," Bill shot back as he angrily grabbed at his bedsheet, clinching it with his uninjured hand.

When the letter was finished, Lt. Estep read it back to Bill then said, "Man, talk to me. This is crazy."

For the longest time, Bill remained silent; tears rolled down his cheeks. Without ever looking directly at Lt. Estep, Bill shared what the doctors had to say, then abruptly changed the subject with, "Ann will have a family of her own. Hell, she was born to be a mother. Whenever we talked about our future, it always included children — she wants to have lots of children. She deserves them."

"She will have them. There are plenty of children waiting to be adopted, and even though I've never met Ann, I just know that she will love them just as much as her own." Lt. Estep wanted to convince Harry he was wrong in writing to Ann what he'd dictated.

"Ann will have children of her own." Bill paused, then continued. "I'm doing her a favor with this letter, giving her the freedom from me to have what she deserves."

"A favor! Freedom? You're just being a selfish bastard." Lt. Estep picked up his cap, ready to leave. He was furious at Bill and wanted to give him time to think about the second letter, the one that would end his relationship with Ann. "Look, I'm headed to the Orderly Room, and I will mail this first letter no problem," Lt. Estep snapped. "But this letter, this crazy, stupid letter," he said as he waved the second letter at Bill, "I'll be back tomorrow and we'll talk more about it."

Without looking at his friend, Bill coldly offered, "Come back or not, that's up to you. But, you know what I want, what I asked you to do so just do it. Mail the damn letter!"

It was a little after 1:00 the next day when Lt. Estep returned to see Bill. He hoped Bill would have come to his senses and, without further discussion, would tell him to tear up the second letter, perhaps even be embarrassed by the rash words it contained. If not, he was prepared to stay there until he convinced Bill to do so.

Lt. Estep swung open the door to Bill's hospital room and was surprised to find it empty. He felt a flash of panic when his first thought was that Bill had taken a turn for the worse, that maybe he was back in the ICU. He left the room and quickly made his way to the nurses' station. It was the tall nurse, Capt. Bulliner, the one he had seen so many times in Bill's room, who told him. Bill had been evacuated earlier that morning, on his way to Germany.

Just like that, Bill was gone: without good-byes, without time to talk about *the letter*. As the days passed, Lt. Estep thought of Bill, wondered how he was doing, and that maybe he would hear from him. Equally in thought was the letter, that absurd, crazy letter that Bill probably regretted dictating and would have eventually asked him to tear up, the one that he had not yet mailed — the one that he never would.

Chapter Fourteen

"GEEZ!" ANN EXPRESSED IN DISAPPOINTMENT AFTER she opened the mailbox, retrieved the assortment of mail, and realized there was nothing from Bill — again. Almost an entire week had passed since his last letter, which had been nothing more than a short note. Not hearing from him was disappointing on one level but on a deeper level were growing concerns for his safety. Every day, the evening news reported on the war and the increasing number of casualties. Rather than allowing the feelings of disappointment and concern to languish, Ann forced her thinking to seek out the positive: *Tomorrow a letter will be there; Bill is doing just fine.* To further counter these feelings, Ann decided she would reread the latest letter or two from Bill.

Ann removed Bill's latest letter from her desk and headed to the kitchen, where she fixed a cup of tea and then sat down at the small kitchen table by the window to read. She could see that the sky was a beautiful shade of blue, without a cloud, and she could hear the birds chirping. Summertime in Summersville was ideal with long, sun-filled days, sailing on the bay, or swimming with friends in one of the nearby lakes. She thought of Bill and wished that he could be there to share the summer and so much more.

Taking the letter from its envelope, Ann began to read Bill's words again. As she read, she couldn't help but wonder what all had transpired in Bill's life since then. With each word read, she could hear Bill's voice and see the facial expressions he would use to convey his message.

> *Hi Annie,*
>
> *I sure do miss you!! How I miss our conversations, our time together, and all that we share!*
>
> *All is well here, still in-processing and still wondering when I will take my first flight — can't wait!*
>
> *I ran into Lt. Estep this evening. He said to tell you hello, and he is looking forward to meeting you one day.*
>
> *Between my schedule and the uncertainty of mail delivery, the arrival of my letters may be sporadic, at least starting out — sorry. I am writing this one on the 28th, and will write as often as I possibly can.*
>
> *I miss you more than words can describe, and you are constantly on my mind. Ann, there is so much to tell you, so much I want to ask you. I think about the future we will share.*
>
> *It is late, and I am beat, so I will close for now. Take good care and know my love is with you always.*
>
> *Eternally,*
> *Bill*

Ann looked at his handwriting and, as she did, used the tips of her fingers to lightly glide across the paper and touch the words that Bill had written. This was another way of feeling close to him, and Ann sensed his presence with her. She touched and circled the word *Eternally* twice more.

Ann placed Bill's letter back in its envelope and let an emotional roller coaster of thoughts pass across her mind. Lost was the beauty of the summer's moment, replaced with the realities of life: college days gone, Bill — the man she loved and wanted to marry — thousands of miles away in harm's way, her mom's health not the best, and ...her period late. Not real late, and this was not the first time, but late nevertheless. Tears formed in Ann's eyes and slowly rolled down her cheeks. She sat motionless, starring off into the distance, and her thoughts continued to cycle through the procession of realities. The loud, ringing sound of the phone startled her and brought her back to the moment. Ann wiped the tears from her face, cleared her throat, and answered the phone. "Hello."

"Hi Ann, how are you? This is Sylvia."

"Oh hi, Mrs. Weber, I'm fine. How are you doing?"

There was a brief pause of uncomfortable silence then she spoke. "Well, dear, I am fine, did have a little cold last week. But, I was wondering, have you heard from Bill lately?"

The way Sylvia expressed her question caused Ann to feel a surge of panic pass through her, but she controlled it before replying, "It's been over a week, but I'm sure he is fine, just busy, and trying to get settled in."

"Oh, I'm sure you're right. Guess I am just being a worrisome mother. I am so sorry that I bothered you with this call."

"It's no bother! And it's always good to talk to you. I worry too, even though I try not to. Bill knows how to take care of himself and how much we love him, so he'll be just fine over there."

"Dear, you are so sweet, and I know you're right. So, let's just keep him in our daily thoughts and prayers until he comes home. Then we will have a big celebration!"

Sylvia paused for just a second and then changed the subject to ask, "And how is your mom?"

"She's not feeling so well and she still works too much," Ann replied then added, "Yes, we'll celebrate for sure when Bill makes it home."

"Please tell your mom I said hello and come see me anytime."

"I will; thanks for calling, Mrs. Weber."

"Dear, someday you have just got to start calling me Sylvia. Now, you take good care, and we will talk again soon — probably sharing the latest from Bill."

"Talk to you soon," was all Ann could manage to complete the conversation.

"Good-bye, dear."

Ann held the phone to her chest and sobbed freely, her chest rising and falling as she drew the awkward breaths between the sobs. Ann missed Bill so much, and she was scared. Despite her false bravado for Sylvia, Ann had experienced moments of panic when terrible thoughts about Bill being hurt or even worse would surface. This conversation had again brought them to the surface of her emotions. As if in slow motion, Ann allowed her body to slide down the kitchen wall and collapse on the floor; she sobbed and feared the worst.

Two days and two restless nights passed since Ann had spoken with Sylvia; two more days of not hearing from Bill. A new day dawned and, as it progressed, Ann grew more and more impatient for the mail to arrive, but then it did, just a little after 1:00. She hurried to the mailbox, praying for a letter from Bill. Excited at the possibility but also aware of the start of a sinking feeling, the feeling she felt each day if there was no letter from him.

Ann grabbed the contents and raced back to her apartment without looking at what she had received. Only after making it back inside did she realize there was a letter, a letter addressed to her and with Bill's name and return address but not his handwriting. Her hands began to shake as she opened the envelope.

Hi Ann,

I am sure you are surprised to receive this note from me and not your Bill. He asked that I write to let you know he is OK, just unable to write at the moment. He is banged up some from an accident a few days ago. Right now, he is in the field hospital and receiving great care. He misses you and will be in contact real soon.

I am sure Bill will call or write as soon as he can and share all the details. I will say that he is one heck of a pilot and did a great job handling the aircraft.

Bill has told me so much about you as we went through flight school and now here. I am just sorry that my first contact with you is through this letter letting you know about the accident. Please don't worry; your Bill is in good hands and will be just fine.

Sincerely,

Bill Estep

Ann rapidly read the letter over and over trying to make sense of it — *accident, can't write, receiving great care, in good hands.* Each time her eyes raced across the words faster and faster, frantically searching for more than was there.

A wave of nausea overcame Ann as she read. Her body first felt a flash of heat and then the clamminess of sweat over take it. When dizziness made it feel impossible to stand any longer, she collapsed into the adjacent chair and began to cry. Ann remained there until she knew she had cried all that she could; there were no tears left, at least not for now. The living room began to grow dim; evening time was upon her and Summersville. Yet, she thought, the sun was just beginning to rise where Bill was. *Where he was, where he was* — now a hospital for him. That thought was all it took for Ann to again feel a wave of nausea overcome her; this time she headed to the bathroom.

The phone rang and rang again. Ann did not want to talk to anyone. But the ringing led Ann to think about Sylvia. Did she know? Should she call her? What could she tell her? Ann did not call her until four days later, after receiving another note, one that Bill Estep again had written for Bill as he dictated the words.

> *Dear Ann,*
>
> *I am writing (actually Lt. Estep is writing for me) to let you know that I am doing well, just sort of stiff and sore. From the sound of things, I will probably be in the hospital a few more days than what I had expected.*
>
> *I start physical therapy soon and they say it is exhausting. If so, I may not be up to sending many notes, but I will be thinking of you and all that you mean to me.*
>
> *You know that I would do anything for you and anything to make your life complete.*
>
> *Eternally,*
>
> *Bill*

It took courage for Ann to phone Bill's mom and, by the third ring, Ann was hoping that Sylvia would not answer.

"Hello," Sylvia finally answered. Her voice sounded tired and flat.

"Hi, Mrs. Weber. It's Ann." Ann paused, still struggling to find the words. But then she heard Sylvia start to cry. Ann now knew that word had reached Bill's mom.

Mrs. Weber tried to recover her composure, not wanting to alarm Ann, but all she could say was, "Have you heard?"

"Yes," Ann responded as her voice cracked and she fought back the tears. Then she added, "Did you get a letter?"

"No. I first received a telegram but it said so little. I spent the next 24 hours trying to get more information through the Red Cross. Finally, I received a call two days ago. It was from a captain, think he said the battalion adjutant, but I couldn't understand his name. The connection was terrible, and he couldn't tell me much more than what was in the telegram." Sylvia paused, she could hear Ann's muffed sobs in the receiver. "Ann I am so sorry that I didn't call you. I didn't know what to do. I kept thinking I would get another call with more information or maybe Bill would call, but nothing."

"That's OK. What did the captain say?" Ann's words sought to mask her feelings of anger and confusion.

"He said Bill was in a crash that was caused by enemy fire. He is stable and improving but has several broken bones and internal injuries."

Ann was both stunned and angry to learn that Bill's *accident* was from enemy fire and the severity of his injuries — nothing like that was indicated in the letters she had received.

Sensing Ann's silence, Sylvia continued. "I asked the captain if he had called you, and he said he could only notify an immediate family member." Mrs. Weber paused and then asked, "Did you get a letter from Bill? What did it say?"

Ann began to respond — answering Sylvia's questions — but feeling numb all the while. Though she spoke words about the letters she had received and about Lt. Estep, Ann had mentally disconnected from the conversation. She had overwhelming thoughts racing through her mind, frantic to know more and intense anger mounting. *What really happened and would Bill really be OK? Why was Bill keeping the truth from her again? Why couldn't the captain call her? Why hadn't Sylvia called as soon as she spoke to the him?* Ann wanted to scream; she wanted to strike out at the world.

"I received two letters, not from Bill but from Lt. Estep writing for him. He was Bill's stick buddy in flight school, and now they're assigned to the same unit. The first just said Bill was in an accident but OK. The second didn't say much more, just something about being sore and starting physical therapy. Neither letter mentioned broken bones or internal injuries."Ann turned the conversation back to Sylvia; she wanted to know more about Bill's injuries. "Did the captain say what bones are broken or anything about the internal injuries?"

Sylvia hesitated then answered, "His leg — I believe his left one — and his right arm. All he said about the other injuries is that they are in the abdominal and groin region."

"OK," Ann responded, but she had a feeling that Sylvia knew more than what she was saying. Trying to subdue the fears and anger that were overtaking her, Ann continued. "I should have called you as soon as I received the first letter. It was wrong of me not to, and I am sorry. I just thought I would know more soon and did not want to upset you."

"Ann, I understand. Both of us are trying to protect the other, which I know is what Bill is trying to do by not telling you more. I know you know this, but Bill has always been a protector. His dad was like that. The problem with being that way is that sometimes he thinks he is protecting when he is really just hurting either the other person or himself. Ann, I know he loves you so very much. He may think he is protecting you, but you know and I know that is not what you feel right now."

The conversation ended with each promising to call and keep the other informed of any new information that each might receive. Ann hung up the phone then stood motionless, trying to comprehend what was happening to her world, to Bill, to them. Bill was hurt, *seriously hurt,* lying in a hospital bed thousands of miles away. He had purposely not told her everything, and Ann felt furious at him. Bill was doing the very same thing that had led to their breakup just before his college graduation. Now Bill was doing it again. But this time, the stakes were even higher.

Ann was certain that she was pregnant.

Chapter Fifteen

ANN AVOIDED ANSWERING HER PHONE FOR SEVERAL days and, when she finally did, wished she had not.

After blowing right past the "Hellos" and "This is your mother," Barbara got right to the heart of the matter. "Ann, I'm worried about you and coming over to see you now." She spoke in a firm but motherly tone to her daughter.

Ann tried to turn the tide. "Mom, I am fine, really. I have had a bug and missed a couple days of work. Right now, the apartment is a mess and I'm still in my pajamas, so why don't you wait until this weekend — maybe Sunday afternoon?"

"I'll be there in 20 minutes." And with that, Ann's mother ended the conversation.

Ann collapsed back on the couch, where she had spent the better part of the past three days. She was a mess, the apartment was a mess, and — at the moment — Ann just didn't care. It was the ringing of the doorbell that finally stirred her from her prone position. With reluctance, she went to the door to let her mother in.

"Ann, you look terrible!"

"It's nice to see, too, Mother," Ann replied as she turned her back to her mom and returned to the living room, plopping down on the couch in a half-reclining, half-sitting position with her feet atop the coffee table. The table was covered and messy — paper plates with uneaten food, empty cups, tissues — new and used – and other assorted items. As Barbara surveyed the mess and her daughter's disheveled appearance, she didn't know what to think other than *this is not my Ann*. In an effort to find a place to sit, Barbara picked up a blanket from the single chair across from the couch.

"Just throw it on the floor," Ann suggested.

Without responding in words, Barbara folded the blanket and, as she did, gave her daughter a look as if to say, *You don't live this way. What is going on?* With the blanket folded and placed on the floor next to the chair, Barbara sat down and waited for Ann to speak.

"What? I told you on the phone that I'm fine, just been sick with a bug. You coming over now was just a waste of your time."

"Ann, I am your mother. You can stop this charade at any time, and tell me what is going on with you."

"Why do you think anything is going on?" Ann spoke in a firmer tone.

"Oh, I don't know. Let's see, what would make me think that? It could be you look like hell, your apartment is a mess, you missed work yesterday and today, and you did not return my calls from yesterday or the day before. Think I am on to something here?"

Ann did not answer, but slumped further into the couch, her head resting on the back, and stared at the ceiling. A tear rolled down her cheek.

"Ann, please talk to me," Barbara asked, this time in a softer, concerned tone.

"Bill." Ann spoke a single word without looking at her mom.

"What about Bill?" Barbara knew that he had been injured and that Ann had not been hearing much from him, but Barbara had no idea why. As far as she knew, everything between the two had been going great. Until recently, Barbara was sure they would be married as soon as Bill made it home.

"He's an asshole."

"I see. How about telling me a little more than that," Barbara said in reply, waiting for Ann to open up.

For the next hour, Ann talked and talked — her words a mixture of insight, confusion, anger, frustration, a little laughter, concern, and fear. She told her mom just about everything there was to tell: about Bill, more about the crash and his injuries, Bill not telling the truth, his habit of always trying to be the protector, and now his withdrawing. Actually, it wasn't withdrawing; it was total absence. Ann had not received a letter in over two weeks. She had spoken with Sylvia a couple of times recently, but as it became clear that Bill wasn't reaching out to Ann, their conversations had grown difficult and uncomfortable for both of them. Ann did not plan on calling Sylvia again.

As Ann talked, Barbara listened. She did ask a couple of questions to prompt her daughter or to clarify something that Ann had said, but most of all she listened as a mother. Though Ann had shared a great deal since she began opening up, Barbara believed there was more. "I need a glass of water," she said as she stood in front of the chair and stretched. "Can I get you one, or would you like something to eat?"

"Maybe a glass of water. The thought of food makes me feel sick," Ann answered.

Barbara returned from the kitchen with two glasses of water, gave one to Ann, and then sat down on the couch, closer to her daughter.

Ann looked at her mom, chuckled nervously, and then said, "What?"

"Anything else you want to share with me?"

Ann looked away and down at the glass, which she had placed between the knees of her outstretched legs, still propped up on the coffee table. "No! Geez! I can't believe I told you all that I did."

"Ann, I am going to ask you something very personal," Barbara said as if to prepare her daughter.

Ann just knew what question her mother was about to ask. This moment had played out over and over in her mind — and each time with dread or denial. Now, there was no stopping; it was about to become reality.

"Are you pregnant?" Ann's mother asked.

Sylvia had just walked in the door from work when the phone rang. Her first thought was to not answer it. The workday had been long and she was dead tired, but then she decided it could be important, maybe even Bill or Ann calling. In recent days, Ann had been on Sylvia's mind a great deal. Over a week had passed since they had last spoken, and even then it was just a brief, awkward conversation, with Sylvia trying to make excuses for Bill not writing or calling Ann.

"Hello," Sylvia said.

"Mom, it's me, Bill."

"Bill! Oh my god! It's great to hear your voice again. I have been so worried about you!"

"Mom, I'm fine. Really I am. Just sore and bandaged up a little."

"How are you *really* doing, and how is the hospital? Are you calling from Germany?" Sylvia wanted to know more than Bill's succinct, protective summary of being *fine*.

"Actually, I'm not in Germany. I made it back to the States two days ago, just outside of D.C. I was only in Germany three days when the doctors decided to evacuate me back to the States for the rest of the care I'll need."

"Do you know how long you will be there? Can I come to visit?"

"It'll be a few days before I know what the long-term plan is. There's a chance I could end up at another hospital, so no visitors for now."

"OK," Sylvia reluctantly acknowledged. Then she asked, "Son, why aren't you writing Ann? Why haven't you called her? She is so worried and loves you so much."

Bill remained silent for a moment then spoke. "I did write her, a few times. Did she say if she received *the* letter?" Bill placed emphasis on *the.*

"I don't know what letter you're referring to. All I know is that it's been several weeks since Ann has heard from you. Why are you doing this to her?"

"Doing what?" Bill's response was abrupt and curt. "I wrote her and told her what she needed to know. It's just better for her this way."

"Bill, you're my son and I love you dearly, but you are wrong. You're wrong to shut Ann out now — wrong for not writing, for not calling. Son, do you think you're protecting her by not telling her what's been happening to you?" Bill remained silent, so his mother continued. "Please call Ann just as soon as we hang up. Ann is a wonderful, caring young woman, who loves you dearly. Don't jeopardize what the two of you have now."

"Mom, you just don't understand!" was all Bill said in response before he began to break off the call. "I have got to go, but I'll call again soon, probably in a couple of days, once I know more."

"Bill, please get well and come home just as soon as you are able. Come home to the people who love you. Come home to Ann, son."

"Bye, Mom. I'll call soon," Bill ended the call. He let his head fall back against the pillow and stared at the hospital room's ceiling, thinking about Ann. He still loved her, that certainly hadn't stopped, and Bill knew that he would always love her. Yet they would never be together, and Ann would find someone else.

When she did, they would have the family that Ann so desired. Her life would be complete, and Bill wanted to believe it was his sacrifice that would make it possible. *Isn't that what we are supposed to do? Sacrifice for the one we love?* he asked himself. A tear rolled down his cheek, which he tried to wipe away by using the side of the cast that enveloped his right arm. The cast scratched at his cheek as much as it wiped away the tear, and when it did Bill let out a sigh of exasperation. "What a damn mess I am — inside and out," he thought as he struggled to maneuver his body in order to reach for the bedstand's drawer.

Retrieving pen and paper, Bill would satisfy the urgent need to feel a connection with Ann by writing, just as he had felt and done while hospitalized in Germany. That letter, the first of its kind, gave him the freedom to express all he felt and wanted to say along with the assurance that Ann would never read his words. A letter written to Ann but used as a means to cope with the loneliness, with the feelings of anger, frustration, and almost losing his mind as the reality of his actions sank deeper and deeper into his being. That letter, this letter he was about to write, and all that might follow would never be mailed. His words would never hurt Ann again.

The first of Bill's letters written to Ann but never to be mailed came about after a difficult day and mostly sleepless night while he was still hospitalized in Germany. Continual gnawing pain from his wounds that never seemed to subside, troubling thoughts of the uncertain future he would face, and a feeling of incredible loneliness had filled his day. When sleep finally came late in the night, he dreamt of Ann until the dream turned into a dark nightmare and his body jerked him awake, startled, his heart racing.

At the start of his dream, Ann was standing off in a distance, yet he could also see everything about her clearly, as if she were right beside him. She appeared so beautiful, a brilliant smile across her lips, and hair glistening in the sunlight, but she was looking off in the distance, not at him. In an instant, it all changed. The person no longer looked like Ann, yet in the dream Bill knew that it was her. She stared in his direction and this time looked directly at him. Her face appeared contorted, as if in deep pain but with no indication of what caused the pain. Her lips moved, but he could not hear the words she spoke. Bill tried to go to her, but he couldn't move. When he looked down, his legs were missing, and then it felt as if he had started to fall into a cavern of black emptiness. Bill grabbed for something to stop his fall, which is when his body jerked and he awoke, gripping the bed guardrail with his good hand. For the next minute or so, he felt as if he were in a fog and tried to orient himself, to calm his rapidly beating heart, and to shake free from the indelible image of Ann that his nightmare had created as it had ended.

Images of Ann as she appeared in the dream were quickly replaced by racing thoughts of reality: how he loved and missed her. Had he done the right thing? Ann was free of him now and could have the family she wanted. What were her reactions to *the letter?*"

Wanting nothing more than to be free of the images and disturbing thoughts from his nightmare, Bill started to reach for the call button. He would ask for another pain pill or something that would make him sleep. But instead of the button, Bill picked up a pad of paper and then the pen beside it. Both were on the tray stand, provided courtesy of the Army hospital. He began a letter to Ann. His written words were scribbled across the pages, barely legible as he held the pen in an awkward position and struggled to make the pen respond to his thoughts. He wrote and wrote, unsure of just how much time had elapsed, until he put the paper and pen down, exhausted but with a feeling of peace within. The letter was four pages in length and not well composed; it bounced from one topic to another and then back again, but it expressed all that he had not shared with her. Bill tried to explain why he had done what he did, that he was sorry and, at times, regretted doing so, but why it was better this way, and that — in his own way — how he would always love her.

At first, Bill was unsure what to do with this letter. Then he reached for an envelope on the tray stand, placed the pages inside and sealed it. He wrote Ann's name on the envelope, as if to address it to her, then stopped. After a little more thought, he wrote the date in one upper corner and where he was when he wrote it — *Army hospital, Germany* — in the other. Bill held the sealed envelope in his hand and closed his eyes to sleep.

Now, alone in his hospital room in D.C., as the conversation with his mom played over in his mind and the weight of his actions seemed to crash down upon him, Bill again wrote to Ann. He wrote about being in the hospital, about the uncertainty of flying again, and his loneliness. He wished her well and, if not by now, then soon that her life would be filled with happiness. Bill again closed the letter with *Eternally*, but then he studied that word on the paper and slowly moved his head side to side as he made a scoffing sound, thinking, *Eternally ...that lasted about as long as my one testicle,* then in an instant, an image of Ann crossed his mind, and the feelings of love he still had for her struck his heart. The image of Ann was from the day before her graduation when he saw her talking and laughing with the other students. How beautiful she was then, how beautiful she would always be to him. Bill placed the letter in an envelope and sealed it. He wrote Ann's name on the envelope. Where the stamp should be placed, he wrote the date, and where the return address would go, he wrote the location, *Walter Reed, Washington, D.C.* Bill opened the bed stand drawer again and placed the letter there, along with the letter he had written to Ann in Germany.

Sunday morning Ann woke up to a beautiful day. Since the conversation with her mom on Friday, she had begun to regain control of her life. Her apartment was a little tidier, her hair washed, and she had put on fresh pj's for the night. She knew what must be done today, and she could do it. But, first item on her list was a brisk walk, and she was soon out the door.

Ann crossed the street in front of her apartment — mostly deserted on a Sunday morning — and made her way to the park. For most of her walk, Ann's focus was on the moment: crisp fresh air, leaves beginning to display their fall colors, and a cloudless, blue sky. It was only when she saw couples jogging or walking together or when she would pass a young mother pushing a stroller, that Ann found her thoughts returning to Bill as well as to what lay ahead for her. Twice she fought back the tears and forced her thoughts to return to the beauty of the moment.

Ann worked throughout the day, playing catch-up with those things that had been neglected over the past few days. After a light dinner, she cleared the few dishes from the kitchen table, took pen and paper from the drawer and, with both immense sadness and resolve, she wrote to Bill.

> *September 21st*
> *Dear Bill,*
> *Through conversations with your mother, I have now learned some details about your crash and your injuries. While this is more than what you shared with me before you stopped writing, I believe there is even more. Knowing you, I doubt you have told your mom everything. I am sorry that you are going through all of this and have faith that your wounds will heal.*

Bill, I don't understand why you are shutting me out. What good does it do you; do us? By doing so, do you think you are protecting me? If so, then you are wrong. You are hurting me and building a wall around you that no one can penetrate.

There are changes going on in my life right now. These changes are because of you, a part of you, but I cannot and will not share them with you when I believe that you are trying to shut me out of your life. If you don't step forward soon to restore what we had, what we have dreamed of, then you are going to get what I guess you are wanting now and that will be a tragedy for you, for me, for us.

Forever,
Ann

Ann placed the folded letter into an envelope and, without leaving her seat, wedged it into the edge of the door frame — sure to see it on her way out the door to work in the morning. Tomorrow, the letter would be on its way to Bill in Germany, to the latest address she had for him, the one she got from his mother. With the letter finished, Ann remained at the table and watched the sun disappear over the horizon. It had been a beautiful day, but it was coming to an end; sadness swept over her as she thought of her relationship with Bill in the same way — beautiful but, as impossible as it seemed, coming to an end. Ann knew she would always love Bill.

Sylvia waited nearly a week for Bill to call again, but he didn't. She did receive one very brief note — written the day after his call — letting her know he was fine and would call again soon.

Since Bill's last call, she had not heard from Ann either and had a sinking feeling that Bill had not called her. If he had, Sylvia was sure Ann would have phoned to let her know. Out of frustration with her son and out of desperation to try to help him not destroy his relationship with Ann, Sylvia decided she would call Ann again. If she confirmed her fears — that Bill had neither written again nor called Ann — she would try her best to convince her that Bill would come around, that Ann just needed to give him a little more time.

As Sylvia dialed Ann's number, she recalled their last conversation — brief and strained. Sylvia had phoned to share the latest from Bill, but also with hope that Ann already knew because she, too, had heard from him. As they talked, it had become clear that Ann had not heard from Bill. Her responses to what Sylvia had shared and questions she had asked were brief and not engaging. It was clear to Sylvia that Ann did not want to talk.

"Hello."

The answer startled Sylvia. It was a man's voice. Sylvia didn't know what to think. Had she dialed the wrong number? "May I speak to Ann please?" was all that Sylvia could get out.

"She's in the shower right now."

"Oh, OK. Will you ask her to call me back? This is Sylvia Weber."

"I will. But we're going out just as soon as she's ready. Not sure when she will be calling you."

"Oh, then that's OK. Thank you." Sylvia hung up the phone. Her heart sank. It was too late; Ann had moved on. There was someone new in her life. Bill had been successful; he had shut Ann out, and now she had found someone new. Feelings of sadness and anger erupted within Sylvia. She was sad that Ann had moved on, and that she had waited too long to try to talk to her. She felt anger as well as sadness for Bill. He was a fool for letting Ann go.

"Who was that?" Ann asked as she walked into the living room in her robe and towel wrapped around her wet hair.

"Just a marketer," Bob answered without looking directly at his sister.

"I wish they would stop calling," was all Ann said, as she disappeared into the bathroom to finish getting ready.

Bob was a little surprised that he had lied to his sister, but he had. After conversations with their mom and some time spent listening to Ann, Bob was now projecting himself as the helpful big brother. Bill had already brought too much hurt to his sister. No need to add to it through conversations with his mother.

Ann was soon ready, and out the door they went. Bob had volunteered to take his sister to her doctor's appointment. She needed the support of her family to make it through this and was grateful they were close. Bob was good at listening to his sister and protecting her when she needed it.

Ann was exhausted — physically and emotionally. The day had been a long one, but also it marked the end of another week without anything from Bill. With a sickening feeling, Ann knew one last thing had to be done before the day came to an end. It was time to write her final letter to Bill.

Sitting at the kitchen table, she saw that it was pitch black outside — no moon shone through and a heavy layer of clouds blanketed the night sky.

September 28th
Dear Bill,

Despite my continued efforts, I have received nothing from you in return. As such, this is my last letter to you.
I will never understand you or your actions.
As sure as life does go on, so too must I without you.
Forever,
Ann

Ann looked at the letter. It was hard to believe that all they had shared, all they had talked about for their future now boiled down to these final, few words and a ... *Forever.* Ann wasn't sure why she wrote it this time. Maybe it stemmed from her anger, and she was using it to remind Bill, ironically, of what he was giving up. How could she possibly love someone *forever* who had been so cruel in breaking off what they had with coldness and then nothing, just an absence, as if he had simply disappeared. Then her thoughts switched. Maybe she did still love him, despite it all, as crazy as that sounded. What did it matter? Bill no longer loved her.

Chapter Sixteen

BILL'S BODY JERKED AND, AS IT DID, HE AWOKE WITH his heart pounding. His hands grasped the bed rails and held on tight. It was the dream, the reoccurring one that shattered his sleep and sent waves of panic tearing through him. In some aspects — usually the setting — each dream was different from one another, but all included Ann, Bill struggling in some way, and falling.

This time, the dream had placed Bill in a cockpit at night — dark except for the glow of the red-tinted lights from the instrument panel. There was another pilot in the left seat, but he couldn't tell who it was, and no words were exchanged. Although he couldn't see her, Bill knew that Ann was sitting in the cargo area behind his seat. He could hear her voice — trying to shout above the noise of the engine and rotorblades but he couldn't understand what she was saying. He wanted the other pilot to take the controls, so he could turn to see Ann, but no matter whatever he tried to do, nothing happened. Bill keyed his mic but his voice was not heard over the intercom. He tried to wave his arm but could not move it. The urgency he felt to understand Ann turned into a panic when he could not. Then he could feel the aircraft starting to fall. It was the falling sensation that always caused Bill to jerk, to reach out for whatever he could hold onto.

As he fought to become fully awake and shake the feeling of panic, Bill tried to focus on the moment. From the diminishing amount of light in his hospital room, he knew that most of the afternoon was gone. Looking out the window, Bill saw a gray sky and snow falling. Not big, white, beautiful flakes, but rather tiny nondescript ones just past the drizzle stage. Pretty miserable, he thought.

Bill continued surveying his small hospital room and realized that his lunch tray had been removed from the stand adjacent to his bed. In its place was a small stack of mail, four or five pieces in all. His first thought was to just let them lie there; nothing much interested him these days, including any mail that he might receive. Bill turned his attention back to the window, to the falling snow. A few minutes passed and, mostly out of boredom, he reached for the mail, laid the pieces in his lap, and with limited, deliberate efforts picked up the first one. Casts, bandages, and jolts of pain when he made the slightest movement continued to make the simplest tasks difficult.

It was from his mother — probably another card — and he laid it off to the side to open later. The next was an advertisement, which he flipped toward the small garbage can by his bed. It was the next envelope that caught him by surprise and brought his senses into sharp focus. It was a letter from Ann, one that had been forwarded to him from the hospital in Germany. The envelope bore the marks of multiple handlings and circuitous routing to reach him. Bill studied the envelope briefly as his hand rotated it upward in an effort to see the next piece of mail; it was a second letter from Ann also forwarded from Germany, and equally tattered. He laid both envelopes on the stand by his bed — unopened.

Bill's stare returned to the dismal weather outside his window, but his thoughts were on the two unopened letters. He tried to calculate when they might have been written and wondered if one or both was after Ann received *the letter*. He also wondered about the two pieces arriving together. Had one letter been held in Germany for a longer period of time than the other? Then he decided that neither the letters nor the timing really mattered. Nothing was going to change.

As time had moved forward since *the letter,* Bill had experienced fleeting thoughts that he would give anything to take it back. But, most of the time, he felt that what he had done was right and that Ann deserved more than he could ever give her. Regardless of which line of thinking filled his thoughts, the ending point was always the same — he was without Ann in his life and it hurt more than he could have ever imagined.

Though he tried to resist, Bill slowly reached for the two unopened letters. As he tried to grasp them in his hand, one slipped from his fingers and fell to the floor. *Guess that answers the question of which one to open first,* Bill thought.

Bill examined the second envelope once again, as he sought to both mentally prepare himself for whatever her letter might say as well as offer himself a reminder that nothing Ann might write would change what he had set into motion. Still, his hands trembled and sadness swelled from within as he opened one end of the envelope, trying to keep it as intact as possible.

September 28th
Dear Bill,
Despite my continued efforts, I have received nothing from you in return. As such, this is my last letter to you.
I will never understand you or your actions.
As sure as life does go on, so too must I without you.
Forever,
Ann

Though he had cast the die with *the letter* to Ann, the finality of it all hit him with a force that took his breath away. He felt stabbed in the heart. Reading Ann's chosen words, Bill was certain *the letter* had reached Ann. *Your actions* was Ann referring to the lie he had written; she couldn't bear to repeat in words what he had said, what he'd done. Just as he wished for her, she was moving on with her life — *so too must I without you.* A wave of emotions and thoughts overcame Bill. *How could it have all gone so wrong? How could it be that two people meant to be together for all time were not? In time, Ann would have another love and a family, but what about me? A broken body, an uncertain future, and an incredible, heart-wrenching void from a sacrifice that seemed a little less noble at times, yet necessary* — so he thought. Bill read Ann's letter twice more before he folded it and placed it inside the envelope. His stare returned to the gray sky that filled his window.

"L-T, time to head to x-ray."

The sound of the voice surprised Bill and broke him away from the thoughts that burdened his mind and ate at his heart. The technician had walked in without Bill hearing the door open.

"Would you do me a favor first?" Bill asked.

"I'll try. What's up?"

"See the envelope on the floor by the foot of my bed?"

"Here you go." In a single, continuous motion, the young technician picked up the letter and extended his arm to hand it to over.

"No, that one goes in the trashcan."

"Are you sure L-T? Looks like it hasn't been opened. Don't you want to read it first?"

"Just toss it. No need for me to read it. All I need to know is in this one," Bill said as he held up Ann's letter, the one he had just read. Then he asked, "Will you stick this one in the second drawer of the stand?"

The orderly opened the drawer and dropped the letter in. "OK, that's done, and now life goes on, my man. Let's get you down to x-ray."

Bill flinched. He felt like he had been shocked by the technician's words — life goes on. The same parting words that Ann wrote. "Yeah, life goes on ... maybe," Though he sought to echo the technician's sentiments, Bill's voice trailed off to a barely audible *maybe*.

As Bill moved from his bed to the gurney and then down the hallway to x-ray, he thought about the past, and his life from this day forward, a life without Ann. Their lives — intertwined since that summer's day by the bay — had now unraveled. She was no more — except in his heart that ached.

Part Two

Through the Years:
Excerpts from a Lifetime of Letters Not Shared

AS THE YEARS PASSED, BILL ALLOWED ONLY A VERY few individuals to get close to him. Then there was Ann; she remained in Bill's heart and often on his mind. When loneliness struck, when his heart ached for her, when his thoughts and yearnings took him back to their time together, or when there was good news to share, Bill would find himself writing to Ann.

As his words unfolded on the paper, he always felt as if he were talking to her, rather than just writing a note. He continued to close each letter with *Eternally*. Though they weren't together, and the word no longer held the meaning that it once did, Ann remained in Bill's heart. He was sure she would be there always.

Each letter written was carefully folded, inserted in an envelope that was sealed, and then placed into a wooden box kept near by his desk. The letters were never mailed; Ann would never read them.

One Year

Dear Ann,

I received very good news today! The medical review board cleared me to fly again. It is hard to believe that fourteen months have passed since the crash and since our lives took different paths. The rehabilitation effort and obtaining approval to fly again have certainly been difficult and, at times, seemed almost impossible, but I made it.

I remember when I first told you about wanting to fly helicopters. It was the night of your winter formal, and you weren't very happy about it. Throughout flight school, I had thoughts of one day surprising you with a helicopter ride along the shoreline of the bay and over the ballfield where we met, but that is not to be now.

Instead, I think about what has taken place in your life over these same months. I wonder if you have met some-one that you will spend the rest of your life with, to have the family with that you desire so much.

Tomorrow, I head back to Fort Rucker for a two-week refresher course — just to get used to the controls again and for an Instructor Pilot's sign-off that I can still fly. I cannot wait to get there and get started. I have missed that incredible feeling of being in the air and that sense of freedom. After the refresher course, my next assignment is Fort Carson. I feel really fortunate to be going there as well, just not sure how long I will stay. A rotation back to Vietnam may be in my future.

I hope you are feeling fortunate with the way your life is now taking shape.

> *Eternally,*
> *Bill*

Five Years

Dearest Ann,
I started a letter to you four days ago — a letter that was going to be very different than what I now write. It was to

say to you that I had met a wonderful woman, maybe even one who I would propose to one day. I was going to bring my letter writing to a close, and planned to destroy all of my previous letters to you. But, all of that has changed.

This evening, as we kissed, I called her Ann by mistake. Of course, she was upset and I apologized. She asked about you and about us. I didn't tell her much but even as I shared what little that I did, I realized that the relationship with her had come to its end. It wasn't right to keep going when I knew my true feelings were not with her.

You really have remained in my heart all this time. How could I ever truly and fully love another when you are always there? You have been a part of me since that day we first met and remain as such — even today.

Even though I had the thoughts of doing so, I really didn't want to stop writing to you or destroy all the letters that I have written. They are a part of me, and the only part of us that exists. It really isn't right to say 'us' — since you are not receiving the letters — but it is us in that you are in my heart to stay.

Eternally,
Bill

Fifteen Years

Dear Ann,
The last week or so has been extra busy for me, but as always you have frequently crossed my mind. My surroundings take me back to a very different time in my life, a time we once shared. Exactly five days ago, I assumed

command of an aviation unit. It's the same unit I was assigned to in Vietnam, but now it's at Fort Hood, Texas.

When I was a lieutenant and assigned to this battalion, I never dreamed that one day I would be its commander. Now I am and have lots of lieutenants working for me. I have thought about Lt. Estep — the two of us lieutenants and fresh out of flight school. We lost contact with one another; someone told me he left the service several years ago.

So much has changed about the Army over the years. An Army career is not for everyone, and it can be hard on families. I have often wondered how you and I would have weathered it. But, one thing that has not changed is me still being called Harry, that is except for family. After flight school, after the crash and what I did to you, I deliberately held onto "Harry." Though it has taken me awhile, I think I know why I did. It was a convenient way to run from or separate out the pain and emptiness I was feeling. Feelings that I brought upon myself through what I did to us.

How I hope and pray that life has been so very good to you.

Eternally,
Bill

Twenty-Five Years

Dear Ann,

Today, this long chapter in my life comes to a close and a new one — not yet clearly defined — awaits me. I am now officially retired from the U.S. Army: twenty-six years' and six months' worth. As with today and every milestone along the way, you have been a part of my thoughts, my wondering.

If you had been present today at the retirement ceremony, you would have heard my commander and others refer to me a number of times as "Harry." As I listened, I had this thought of you standing up in the middle of the ceremony to correct the speaker, "His name is Bill, not Harry." It made me smile. Over the years I really have come to understand that my clinging to "Harry" was really more about hiding or sheltering myself from the past, that time in my life when I was Bill to the world and you were a part of it; you were everything. Foolish — yes, perhaps it was, but now, as if in a blink of an eye, my military career has come to a close and life as it is goes on ...as Harry.

My plan is to remain in the Fort Lewis area for the time being. I may have a job offer that will take me back overseas, which would be fine. For a little while, I did give some thought to moving to Summersville. I haven't been back in all these years, but maybe one day I'll make it there.

Speaking of years, I can only imagine what has taken place with you and your family. Perhaps you are even attending a college or high school graduation for one of your children. So many times, I have wondered how many children you have and whether any or all share your beauty. When I think of you, it is impossible for me to think of anything but the best of life coming your way — no sickness or injuries, just good days like sunshine on the bay.

Eternally,

Bill

Forty Years

Dear Ann,

I am writing this letter while sitting in my living room, which is mostly bare as is the rest of the house. Tomorrow, I pack a few things into my car and then make the drive to my new home in Summersville. While I'm still a little shocked that this move is taking place, it also feels so very right. The move is like coming home, not to the place where I lived before but coming home to where my heart has really been over these many years.

All of this came about because of an article I read. It was in the local newspaper and described the Drake Living Center with all it has to offer as a retirement center. But, even better is that my condo has a great view of the bay and the ballfield. What a beautiful site for my eyes to see!

Of course, as the time has grown closer for me to make the move I have thought of you so much: I am assuming you still live in Summersville but no idea where. Where do you shop and visit frequently? I wonder if one day our paths might cross in a grocery store or maybe at a gas station. Perhaps we will be sitting in our vehicles at an intersection at the same time. Would we even recognize one another?

Even though all these years have passed and youth has given way to these golden years, I believe the feelings of the heart remain forever young. Thank you for making those feelings possible within me.

Eternally,

Bill

Part Three

Answering Love's Final Call

Chapter Seventeen

BILL MADE HIS WAY TO HIS CAR AND, AS HE DID, noticed just how much the temperature had dropped; summer was drawing to a close. He tossed the envelope onto the passenger's seat but made no immediate effort to start the car; rather he was deep in thought. Along the way, Bill had purchased a few houses, but now he wondered — *Would the condo in Summersville be his last?* Age, injuries, genetics, and bouts with cancer were all adding up to cut a crease across his longevity line. At different times, Bill found himself both amazed that he had lived as long as he had — soon to turn 68 — and just how quickly those years had passed.

Tap, tap, tap. The title closer had tapped on the driver's window while speaking in a loud voice that startled Bill and brought his drifting thoughts to an abrupt close.

"Christ, you about scared me to death," Bill let him know in no uncertain terms as he rolled down the window.

"Harry, sorry to have startled you. I forgot to put the last of the closing documents in the other envelope and wanted to make sure you had them before you drove off. " The closer passed the documents through the half-opened window and turned quickly to return to his office. He felt the dropping temperature as well.

Bill glanced at the top document — a title insurance policy issued to Mr. W. Harold Weber. He then added it and the last of the documents to those already in the envelope, pulled out of the parking lot, and headed home. There were quite a few things to get done before he headed to Summersville. Bill grinned when he thought of moving there. The last time he was in Summersville, the old, majestic stone buildings that were now refurbished as the Drake Living Center and housed his condo had stood abandoned and neglected, an eyesore in an otherwise beautiful city. The move to his new home was just a four-hour drive to the north, but the planning to do so and now the completed closing had turned Bill's thoughts and memories back to his youth and, of course, to Ann.

"I'm calling about the ad you placed in the paper — household goods for sale," the female caller's voice was soft and slightly timid.

"OK," was Bill's only response. He had taken three calls before this one and, after they turned out so poorly, really wasn't in the mood to take another one. But he was also anxious to find the right someone to take possession of the household items vaguely referenced in the ad.

After a few seconds of silence, the caller asked, "Can you tell me what all you have?"

"What are you looking for?" Bill asked.

Again, a few seconds of silence before the caller spoke. "Well, just about everything. My husband and I are just starting out, and we don't have much."

"Why don't you have much?"

"Pardon me?"

"I said, 'Why don't you have much?'" Bill's abrupt response sounded part inquisitive and part demanding. This was out of character for him, but he had taken on a temporary persona in his search to find just the right person.

The caller hesitated, trying to decide whether to answer or hang up on this rude person. She decided to answer. "Well, I finished college in August, and my husband just got out of the military. He was overseas until last week. We had a few things in storage, but someone broke into the storage locker and stole everything." She paused, and when Bill said nothing, she added, "We have a small place rented, but nothing to put into it."

"What's your name?" Bill asked in a different demeanor — softer and friendly. He figured as gruff as he had been, this young lady was probably having her doubts about him, and he didn't want her to hang up. Bill had decided this couple were the ones.

"Helen, Helen Thomas, and my husband is Ben," she answered, without understanding what was happening.

"Let me give you my address. Got pen and paper handy? Can you and your husband be here at 8:30 tomorrow morning?" Bill rattled off quickly.

"But I still don't know what you have to sale."

"Don't worry about that. I plan on giving you everything I have in the house and garage, except for a couple of things I have set off to the side."

Helen was silent; she did not know what to say or think. She had called expecting to find a lead on a few things for their apartment, been spoken to by a rude man, and now this same man — this stranger — said he would give everything to them.

"Well, can you be here or not?" Bill asked, filling in the silence.

"I am sure we can, but I don't understand."

"Don't need to right now. Just be here in the morning and plan on making a day of it. You may need a few friends a little later in the day to help you load the stuff. My address is 1801 Stone Creek, which is off Highway 31, just south of town."

Still uncertain, Helen answered, "I know where Stone Creek is. Thank you so much. Whatever you have, we appreciate it. And umm ... Well, see you tomorrow."

Bill could hear the uncertainty in her voice and wondered what she'd say to her husband to convince him to make the drive over to a place where a really odd man wanted to give all his things away. "See you in the morning, Helen," was all Bill offered in response.

He hung up the phone and his eyes scanned the room. Within 24 hours or so, all of the furniture and furnishings he owned would be gone. The exceptions had been carefully packed in a few boxes and, along with a couple of other items, collectively set off to the side of his living room. They would accompany him to the Drake.

Bill's doorbell rang precisely at 8:30. "I'm coming," he called out as he made his way to the front door and opened it. There stood the caller and her husband — he was sure it was them — both looking a little unsure of what might happen next.

"Good morning," Bill offered with a smile. "I bet you are Helen and Ben. Am I correct?

"Yes sir, I'm Ben Thomas and this is my wife, Helen."

"Well, it's nice to meet you. Come on in." Bill opened the door and motioned inward.

Ben and Helen surveyed the living room contents then looked at one another. They were stunned at what they saw: beautiful furniture that appeared almost brand-new.

"Have a seat." Bill motioned to offer them the couch as he took a seat in his chair by the window. "Ben, Helen said you just left the service. What did you do?"

"Sir, I was in the Army and spent three years as a medic."

"How about we drop the *sir* and just call me ..." Bill paused and then lightly smacked his forehead with his hand before he continued. "My gosh, where are my manners? When you came in, I forgot to tell you my name. Weber is the last name, but you can call me Bill or Harry. It' a long story, but it was Harry when I was in the Army and most of the time I worked after retiring from the service. Bill takes me back to my youth."

"You were in the Army?" Ben was surprised but also felt an immediate connection.

"Yep, 26 years' worth. I flew helicopters, except when they made me fly a desk; I hated that."

"Wow! That must have been exciting. I got to go up in a chopper a couple of times, once during basic training and once in Germany. I loved it. Bet you have some incredible flying stories." Ben leaned forward as if eager to hear about his flying.

Bill did not respond to Ben's statement, but rather turned the conversation. "Helen, you said you just graduated from college. Where'd you go, and what was your major?"

"I was a sociology major at Central State. It's a pretty small college, so not a lot of people know about it. But, it's only about a hundred miles from Summersville, and a lot more people are familiar with it. Have you ever heard of Central or Summersville?"

Bill chuckled then answered, "Yes, I'm familiar with both; made quite a few trips to each way back when. Actually, I'm headed to Summersville. That's where I am moving to."

"No kidding! I have a sorority sister from Summersville, and after college she moved back there. Sarah was a couple of years ahead of me. I visited Summersville once to see her, and it seems like a real nice town. The bay is so beautiful."

"As you kids get older, you'll see just how much the world shrinks. Here we just met and already made a connection through the Army, Central, and Summersville." Though Bill spoke the words and smiled at Helen and Ben, his thoughts were of Summersville, the bay, and how his life had been shaped by what took place there so long ago.

"Sir, about the furniture ..." Before Ben could continue, Bill cut him off.

"Nope, got to drop the *sir*."

Ben smiled, thought for a moment, and then said. "OK, I'll try. Since you were Harry in the service, and I was in the service, I will go with Harry *if* that is OK with you."

"Sure."

"Well, we have enough money to pay for a couple of items, but it looks like you may have a whole houseful of really nice stuff." Ben paused, not sure how to say what was on his mind, but then continued, "Helen said you mentioned something about just giving it to us." The closing part of Ben's words was spoken more as a question that he was embarrassed to ask. "We don't understand."

"Are the two of you good people?" Bill asked.

Ben wasn't sure what he was asking or why, but he looked at Helen as he answered the question. "We try to be."

"I think you are and think you could use a little bit of a break just starting out." Bill paused, then continued. "As for me, I'm winding things down. No wife and no kids; a brother and sister, and both have plenty. So, I figured that I would run the ad — vague as it was — and try to find the right someone that could benefit from what I have." He paused for a moment, then continued. "You interested?" Bill asked but already knew from the looks on Ben and Helen's faces that they were excited about their good fortune.

"Mr. Weber, how can we ever thank you enough or repay you in some way?" Helen asked as she was almost moved to tears by his generosity.

"First, you can stop calling me Mr. Weber, and second, maybe send me a Christmas card with a picture of you two in your apartment," Bill responded in a joking manner as he chuckled, then added, "But mostly, just enjoy the things, and remember what I'm giving you are just things — not real important. What's important in life is what you have in one another.

"Now, let me show you what I have, what's about to become yours," Bill said as he rose to his feet and headed toward the hallway. As the three made their way through the house, he pointed out the items in each room and the couple remained speechless, often glancing at the other or squeezing one another's hand as shared signals of excitement. After entering the kitchen, the last room of the tour, and seeing the assortment of dishes, pots and pans, utensils, and other items, Ben was the first to speak.

"Are you sure about this? You could have a garage sale or even get an auction company to clear out the house for you. You must have several thousand dollars worth of furniture and everything else in the house."

Bill just looked at Ben and then Helen. The young couple stood arm in arm, leaning against the kitchen counter. He knew he had found the right ones; he wanted them to have it all. He chose to ignore Ben's question about being sure.

"You ready to look in the garage? I have some things there, too," Bill said to the two of them as he picked up the garage door opener from the counter. By now, he had a twinkle in his eyes and was enjoying seeing the excitement that Helen and Ben could barely contain. The two were right behind him as they headed out the side door to the detached garage.

Standing in the driveway, Bill pushed the button on the garage door opener, and it began to slowly lift. As it did, the overhead light came on, which helped showcase all that was there. Ben had never seen a garage so organized, so bright. Gardening tools hung on the walls, and power tools of every assortment were lined up on the workbenches. Parked in the garage was a Ford pickup truck. Ben figured it to be about 10 or 12 years old, but it looked as if it had just come off the showroom floor.

"That's a great-looking truck," Ben said as he made his way to the driver's door to take a look inside.

"Only has 47,000 miles on it," Bill let Ben know.

Ben looked the truck over, as did Helen, although clearly not with the same enthusiasm, before he asked, "What's here in the garage that you would like us to take?"

"Everything." Bill smiled at Ben and tossed him the ignition key to the truck that had been in his pocket.

Ben snagged the key out of the air, looked at it with disbelief, and asked, as if dreaming. "Everything?"

"Yep, it's all yours."

In excitement and celebration, Ben picked Helen up and spun around twice before he kissed her and then set her back down. As far as he was concerned, he had just won the lottery: a pickup truck in pristine condition and more tools that he could have ever hoped for in his lifetime.

"There are boxes and tape in the back of the garage. Should be everything you need to start packing," Bill said. "That's part of the deal: You pack, you move it all." Then he smiled as Ben and Helen stood facing one another, holding hands; first glancing at one another — expressing love without words and gratefulness at what the world had brought to them this day — then back at Bill with gratitude and as if to make sure they weren't dreaming.

Helen walked to where he was standing and gave him a big hug, which caught him a little off-guard. "Mr. Weber you are a wonderful man. You have no idea just how much this means to us. You have changed our lives forever."

"I don't know about being wonderful, but I do know for sure that you aren't supposed to be calling me *Mister Weber,* and you best get to work," Bill joked, trying to mask his uncomfortable feelings at being hugged and referred to as wonderful.

Helen, Ben, and the friends they were able to recruit worked steadily as they moved about the house and garage to pack and remove what once was Bill's. All now belonged to the lucky couple. Ben had found a larger storage unit in a more secure part of town, and everything was being moved there for now. The bed of the pickup was filled over and over again with boxes and furniture as the moving crew took things to storage only to return and immediately fill the truck again.

"Pizza's here. Time to take a break," Bill called out twice, once to Helen and her friends who were in one of the bedrooms packing and once at the side door to Ben and his friends in the garage doing the same. Using the folding lawn chairs and packing boxes as temporary tables, they gathered in the living room.

"Mr. Weber, Ben says all you're taking with you is stacked over there in the corner. You're traveling light." It was one of the young men, Tyler, helping with the move, who commented between bites of pizza.

"There goes that *mister* again ... and you're correct. Don't need much there; and what I do need mostly comes with the place."

"Where are you moving to?" Tyler asked.

"Summersville, into a small condo located at the Drake Living Center." Then Bill chuckled. "But the living part is a little suspect; mostly old people getting ready to kick the bucket."

"You're moving to Drake?" Helen asked in an excited fashion. "That's where my sorority sister works. The one I mentioned to you this morning, Sarah. Now I know where to send your Christmas card." Helen smiled. Only she, Ben, and Bill knew what she was talking about.

"Did you make those two wooden boxes?" Ben asked, as he used a slice of pizza to point in the direction of the corner. The boxes Ben pointed to were made of cherry, simple in design, but eloquent in their craftsmanship. Each top was held closed with a small locking mechanism built into the front side. Though he asked the question, Ben was pretty certain of the answer based on the assortment of woodworking tools in the garage.

"I did."

"Do you have treasure stored inside them?" Tyler asked, trying to make a joke.

"Sort of. At least it is treasure to me, but just paper and envelopes to everyone else."

"They're full of bills?" Tyler continued to try to joke, but no one laughed.

"No, just letters, lots of letters."

Helen set her paper plate down, stood, and walked toward the corner of the living room where the two wooden boxes, a few cardboard boxes, and a garment bag had been placed; the items that would accompany him to Drake. "I'm going to hang your suit bag up in the closet. Don't want your clothes to wrinkle." The garment bag Helen was reaching for was lying across the boxes.

"That's OK, you don't —" Bill tried to stop her, but it was too late.

As Helen picked the bag up by the protruding hangars, the front of the bag turned to face all who were sitting in the living room. While the back of the bag, which had been previously visible to the group, was black, the front was a clear plastic — allowing the contents to be seen. The bag held only two items, and the front item was Bill's Army uniform — a set of dress blues. His nametag, insignias, silver wings, and rows of medals adorned the uniform as if ready for inspection.

Ben stood to take a closer look, and when he did, he recognized the Purple Heart and Silver Star medals. He was pretty sure the highest-ranking medal on the uniform was the Distinguished Service Cross but wasn't positive. Ben looked at Bill, and each acknowledged what was known only to them at that moment: the sacrifices of their brotherhood.

"It's wonderful that you still have your uniform after all these years," Helen innocently stated.

"Yeah, I keep it ready," was Bill's only comment.

"Do you ever wear it?" Helen asked, as she continued to look at all that adorned the uniform.

"Not lately. But I plan on wearing it to the last formation."

Helen looked at Ben as if not understanding Bill's response and not certain if she should ask further. Ben returned a look that said, *Let it go. I'll tell you later.* Helen handed the garment bag to Ben for him to hang in the closet. As he took the bag from Helen, he looked at her then turned to Bill, and rendered to him one of the sharpest salutes he had ever executed. No one else understood, and no one asked.

Little remained; left in the house were a single bed from one of the guest bedrooms, an old rocking chair, a lamp, and those items accompanying Bill to the Drake Living Center. Bill, Helen, and Ben stood in the driveway watching the others drive away after a full day of packing and moving. The sun was setting, and part of the sky blazed with the last of its rays while darkness began to creep its way across the eastern sky.

"So, you kids will be back in the morning to get the last few things?" Bill asked.

"8:30 again?" Ben asked.

"Since it's Sunday, let's make it 10:00. Give you a chance to sleep in. This has been a long day for you." Bill didn't say it, but he was exhausted as well and looking forward to sleeping in a little.

"OK, we'll be here at 10:00," Helen spoke as she gave Bill another hug. This one even tighter, more sincere, as if they now shared a bond that took hold much faster than anyone could have expected that morning.

Bill waved good-bye, walked back into the house, and lowered himself into the chair. From the window, he saw the last of the sunset and then sat in darkness for a few minutes until reaching for the table lamp beside his chair.

He opened his worn briefcase beside his chair and took out paper, pen, and an envelope. It had been a good little while since he had last written, and now he felt as if it was the time to do so again — getting rid of his stuff, making Ben and Helen happy, heading to Drake tomorrow. These were the things that he liked to share in his letters.

Dear Ann ....

With the letter complete, he folded it in thirds and placed it in the envelope. Slowly rising from the chair, tired from age and the day's activities, Bill opened one of the two wooden boxes and placed the envelope in a long line of them arrayed in the top tray of the box. This box, like the other one beneath it, was full of letters to Ann. He wasn't sure just how many more envelopes would fit, but probably 25, maybe even close to 40 if he jammed the last few in. Bill closed the lid, returned to the chair, and looked at the small array of items headed to Summersville with him. He let out a soft chuckle. Life all boiled down to this now. As he leaned back in his chair to rest, Bill's thoughts were on his move to Summersville, his new place, and how long he might live there. Just as the space was limited in the box, so too did Bill's sense of his time on this Earth. He wanted to be in Summersville when that time came.

Chapter Eighteen

"JUST A MINUTE AND I'LL GIVE YOU A HAND," CALLED out a loud, friendly voice.

Bill had noticed the man working around the shrubbery as he pulled into his assigned parking space at the Drake Living Center for the very first time. Just as he opened the back hatch of his vehicle to begin unloading boxes, the stranger's offer led him to stop and turn around. "Believe I'll take you up on that. Thanks."

"Hi, I'm Frank, maintenance supervisor here at the Center, but sort of a jack of all trades, including helping folks move," he offered as he walked toward Bill. "You must be the new owner of 701?" Frank smiled and extended his hand to Bill after removing his well-worn work gloves and placing them in his back pocket.

Bill shook Frank's hand. "It's nice to meet you, Frank. I'm Harry or Bill — go by either one. He could see the quizzical look on Frank's face, so he added. "Long story, but it was Bill in my youth, then Harry during my time in the Army and pretty much all the time since. 'Harry' will work fine here, in my new home. But, hey, I do appreciate your offer, wasn't looking forward to making several trips between my new place and the car."

"No problem. We'll get you moved in; it won't take any time at all. I'll go get the platform dolly and then we can use the service elevator. Bet we can make it all in one trip." Frank had casually surveyed all that was loaded in his car — not much and nothing too heavy-looking.

"I'll wait right here," was all Bill offered in response, but he had also been looking at Frank and could not help but fixate on his size. Frank was probably 6-feet-6 or 7 and pushing 300 pounds, with a massive chest and arms to match. His shirt was labeled with a weathered decal offering up his name — *Frank* — in red, cursive letters now faded almost to the point of being illegible. He looked to be in his forties and seemed to have a constant smile on his face.

As he waited on Frank to return, Bill leaned against his car and let his eyes take in all that was now to be called his home — the Drake Living Center — "a sprawling complex of stately housing and support facilities catering to citizens with senior status." At least that is what the newspaper article said, the one that had caught Bill's eye one Sunday morning almost a year ago. The article became the catalyst that started the chain of events leading to Bill now calling Drake home.

The history of Drake's land and buildings was rich; it had first served as a military academy before the Civil War, eventually becoming a private, liberal arts college at the turn of the century until it closed in the 1930s. It was named in honor of Gen. James Madison Drake, a prominent local citizen and a tireless proponent of restoring the buildings and grounds to their former glory. Restoration was complete, and the beautiful stone buildings stood as sentries on the hilltop overlooking the town of Summersville.

"OK, let's get you moved in," Frank announced through a big smile as he made his way toward Bill with cart in tow. Frank was right; everything packed in his car did fit on the dolly.

Once loaded, Frank led the way to the service elevator and talked nonstop, telling Bill about Drake and the former owner of 701: Mrs. Washington. Frank first asked if he knew Mrs. Washington, and when Bill said that he did not, proceeded to tell him all he knew. She had passed away over a year ago, after living in the unit less than two years. Most residents at there thought the reason it had taken so long for her daughter to sell the place was that the asking price was too high.

In his initial offer to buy the place, Bill had made a modest reduction in the asking price, which was rejected. He then immediately made the full-price offer. Though he had not set foot in the condo before purchasing it, he was confident of his decision. Bill's new home was the corner unit on the top floor of a seven-story building located on the highest point of Drake's grounds. It encompassed 900 square feet of living space, divided among a galley kitchen, dining area, living room, one bath, and two bedrooms, one of which would be his study. From the study, he had a picturesque view of the bay and the adjacent ballpark. It was that view, captured in a couple of the twenty-some photos sent to him by the listing agent, that had sold him on the place — sight unseen. As soon as Bill entered the condo for the first time, he walked past the kitchen and living room, making his way to what would be his study. Frank followed.

"Where do you want these?" Frank asked, as he stood at the doorway holding the two wooden boxes, one stacked on the other.

"Those go in here. Just set them on the floor beside the desk."

"Did you make them?" Frank asked as he held the two boxes slightly away from his body — emphasizing his question concerning the boxes.

"Yes, but a long time ago."

"Nice work," was Frank's only reply.

"You sure you don't want me to help you unpack or move any of the furniture around?" Frank had quickly unloaded the cart and placed each of the items as Bill directed.

"No, I'm good, but you've been a great help." Bill extended his hand to shake Frank's and to pass him a fifty-dollar bill tucked in his palm.

"Oh, I can't take that, just part of my job," Frank offered in protest.

"And this is part of my job, being appreciative of a helping hand. You earned it, and I would like for you to accept it."

"Well, OK, thanks," Frank conceded, slightly embarrassed. " Let me know if you need anything else. My wife — Pam — and I live in the old caretaker's quarters down by the administration building, so I'm always around."

"Thanks, Frank. I'll be sure to find you if something comes up."

Bill closed the front door, turned, leaned back against it, and let his eyes take in that which was now his new home: small but all that he needed. A combination of some items left from Mrs. Washington's estate and a few new things arranged for by the real estate agent provided the furnishing. All furnishings that once filled the second bedroom had been removed, and a desk, two chairs, and a tall bookshelf now filled the space. Bill made his way back to the study and sat for the first time at his new desk. The chair was comfortable, and by swiveling to his left, he could see the view that had drawn him back to Summersville: the bay and the ballpark. The ballpark lay dormant, bats and gloves put away for now, but with the arrival of spring he would have a bird's-eye view of the ballpark's activities and the sunshine sparkling on the bay.

Within an hour of his arrival, there were only two cardboard boxes left to unpack. One held the last of the books, and the other a few irreplaceable, personal treasures. One was a photo from days gone by. It was housed in an aged frame, worn along the edges from repetitive handling. He placed the photograph on the right side of his desk, strategically located so that it was visible whether he was entering the study or walking by its doorway. The next item from the box was placed eye level on the bookshelf. As he laid the baseball glove on the shelf, he lifted its fold just enough to see what remained of Ann's signature — faded to the point of almost being illegible, but the memory as crisp as the day she had signed it.

"Mr. Weber, please come in." Sarah James, Drake's activity director, offered a welcoming smile as she stood where the short hallway intersected the waiting room. As part of the Drake Living Center's orientation, Sarah met with new residents to welcome them and share information about all the activities available.

Bill slowly rose from the couch where he had just sat down, offered Sarah a smile, and said, "How about just calling me Harry, which is actually my middle name. But I have used it for so long that now I prefer it to Bill."

"Well, I'm Sarah, and it's very nice to meet you." She extended her hand to shake and when their fingers touched, each reacted to the static shock by quickly pulling their hand away.

"Wow, do you greet all the residents that way?" Bill asked as he chuckled and again extended his hand.

"Just the special ones." Sarah laughed and took his hand in both of hers.

"Let's go into my office and I'll tell about what we have to offer." Sarah was proud of the activities. She began with one that she hoped would catch his interest. "I got wind that you're a woodworker. Did you know that we have a first-class woodworking shop here?"

"What, how did ..." Bill started to ask then caught himself; he figured out the answer. "Frank must have said something."

"Yes indeed. Our Mr. Frank was telling me about the beautiful wooden boxes you made." Sarah liked that she was able to start the conversation with a little inside information. "Frank is a great guy, and he keeps a close watch on all the residents — and the staff," she added, chuckling. "We're lucky to have him here."

"Sure would hate to pay that man's grocery bill," Bill replied, and they both laughed. He noticed how Sarah's eyes sparkled when she laughed.

"Wait until you meet his wife, Pam. She's so tiny." Sarah continued, telling Bill all about the litany of activities.

While he listened and asked a question or two, Bill really wasn't too interested in participating in any of the activities, not even the woodshop.

"Are you on the meal plan?" Sarah asked in reference to the dining hall available to the residents as an option.

"Oh yes, not much of a cook and too old to start learning now."

"Well, in the spring, we offer a series of cooking classes, so you never know."

Before Bill could respond to Sarah's cooking class offer, their conversation was interrupted. Beth, an administrative assistant, had opened Sarah's door just enough to lean in.

"Sarah, Mr. Wilkins asked if you could step in his office for just a minute. I'm sorry, Mr. Weber."

"OK," Sarah said to acknowledge the request, but her facial expression showed she was not pleased. "I'll be right back, and I won't let you leave until I have you signed up for at least *one activity*," Sarah said, jokingly pointing her finger at Bill.

He just smiled at Sarah as she stood to follow Beth to her boss's office. Bill really wasn't interested in the Center's activities, but he was enjoying the conversation with Sarah. As he sat in Sarah's office alone, awaiting her return, he took further notice of his surroundings. Her office was small and the furniture not the newest, but it was warm and inviting, just like his first impression of Sarah. Except for one lithograph print of the Drake Living Center as a college, the rest of the artwork on the walls was more an eclectic combination of everything from abstract to children's artwork to a couple of inspirational illustrations — the wisdom of the aged and one urging the viewer to embrace the moment.

Behind her desk was a bookshelf housing books, a couple of plants, and three photos in frames: one large and smaller ones on each side. Bill's aging eyes strained to see the details in the smaller photos. Though not clear, in the larger photo he could make out what he thought to be the images of two women and a baby on one of their laps. Bill wondered if maybe one of them was Sarah. He had noticed that she was not wearing a wedding band on her finger but no idea if she had children or not.

When Sarah did not return to her office within a few minutes, Bill decided he would leave; she was busy, and he really wasn't interested in the activities. As he stood and momentarily paused to steady himself, his gaze again focused on the larger photo behind her desk. There was something about the photo that drew him in, seemed somehow familiar, but he wasn't about to walk behind Sarah's desk to take a closer look. Bill made his way out of Sarah's office and down the hallway without seeing her or Beth. It was time for lunch, anyway.

"Carl, today I think I will have the turkey with mashed potatoes and a side salad," Bill said as he handed the menu back to Carl.

"Yes, sir. That will just take a minute."

Bill had quickly come to enjoy eating in the Drake's dining hall and, like everyone else who dined there, had learned a few of the names of the waitstaff and some of the other diners. The food served was quite good and the ambiance to his liking: linen tablecloths and napkins, courteous waiters in bow ties, and a wall of windows overlooking the Drake's manicured grounds and garden. The setting reminded him of the officers' club at Fort Hood. It was the nicest one of all the places he had been stationed during his career, and one that Bill frequented on a regular basis.

"Mr. Weber, I brought you a little bowl of tomato basil soup to sample. Have you tried it yet?" Carl began moving Bill's lunchtime selections from his tray to the table.

"I don't think I have, but it sounds good. It was feeling pretty chilly on the walk over here. Turning into soup weather."

"Anything else I can get for you right now?"

"Think this will do me for now, but I could probably be persuaded to have a piece of pecan pie a little later on."

"Somehow I knew that request was coming," Carl joked with Bill before turning to walk away. Then Carl paused and turned back toward Bill. "Mr. Weber, you have a visitor, and it looks like you might be in trouble."

Bill looked up and saw what Carl was referring to: Sarah was walking toward his table, smiling, but shaking her finger at him. Almost a week had passed since their brief meeting, and he figured she was coming to give him a hard time about slipping out of her office while she was with her boss.

"Mr. Weber!" Sarah stated in a teasing, exasperated fashion as she now stood beside Bill's table with her hands on her hips.

He had laid his napkin off to the side and stood to greet her. His thoughts were of her smile — so radiant — and making up an excuse as to why he'd left her office while she was out. Just as he started to speak, still not quite certain what excuse he would offer, he was caught totally off-guard by Sarah's action.

She extended her arms and gave him a warm, sincere hug, then squeezed his hand affectionately before letting it go, and then said, "Mr. Weber! Why didn't you tell me about meeting Helen and Ben? I can't believe what you did for them!"

For just a second, Bill drew a blank from what Sarah said, but then smiled. "Please have a seat," he offered as he pulled the chair out from the table for her to sit.

"Helen phoned yesterday, telling me all about how you met and all that you did for her and Ben. She sounded so excited and thinks you're the most wonderful man on earth! Ben does too, and he told Helen that you are a real hero from your military days. They were so moved by you and your generosity. That really was so very kind of you!"

"It's a long story. Besides, their taking most of my things helped me out." Bill sought to downplay what had taken place and wanted to change the subject. "Say, after you *abandoned* me in your office, I was looking and noticed the larger photo on your bookshelf."

Sarah cut him off, "That's me as a baby with my mom and grandmother. It's the only photo of the three of us together." Sarah then turned the conversation back to their meeting. "But, I did not *abandon* you! I was only gone for 10 minutes — Mr. Wilkins is quite a talker —and when I returned *you* were gone." Sarah, too, was teasing Bill about his stealthy departure from her office. Continuing, she raised one eyebrow as she asked, "So when are you returning to my office? We have an unfinished conversation —like when you plan to participate in some of the activities just waiting for you."

"I do believe I'm free on just about any day next week that doesn't end in a *y*. Will that work for you?" Bill continued the teasing; each now seemed comfortable with passing it back and forth, but he also avoided any further discussion about the activities.

"Mr. Weber, I'm not giving up. I can be pretty stubborn myself." Sarah leaned back slightly in her chair and decided to take a little different approach. "So, what brought you to Drake? Surely it must have been all the activities I have so *tirelessly* put together just for you?" Sarah held the back of her hand against her forehead in a mock fashion as if about to faint from exhaustion.

"It was the view, and any chance you can can you call me Harry, not 'Mr. Weber? Mr. Weber sounds so formal. All my friends and Army buddies call me Harry. Is it a deal?"

"The view?" Sarah paused, not sure she understood his response. "And I will call you Harry *after* you show back up in my office to continue our discussion, but for now it is *Mr. Weber.*" Sarah smiled; she thought her strategy was pretty clever. He didn't want to be called Mr. Weber and she wanted him back in her office.

Bill ignored Sarah's reference to another office visit . "It's a long story about how I got here. Too long," he said.

"I'm listening," Sarah offered along with a smile.

"Well, I read about Drake in a newspaper article several months ago..." Before Bill could explain further, Sarah cut him off again.

"No kidding! I wrote that article! And if you recall, the article's focus was on all the activities. See, it was *destiny* that we'd meet and you'd participate in lots of activities," Sarah teased.

"Now, about the view." Continuing with the teasing, Bill chose to ignore further discussion about the article and Sarah's comment. "When I started looking into the Center and what might be for sale, I contacted a few Realtors about their listings. The one for Mrs. Washington's place was very helpful, and he sent me quite a few pictures of the place. A couple of them showed the view from the second bedroom."

Sarah gave him a quizzical look.

"The bay and the ballpark," Bill offered as clarification.

"Oh, that is a nice view. But why did that view convince you to buy? Have you lived in Summersville before?"

"Never really lived here but spent quite a bit of time visiting a long time ago. Even played baseball on that field." Bill's words seemed to trail off as his thoughts briefly drifted back to those days.

Sarah knew there was more to the story. "I need to run, but I want to hear more about the bay and the ballfield. Right now, I have an appointment with the Clarks — a couple that just moved into 403 — and I'm certain that they will not *abandon* me." Sarah smiled as she continued the teasing, but she really did want to know more about Mr. Weber. There was something a little different about him, something that seemed to draw her a little closer.

"Don't get up. Finish your lunch," Sarah said as she quickly stood and realized that he was also starting to stand out of politeness. As she spoke, she placed her hand on his shoulder. "We have lots more to discuss, you and me. That is, Sarah and *Mr. Weber,* until you show up at my office." She smiled again then turned and left.

Bill watched her walk away and, as he did, noticed her blond ponytail bouncing and that her step had quite a real pep in it. Based on first impressions, he really liked Sarah. It was his intent to not get too close to folks, and he was surprised at how open and relaxed he felt talking to her. In some ways, she reminded him of that piece of his past that now brought him to Summersville.

Chapter Nineteen

"YOU READY FOR A PIECE OF PECAN PIE?" CARL ASKED Bill as he began to clear away his lunch dishes. Then he added, "Mr. Weber, you sure didn't eat much today; it seems as if your appetite has been on the light side lately. You doing OK?"

"Think I will pass on the pie today. Trying to keep this manly physique of mine from going to pot, you know?" Bill tried to make light of his diminishing appetite, but Carl was right; food had lost its appeal to him. Then he asked, "Say Carl, has Sarah been in the dining room today?"

"I don't think so, but I've only been here about 30 minutes, so she might have come in earlier." As Carl continued to clear the table, he looked up to see Sarah coming through the dining room entrance. "Well, speaking of the devil." He spoke loud enough to ensure that Sarah would hear what he said.

"Are you calling me the devil?" Sarah joked as she responded to Carl.

"No ma'am — at least not today," Carl joked right back.

As was his custom, Bill rose to greet Sarah and then pull her chair back for her to be seated. Over the past eight weeks or so, Sarah had often eaten lunch with Bill or at least stopped by his table for a few minutes, especially if he was eating alone. When she first started doing so, Sarah told herself *He's new and doesn't know anyone.* Then it was *He still hasn't signed up for any activities, so I will keep after him.* However, as time passed, she realized it was more than that. *There was just something about him that she really liked and enjoyed being around him, hearing his stories.*

Bill had opened up to Sarah some, telling her about his life and his adventures. Though he had shared a great deal, Sarah always had the feeling that there was more to his life, a piece he kept to himself. A couple of their lunchtimes went well past the hour that Sarah had allotted on her schedule. In each conversation they shared, Bill tried to turn it away from him in an effort to find out more about Sarah. Most of the time she would try to paint her life as boring — pretty much limited to Summersville except for college — and then volley the conversation back to him. He did learn that when Sarah was just 3, her mother was killed in an automobile accident. Her grandmother — Nana to Sarah — had raised her. Bill could tell that Sarah did not remember much about her mother and that this bothered her a great deal.

"What's the deal with your appetite? Looks as if you barely touched your food." Sarah had noticed the still-full plate Carl was placing onto the tray.

"Tell her, Carl."

"Well, he says he's watching his manly physique, but I'm not buying that. He's even passing on his pecan pie."

"So, what's up with your eating?" Sarah asked in a way that seemed to say, *I am looking for a serious answer.*

"Coffee?" Carl asked Sarah, interrupting.

"Please, but make it black. I have a crazy schedule this afternoon and am exhausted already. I need a boost."

"Maybe it is *your* eating habits we should be talking about, young lady. Why are you so tired already today?" Bill asked.

"Nice try, but let's stick with you and *your* eating habits. The only reason I'm tired is because I stayed up too late last night.

Your appetite has been on the fritz for a couple of weeks. When is your next doctor's appointment?"

"Oh my gosh, now you're trying to be my nurse!" Bill protested to Sarah.

"No, really, I am concerned about you. No appetite and I'm pretty sure you're losing weight. Are you?"

"Really, I'm fine. But I do have a doctor's appointment either next week or the week after. It's marked on my calendar."

Sarah didn't inquire further but sat looking at Bill as if to figure out what he was not telling her. He used the opportunity to change the subject.

"So, why were you up so late last night?"

"Nana and I were talking, and before I realized it was after midnight."

"What were you two talking about that kept you up so late?" Bill asked.

"Mostly about life. Me trying to figure it all out and getting Nana's perspective on the unexpected twists and turns life seems to take."

"It's nice that you value her opinion. She must have a good head on her shoulders."

Without Sarah saying so, Bill had a pretty good hunch that the topic of conversation for Sarah and her grandmother was men. Over the course of their lunchtime conversations, he had learned that until about six months ago Sarah had lived with her boyfriend. That relationship had ended abruptly, although Sarah never did say why. After the breakup, Sarah moved back in with her grandmother, at least temporarily, until she could save enough money to afford a place of her own.

"She is. My Nana is something else. I don't know what I would do without her." Sarah left it at that, not sharing anything more about their late-night conversation.

"How was lunch?" Frank asked as he ran into Bill just inside the entrance to the Center's main building, the one that housed the dining room.

Before he answered, Bill noticed Frank's smile again — always smiling. "It was good, real good. Are you headed there now?"

"Yes, but to try to fix a clogged drain, not to eat."

"Well, you should take time for a bite. Tell Carl to treat you to the piece of pecan pie that he tried to give me."

"I'll do that. You best stay bundled up. Weatherman says we may have the first snowfall of the season late this evening," Frank said.

"Good advice. After I make it back to my place now, I'm probably in for the rest of the day. See you later, Frank."

As Frank disappeared inside the building, Bill pulled his collar up and stuck his hands in his pockets. The walk back to his condo was only a half-block, and he would be there in just a few minutes. On some days, he extended the walk or climbed the stairs rather than take the elevator to the seventh floor, but today he would do neither. Though he had said nothing to Carl, Sarah, or Frank, Bill had certainly felt better in his life than what he was feeling today — just not much energy and a little unsteady on his feet.

"I think the electric eel will take care of this, but I need to go back to the truck for the extension." Frank told Elizabeth, the dining room manager, but he was also talking out loud to himself. He did not like unclogging drain lines and had told Elizabeth several times that her kitchen staff should be more careful with what they tried to wash down the sinks. "I'll be right back." Frank grabbed his coat, headed down to the first floor, and then out the door to his truck. As he walked toward the truck, Frank tried to remember where the extension was stored. He thought it was in one of the two exterior storage boxes on the left side of the truck, but wasn't positive.

Frank walked toward his truck as fast as he was able, motivated by the chill in the air and his annoyance with another unclog job. As he touched the left front corner of the truck's hood with his gloved hand and started to step off the curb, Frank abruptly stopped in mid-step and, for just a second, was stunned with what he saw: Bill lying next to the truck's front left fender, face down. Since there was a car parked next to Frank's truck, he was hidden to anyone who might happen to walk by.

"Oh my God! Mr. Weber, what's wrong?" Frank asked as he knelt by Bill's motionless body and tried to assess the situation. He was unconscious, his breathing shallow, and blood streamed from a gash on his forehead. "I'll get help. You'll be OK." Frank spoke in a loud and deliberate voice, trying to sound calm and reassuring. He grabbed for his phone and then realized he had left it inside. Frank stood, looked around, and no one else was in sight. He had to go back inside, but first took off his jacket and laid it across Bill's back.

"I'll be right back. I'm going inside to call an ambulance." Frank raced to the building door and flung it open. Margaret, one of the kitchen staff, had just gotten off the elevator and was now standing in front of Frank.

"Call an ambulance! Mr. Weber is down on the concrete, unconscious, by my truck!" Frank spoke with excited bursts to Margaret and then as quickly as he had appeared to her was gone again, racing back out the door.

"Don't try to move. The ambulance'll be here real soon." As Frank knelt by Bill again, he heard a few mumbled words, and saw him move his right leg some, as if trying to make an effort to get back on his feet.

"Just lay still. Please don't try to get up." Just then Frank heard the sound of the sirens, distant, but growing closer. "The ambulance'll be here in just a minute. I hear them coming."

This time, Bill's voice was a little stronger and Frank understood what he was trying to say — "No damn ambulance."

"Mr. Weber is in Exam Room No. 6, waiting to be admitted. Unless you're family, you are not allowed back there." The nurse's response to Sarah's inquiry about Bill was curt and given without looking directly at her.

Sarah had not heard the ambulance arrive. She was in a meeting in one of the buildings farthest from the dining hall, and it was nearly 45 minutes later before she got word that one of the residents had been taken to the hospital. When she learned that it was Harry, she grabbed her coat and raced to the hospital's emergency room entrance. Her thoughts were of the worst.

Sarah was annoyed with the nurse's attitude and thought about telling a lie, saying she was family. Instead, she spoke with authority in response, "I am on the staff at Drake, where Mr. Weber lives. He does not have family. I must speak with him to assess his situation."

"OK, but make it brief — five minutes." The nurse didn't want to give into Sarah but was certain that if she said no, the conversation would not end there. Sarah made her way to the examination room, not knowing for sure what to expect when she announced her arrival and began to slowly pull back the curtain.

"Hi Sarah! Come on in. We're having a party." Bill was partially sitting up in his bed, his head bandaged with signs of blood showing through, and Frank standing next to the bed but without his usual, ever-present smile." The look Frank passed to Sarah was serious despite Bill's attempt at humor.

Sarah studied Bill for just a second then asked, "What in the world happened to you? I was scared to death when I heard that they'd carted you off in an ambulance!"

Before Bill could answer, Frank interjected. "I've got to get back. If I don't finish up in the kitchen, dinner won't be served this evening." He paused as he slipped on his coat then added, " Just so you know, he's been a bit cantankerous with the staff," as he rolled his eyes at Sarah.

"How are you getting back?" Sarah asked.

"I'll give Pam a call. By the time I grab a cup of coffee from the snack bar, she'll be here."

"Are you sure? I could take you." Sarah offered but really did not want to leave Bill.

"No, Pam'll come get me." Frank placed his hand on Bill's shoulder and gave it a gentle squeeze. "I'll see you back at the Center real soon. And listen to what the doctors have to say."

Bill placed his hand on Frank's. "Thanks so much for getting me here and sticking with me. Without you, I might still be laying on the pavement."

"Glad I came by when I did. You take good care." And then Frank was out the exam room door. He was not a fan of hospitals.

Sarah stood at the end of Bill's examination room bed, turned her head just a little — giving him that look of *What's up with this?* — then asked, "How are you?" She was concerned, very concerned, but did not want to come across as such.

"I'm fine; just managed to step off the curb the wrong way and down I went."

Sarah wasn't convinced. "So, if you just took a little tumble, why are they keeping you here for observation?"

"Because I am old and they want my money!" Bill responded, both in jest and with a degree of truth. On days like these, he was feeling old.

"What did the doctors say?" Sarah ignored his efforts to make light of the situation.

"Not much really. They want to run a bunch of tests. If it wasn't for the weekend coming up, I figure I could be out of here tomorrow."

Sarah decided not to push her questioning for now. Before she spoke again, the door opened, ushering in a nurse, an orderly, and a gurney.

"Let's get you up to your room, Mr. Weber," the nurse said.

"How about going home instead?" Bill replied.

"Not today, besides you know you want to stay here for the weekend — just kicking back, watching football, and eating some of our *delicious cuisine.*"

As the nurse and orderly maneuvered the gurney into position, Sarah felt both in the way and out of place. Trying to be useful, she asked, "Is there anything you need? I'll be back this evening and glad to bring it."

"I don't think so," Bill paused then changed his mind, "Well maybe, but I hate to ask."

"What can I bring you?"

Before Bill could answer, the process of transferring him to the gurney began and he was momentarily silenced. As he was being transferred from the bed to the gurney, he grimaced. Sarah could see that he was in pain and weak. She knew that there was more to his situation than a bump on the head. Sarah also saw signs of much more than Bill had ever shared with her.

His hospital gown had dipped off his right shoulder as well as exposed the lower half of his left leg. Both showed extensive scaring from injuries, surgeries, or both; she wasn't sure. Sarah had noticed he walked with a slight limp but had never imagined that it might have been caused by such traumatic damage to his body. He had never mentioned any surgeries or significant injuries to her.

Now that he was on the gurney, Bill responded to Sarah. "In my coat pocket are my keys."

The nurse interrupted, "It's best you take all of Mr. Weber's valuables with you, if you're OK with that." The nurse looked at Bill for approval. "Otherwise, we'll need to inventory and put them in the safe."

"That will be fine. Sarah, do you mind?"

"Of course not. What about the keys and what would you like me to bring to you?"

"If you will, stop by my place. I need a few things — my toilet articles, like shaving gear and toothbrush. You know. All of it's in the top drawer, just to the left of the bathroom sink. Also, in my study is an old leather briefcase. Think it's beside the desk on the floor. Will you bring it too? But don't make a special trip. Just when you have the time."

"I'll be glad to go by your place for what you need. Right now, you're headed to your room, and I am going back to the office, but I will see you this evening." Sarah now stood closer to Bill's gurney, which had been moved out the door and pointed down the hallway. She added, "Please listen to what the doctors tell you. I want a full report on everything they had to say when I see you this evening." Without thinking about it, Sarah had taken Bill's hand and lightly stroked the back of it with her thumb.

"I will." Bill squeezed Sarah's hand then closed his eyes. She watched as he was rolled down the hall and into the elevator. She turned and began walking to her car. Sarah wiped a tear from her eye.

"How is Mr. Weber, dear?" came the probing question from behind.

Sarah was startled. She had just put the key into the front door lock of Bill's condo when Mrs. Sadler spoke. Sarah had not heard her door open, but Mrs. Sadler — whose apartment was across the hall — must have heard the elevator and Sarah walking down the hallway. Though Bill had not said a great deal, Sarah knew he did not care for Mrs. Sadler and went out of his way to avoid her. Unfortunately, she kept an eye and ear on the hallway, trapping him and others into unwanted conversations.

"Oh ... hi, Mrs. Sadler. He's doing OK, and I'll tell him you asked about him. I'm here just to pick up a few of his things." Sarah turned back toward the door in an effort to both wiggle the key — it didn't seem to work well — and to terminate the conversation, but Mrs. Sadler was not finished.

"They say he fell, may have been drinking." Drake had a gossip cell, and Mrs. Sadler's phone was kept hot serving as gossip central.

"No, he may have stumbled or perhaps fainted."

"Do you know if his family has been notified? Maybe it's real serious."

"I think he will be fine." Just then, the stubborn lock gave way and Sarah twisted the knob to open the door. "Bye, Mrs. Sadler. I'll tell Mr. Weber I saw you," Sarah said as she entered Bill's condo and quickly shut the door to stop any further discussion.

Her first task was to gather the toilet articles he asked for. She had not been in his home previously and did take a minute to glance around as she made her way to the bathroom. The living room was sparsely decorated but clean and orderly. The same was true for the small kitchen to her left and then the bathroom as well. It took just a minute to assemble the toilet articles, and then she headed to the study. It was just a few steps from the bath to the bedroom he had converted to his study, but by this time Sarah's thoughts were not on the study. She was wondering if she could make it out of the building without seeing Mrs. Sadler again.

Sarah felt for the light switch. When she flipped it, a desk lamp came on rather than an overhead light as she had anticipated. This room was different. It wasn't cluttered but contained a great deal more than the other rooms. Books filled the bookshelves to capacity, with the exception of a few decorative items strategically placed on two of the shelves. The walls were richly painted and adorned with mementoes of days gone by; mostly from his days in the Army, or so she thought with her first glance.

Sarah stepped toward the desk, her eyes searching until she saw the briefcase, just as he described it, where he said it would be. Sarah wondered why he wanted it, but had not asked. As she bent over to pick it up, her peripheral vision caught sight of the photo on his desk. Immediately Sarah stood back up, her eyes never leaving the photo. She could not believe what she was seeing.

The photo, mounted in a silver frame, was old and showed signs of fading with time, but Sarah knew it well. She had seen the photo many times before. It was of her grandmother — forever captured as a young woman emerging from the water and pausing on the last step of the dock's ladder. The background showed the beauty of the bay as well as ominous dark clouds that foretold a summer storm brewing. She was beautiful in her two-piece bathing suit — her skin tan, her wet hair pushed back. Her hands were on her hips and her head cocked slightly to the left, both gestures accentuating the expression captured as she looked into the camera. It was one both happy and sad, smiling in happiness but a sadness in her eyes that could not be denied.

Sarah picked up the photo, her hands shaking as her mind raced for answers. It made no sense. Why did he have this picture? And why on his desk after so many years had passed? Sarah was 4 or 5 years old the first time she had seen the photo. It was in a box of old family photos — some of Nana and some of her daughter, Carol, Sarah's mom. Once discovered, Sarah would look at the photos for hours on end and always ask her Nana to tell the story that went with each one of them, especially the photos with her mom. When Sarah first saw the picture of her Nana in a bathing suit, she had giggled. But, as she grew older and studied the photos more throughout the years, she became drawn to and fascinated by this particular photo and the unspoken story behind it. Her Nana would not talk about it.

As Sarah stood by Bill's desk and held the picture, she was overcome with a sick feeling within her. Quickly, she set the picture back on the desk and stepped back, as if trying to separate herself from it. She grabbed the briefcase, picked up the bag of toilet articles, then rushed to leave his condo as quickly as she could. Mrs. Sadler was waiting for her when she opened the door.

"Do you think Mr. Weber will come home soon?" Mrs. Sadler asked.

"Not now," was all Sarah offered in response as she hurried to the elevator. As Sarah left the building, the cold wind struck at her face and made the tears on her cheeks sting. Sarah stopped and looked at the night sky — dark but with stars shimmering. It displayed both its brilliance and an emptiness that could swallow all. She didn't understand any of this: Why did he have the photo? Why had Nana refused all these years to tell the story behind it?

Chapter Twenty

SARAH PULLED INTO THE HOSPITAL'S PARKING LOT entrance then rolled down her window to take the ticket from the dispenser. As she did, a gust of cold air struck her face and brought her thoughts back to the moment. Even though the drive had been less than 20 miles, it was still a scary thought to Sarah that she had driven the distance without fully being aware of doing so. She could not remember driving from Drake to the hospital. Throughout the drive time, her thoughts had remained fixated on the photo and trying to put together pieces that did not seem to belong.

"Mr. Weber is down the left hallway in room 414." The nurse at the central duty station's desk answered Sarah's question without looking up.

"How is he doing?"

"He's resting." A second nurse, standing at the counter, offered in a flat, tired voice without looking at Sarah.

"Thanks," Sarah responded then made her way down the long, sterile-looking hallway to room 414. It was the last room on the left, just before the hallway ended. In the end wall stood a large window that now framed nothing but the blackness of the night.

Sarah touched the door handle to Bill's room but then let go, stepping away, and turned to face the window. She still did not know what she was going to say or ask of him about the picture. Sarah also had thoughts that perhaps she should say nothing until he felt better — no need to raise the question or maybe upset him while he wasn't feeling well. Obviously, the photo meant something to him when it was taken but that was a very long time ago. Why did he still display the photo?

Sarah took a deep breath, stepped toward the door again, and as she turned the handle realized that the sick feeling in her stomach had returned. Sarah prepared herself to offer a pleasant, smiling face with no hint of the deep, questioning thoughts it masked. "Hi ..." She started to speak but abruptly stopped. He was asleep. The last thing she wanted to do was wake him from the rest he needed, but his sleeping also postponed their conversation.

Sarah stood just inside his door and studied him. A light above his head cast a pale, yellowish glow across his face and shoulders. She was both surprised and alarmed at just how tired and old he appeared. Until today, he had always appeared spry, well-groomed, joking, and active. As she watched him sleep, her thoughts returned to the photo on his desk. Over and over again she tried to imagine the connection he and her grandmother had shared so long ago and why he still had the photo displayed.

Stepping across the room, Sarah placed the bag containing his toilet articles on the tray stand located at the foot of his bed. As she started to place the briefcase beside it, the corner bumped the stand, knocking if from her hand. The briefcase bounced off the edge of the bed and then hit the floor, spilling the contents.

Sarah just knew the noise would wake him. It did not. The noise had not fazed him but she stood motionless for just a minute to make sure. Then Sarah bent down to pick up the briefcase and its spilled contents. At first glance, the items that had fallen out appeared as might be expected: a tablet of lined paper, two pens, and a few envelopes. She picked up the pens and paper then started reaching for the envelopes. Two envelopes on the floor closest to her appeared unused. Similar ones had remained stuffed in one of the pockets in the briefcase, and Sarah placed these two back into the stack. The last envelope was the farthest away and lying facing down on the floor. Reaching with her out-stretched arm and hand, Sarah grasped the envelope and pulled it toward her. Unlike the others, she could tell by the feel that it had papers inside and had been sealed. She started to rise from the floor and, at the same time, turn the envelope over in order to place it back in the briefcase, similar in position to the others.

Sarah let out a slight gasp. *Ann Marie O'Connell* — Nana's full name — was written on the front of the envelope. In addition, where the return address would be placed, it read *Drake Living Center.* Instead of a stamp, a date was recorded there — two days ago. She had no idea if this envelope had been in the same sleeve with the others or not. Sarah decided to add it to the stack of unused ones, placed the briefcase on the tray table, and turned to leave the room as quickly as possible. As she opened the door, she thought she heard Bill stir but did not turn to find out.

"Nana, I'm home," Sarah announced as she opened the front door.

"I didn't expect you home quite this early, dear. I thought you were going to the hospital to visit one of your residents," Nana called out from the kitchen after she heard the front door open and Sarah's voice. "Do you want some dinner?" Ann asked.

"No dinner, thanks. He was asleep when I got there, so I didn't stay. I'm going to change clothes." Sarah's recurring thoughts played over and over again — images of the envelope addressed to Ann as well as the photo of her on Bill's desk. Why did the envelope have her name on it? How could she possibly convince her grandmother to talk about the photo? Ann had always remained steadfast throughout the years in her unwillingness to tell Sarah anything about it.

"Hey, Nana," Sarah started off as she made her way to the family room.

"Yes, dear?"

"Where is that box of photos? You know, the one that has all the pictures of you and Mom, a few of the three of us, and some others." Sarah did not look at her grandmother when she asked, but stared at the TV as if intently watching the news.

"I'm not positive but believe that it's in the attic. What in the world got you to think about them? It's been a long time since you dug those old photos out."

"I don't know, just want to look at some of them again." Sarah turned to look at her grandmother. "Will you hold the ladder while I go up into the attic?"

"Why don't you wait until tomorrow, dear?"

"No, I think I want to get the box now while I am feeling brave enough to go up there."

Ann reluctantly followed Sarah as they made their way to the utility room. Sarah reached for the pull-down cord and tugged at it to lower the folded stairs.

"Sarah, are you sure you want to drag that box out of the attic? You know what a mess it is up there and cobwebs galore." Ann offered one last caution, hoping Sarah would change her mind. But she also knew her granddaughter well enough to know something was up. She just had no idea as to what it might be.

"Yes, I'm sure. Just hold the ladder, please. So, you think the box is back in the far corner by the old trunk?"

"I think so. Please be careful."

Sarah started up the ladder and, with flashlight in hand, soon made her way from the ladder to stand on the floor of the attic. The attic was neither Sarah nor Ann's favorite place to venture, but this time Sarah was on a mission. It did not take her long to locate the box, wipe off some of the dust that had collected on the lid, and then make her way back down the ladder. Sarah handed the box to Ann to hold as she folded the stairs back into the attic, then asked. "How about after dinner tomorrow we get the fireplace going and spend some time looking at the photos?"

"OK, if that's what you would like," Ann replied.

"I would like that, and to sweeten the deal, I'll fix dinner as well."

Sarah took the dusty box from her grandmother and carried it to her room. She spent the rest of the evening looking at the pictures and trying to figure out a strategy for the following evening. As Sarah searched the box of photos, she paused to study each selected one, especially of her mom. Nana had shared so much about her, often with Sarah clinging to every word, but very little about her mother's dad, Sarah's grandfather. It was another topic that Nana would not discuss, but rather would offer a vague comment about *it was the war,* then turn the conversation elsewhere. Sarah located the bathing suit photo and studied it intently and with a very different interest. Her Nana was a beautiful young woman in the photo, but why such a look of sadness in her eyes? What was that about? Was Harry in some way connected? How could she convince her Nana to share the story behind the bathing suit photo?

Sarah began placing the selected photos back in the box and strategically placed the bathing suit photo so that it would be discovered after five or six other photographs were taken from the top of the pile. Until sleep overcame her, Sarah continued to struggle with how she would convince her Nana to talk about the photo. Should she first tell her about seeing the photo on

Harry's desk or wait until after she was able to convince her grandmother to tell her about the photo? Over and over Sarah tossed the two approaches about in her thinking — which should come first?

"Do you want a cup of tea?" Sarah called out to Ann from the kitchen. Dinner was over, and Sarah had finished the last of the dishes. Ann was in the family room, enjoying the warmth of the fireplace.

"Yes, please, Earl Grey."

"Here you go. But let me set it down first. The cup's hot." Sarah placed Ann's cup of tea on the coaster, took a seat on the couch, and then turned to pick up the box of photos that she had placed near the couch earlier in the day.

"You dragging out the photos already?" Ann stated in a minor protest.

"Sure, this will be fun!" Sarah hoped some enthusiasm would hide her nervousness. She pulled the first photo from the box. "Didn't you say Mom was about six when this one was taken?" Sarah handed her the first photo from the box.

"I believe so, or maybe seven."

"Tell me again — Why did you have her hair cut so short? She looks like a boy!"

"Oh Sarah, you know the story. Your mother decided to cut her own hair and before I could stop her, she had chopped off a couple of really big pieces. What you see in the picture is the best the stylist could do after the damage was done."

"What about this one?"

"That's my mom, your Great Uncle Bob, and me. I was only two or three months and Bob about 18 months or so. Mom definitely had her hands full with two in diapers."

After three more photos were pulled from the box and discussed, Sarah made it to *the* photo. "Nice bathing suit," she stated in a kidding fashion as she handed Ann the photo.

"It was at the time." Ann stated then started to pass the photo back to Sarah after a cursory glance at it.

Unlike with the others, Sarah didn't hold out her hand to take it from Ann, but asked, "Will you please tell me about that one?"

At first, Ann said nothing but looked at Sarah, trying to figure out what was behind her request and sensing she would not let it pass. "Why? That was a long time ago." As Ann spoke, still holding the photo, she looked away from Sarah.

Sarah decided she would take the lead. "I need to tell you something, but it would be better if you told me about the photo first."

Ann said nothing, just stared at the fire. After a moment longer, she spoke. "Sarah, I'll just say it was at a time when I was young, foolish, and very much in love — deeply in love with the man who took the picture. He was leaving for Vietnam, and I hated the thought of him going away, of spending one moment without him. The day after the photo was taken was when he left. That was the last time I ever saw him."

As Ann spoke, Sarah saw sadness in her Nana's eyes, the same sadness captured in the photo so long ago.

"But what does this photo have to do with anything you need to tell me?" Ann asked. She wanted to say no more about the photo.

Sarah hesitated, then answered, "I saw a copy of this photo yesterday."

"Surely not this one. Maybe what you saw just reminded you of it."

"Nana, I am sure. It was this same photo."

"Where did you see it?" Ann asked.

Again Sarah hesitated in responding, but then answered. "Yesterday, I went by Harry's apartment to pick up a few things that he asked me to bring him."

"Oh yes, he's the man who fell. I remember you telling me."

"One of the things he wanted was his briefcase. I went into his study to get it for him and there was your picture. It was in a silver frame sitting on his desk. "

"I don't understand." Ann looked puzzled.

"I don't either. I was going to ask him about it when I went to the hospital last night, but he was sleeping."

Ann said nothing.

Watching her grandmother stare into the fire, Sarah decided to tell her the rest. "There is more. As I was placing his briefcase on his tray stand, I dropped it. Everything in it scattered across the floor, including some envelopes. When I picked one of them up, I noticed it was sealed and then saw that it had your name written on it — *Ann Marie O'Connell.*"

Ann turned toward Sarah, her face now visibly pale. "What's his name?

"Nana, I told you. It's Harry."

"No, what is his full name?"

"Oh. His last name is Weber; I'm pretty sure it's William Harold. He told me a funny story about being in the Army and his flight instructor started calling him Harry because there were too many Bills in the class or something like that. Anyway, the middle name stuck and he has been Harry to his friends ever since. He introduced himself as Bill or Harry when he moved into Drake."

Ann was visibly shaken by Sarah's answer. She held a paper napkin in her hands, a remnant from dinner, and twisted it over and over, using that gesture to control the shaking of her hands. Finally, Ann spoke. "That man isn't Harry, he's Bill, and he is the one who took the picture." She then rose from the couch, turned to leave the room, but paused — placing one hand on the back of the couch as if to steady herself. She spoke again without looking at Sarah. "I don't know what you intend to do with this information; you must decide. But I want you to know that I don't want to see him or have anything to do with him." With that declaration, Ann continued to her bedroom, mumbling, "Good night," as she left the room.

Sarah sat motionless, starring at the fire — now nothing but ambers with no flame visible — and holding the picture in her lap. Sarah was stunned at what Ann had finally shared, and she felt terrible, terrible that her Nana was so upset and that she, with her questions and the photo, had opened a wound from so long ago.

"How was your weekend?" Beth looked up from her desk and greeted Sarah as she came through the office door.

"Fine. And yours?" Sarah answered with a smile, even though the weekend was not fine. She had upset her grandmother and now had no idea what she was going to do to try to fix things. Even though Sarah and Beth were good friends, this was not something she would mention to her.

"Same ole, same ole. Say, have you heard how Mr. Weber is doing?"

"Not really. I went to see him Friday evening, but he was sleeping when I got there. I should have gone yesterday, but didn't. I plan on going today at lunchtime."

"When you do, tell him the office gang said hello and get well soon." With that, Beth looked down and returned to sorting the stack of invoices.

Monday morning slipped away without Sarah accomplishing a great deal. She was distracted by thoughts of going to see Harry — or Bill, as her Nana called him. To Sarah, he was Harry. Helen had spoken of Harry being such a wonderful man and, ever since then, it just seemed right to call him that. As far as Sarah knew, everyone at Drake called him Harry.

Sarah drove to the hospital with a sinking feeling. It was 12:45 when she started down the hallway to his room. As she approached the room, two thoughts passed through her mind. The first was that maybe he wouldn't be there; maybe he'd be in X-ray or some other department for testing. The second thought was figuring out a way to talk to him about the photo and envelope. The first thought quickly evaporated: Harry was in his room.

"Hi Harry. How are you feeling?" Sarah asked, trying to sound cheerful.

"Well, hi Sarah. Oh, I'm fine. Say, thanks for dropping off my things Friday evening. Guess I had dozed off early and missed your visit."

As he spoke, Sarah realized she was seeing him differently. She felt herself begin to blush and looked away, out the window.

"Doesn't look like a very nice day out there. I think I saw snow flurries earlier."

"You did, and there's more on the way tonight," Sarah answered, feeling uncomfortable. She didn't know whether to stand or sit in the chair near his bed. Finally, she sat.

"You doing OK? You look pale," he commented.

"I'm fine. And here you are up to your old tricks, trying to change the subject." Sarah smiled. "Back to my question — how are you?"

He chuckled at Sarah and her persistence. Then he sighed and turned away from looking at her as he answered. "Guess I could be better. I had tests yesterday and most of this morning.

The doctor seems to be a little concerned about my heart and a couple of other things."

"And what does that mean, 'a little concerned'?"

"I really don't know and won't for a couple more days, but probably nothing. I feel OK, just a little weak. But that's from lying here all weekend."

The word *weekend* brought Sarah back into the reality of the moment and why she was here. She thought of her Nana sitting on the couch, her hands wringing the napkin and her lip quivering. She saw the briefcase lying on the traystand by the bed. The time had come.

"Harry, it looks like your briefcase has been around for a while," Sarah said to begin the conversation.

"Yes, it sure has, probably 40 years or more."

"When I picked it up from your study, I couldn't help but notice all of your books and the mementos on the walls. You have a nice study."

"I spend a lot of time in it. I like being surrounded by the books and reminders of my younger days. Plus, it has the view I mentioned to you."

"Your younger days, you mean when everyone called you Bill?"

He looked at Sarah, not exactly sure what she meant, not sure how to answer.

Sarah continued, "It was dark outside when I went to your apartment, but I can imagine what the view must look like from the study. Hey, I also saw Mrs. Sadler —twice — and of course she was asking about you."

He said nothing, just rolled his eyes when Sarah mentioned his neighbor. A moment of silence overcame them, Harry searching for a topic or question to ask of Sarah and Sarah hesitating to take the conversation farther.

"When I was in your study, I couldn't help but notice the photo on your desk."

"Beautiful lady, don't you think?" His voice perked up.

"Yes, she is beautiful. The picture looks like it was taken quite awhile ago."

"It was, but at times I remember it like it was yesterday."

Sarah could feel her heart start to race as she pushed the conversation further. "Do you mind if I ask you her name?"

Harry looked at Sarah for just an instant then answered. "Sure, it's Ann. But sometimes I called her Annie."

"Can you tell me her full name?"

"Ann Marie O'Connell to be exact. But why do you ask?"

Sarah ignored his question and continued, "Friday evening when I stopped by to see you and leave your things, I accidentally dropped your briefcase as I started to set it on the tray. All of its contents spilled onto the floor. I thought the noise would wake you, but it didn't. When I picked up the envelopes, I couldn't help but notice that one of them was addressed to that person. So, you write her?"

"Yes, I do and have almost all of my life."

"Does she write you back?"

Harry wasn't sure what Sarah had on her mind or why she was asking. In all the years, he had only told one person about his letter-writing, and that was his mom just before she passed away over 30 years ago. Now, he was telling Sarah without hesitation. As he tugged at the bed sheet, he contemplated how to answer Sarah. "No, she doesn't, because I don't mail them."

Sarah's head was reeling from what he was telling her, but she tried her best to keep a calm, outward appearance.

"Why do you write the letters, then?"

"Sarah, if you are fortunate, perhaps with a little luck and grace thrown in, you will meet someone so incredibly special to you that your love for them never goes away. You feel it from the day you meet until the day you die. That kind of love is the sweetest part of life. Frankly, I'm convinced it goes on after that.

If we have souls and they are eternal, then I think that they carry that love with them. Well, Ann is that love for me, and I have loved her since the day we first met. Do you know where we met?" he asked.

Sarah looked at Harry without answering. She could see the sparkle in his eyes. He had come alive when he spoke about Sarah's grandmother.

"Of course you don't," he offered and then continued. "We met at the ball field by the bay, the one I can see from my study window. Well, actually we met in the parking lot."

"If she is the love of your life, why aren't you together?" Sarah asked with a directness that surprised him.

"Because loving someone sometimes means letting them go. I let go of Ann, and I wish I could say that I did so for all the right reasons, but that's not true. I was just a stupid, selfish, young man having a hell of a pity party. It was a bad time in my life. I knew it was impossible for me to give her what she wanted, what would make her life complete. Hell, I even lied to her in a letter that ended it all. But all of that is a great deal more than you wanted to know. You didn't come here for that."

"Well, actually I did," Sarah replied.

Each looked at the other without speaking before Sarah broke the silence.

"Harry ... the picture on your desk. I have seen it many times before."

"I don't understand. Where could you have seen the picture?" His voice now carried seriousness and concern. Gone was the sparkle from his eyes.

"I saw it as a child growing up and then again just this Saturday at my grandmother's house. Ann Marie O'Connell is my grandmother."

His eyes blinked in disbelief as he struggled to comprehend what Sarah had just revealed. His jaw dropped slightly, and his mouth stood open. He was trying to come to grips with it all. Then he looked down.

Sarah could see tears in his eyes.

In a quivering voice, he began to speak. "I was injured pretty bad the first time I went to Vietnam, chopper crash almost killed me. Right after that I made a terrible decision — lying to your grandmother — it has haunted me ever since then. After I lied, it didn't take long for me to realize how foolish I had been, but it was too late. Ann had moved on with her life. She told me so in a letter. But, I never stopped loving her and, for whatever reason, me writing all the letters over the passing years seemed to help ease the pain. The letters are nothing more than me describing my life to her, as if we are having a conversation. I think it was these conversations that helped keep me from going crazy from loneliness or from my regret for being so foolish, and I used them to recall wonderful times when we were together." After pausing to wipe the tears from his eyes, he looked at Sarah for just a second, and then continued. "Sarah, I'm not sure why I've told you all of this. I was just sure I was taking it to the grave with me, never planned on sharing it with you or anyone else. I'm sorry to have burdened you with this, but now I'm going to add to it. Please don't tell her about me or the letters."

Sarah did not immediately answer him. She felt terrible. She had opened another very deep wound, this time in Harry. What could she do? Now the truth was out, or at least the little amount that Ann had shared, and now a little more so from Harry. Sarah wanted to ask him and her grandmother so much more, but each sought to remain estranged from the other. She wondered if there ever would be a time that was right to ask. Sarah had a feeling that there was much more to what both had shared with her.

Sarah stood and fidgeted, then spoke. "I'm sorry that I brought this up, but I appreciate you sharing with me what you did. And

I will respect your request not to tell my grandmother about you or the letters." She knew this would be difficult, but it was what he was asking of her. After making such a mess of things, she would at least honor it. "I need to get back to Drake now. I'll be back tomorrow." Sarah moved closer to the bed and gently squeezed Harry's hand. His cheeks were shiny with tears and, at first, it was difficult for him to look at Sarah. He took her one hand in both of his, looked at her — differently than ever before—and softly spoke. "I see your grandmother in you, Sarah, and I am grateful, grateful that you are such a good person to me, and grateful that we have a connection, a very special one in your grandmother."

Sarah's lip quivered as she looked at him, and she then turned to leave the room. It was difficult for her to speak, but she managed to say in a weak, broken voice, "I am grateful too."

Chapter Twenty-One

"HEY SARAH, I HAVE A FAVOR TO ASK." IT WAS FRANK.

His rapid knock on Sarah's open office door surprised her. She had been deep in thought elsewhere. "Hi, Frank. What's the favor you need?"

"Go to the hospital to pick up Mr. Weber," Frank first replied, then added, "He called about an hour ago and asked if I would pick him up. Said he is being discharged this afternoon. I told him I would be there at 12:30, but just now I got a call from the kitchen. There's a problem with the drain line *again.*"

Sarah was surprised that Harry had not called her but tried not to show it when she answered, "Oh sure, I can go. Sorry that the kitchen drain is a problem *again.* Sarah sided with Frank about the drain problem, but her sympathy was lost on Frank, who just mumbled, "Yeah," as he headed off to the kitchen.

Sarah looked at her watch: 11:05. To make it to the hospital by 12:30, she had enough time to finish the paperwork that had consumed most of her morning, but not enough time to still go to lunch as planned. She was to meet her grandmother at O'Kelly's. The two often met for lunch, sometimes at a restaurant and sometimes at the Drake's dining room. On occasion, Sarah would need to cancel at the last minute, usually due to something coming up at work. Ann was always fine with the last-minute changes, but this time might be different. This time it involved Harry. Sarah picked up the phone to call her grandmother but hesitated. She felt uneasy about making this call, but it had to be done, so she dialed and waited.

"Hello," Ann answered on the third ring.

"Nana, it's me. Something's come up, and I'm not going to be able to meet you for lunch. Sorry."

"Oh, that's fine. Is everything OK?"

"Yes, but Frank just stopped by and asked if I would run an errand for him." Sarah paused and wondered if she should stop there but decided to continue. "He was going to go to the hospital to pick up Harry, but a problem came up in the kitchen, and it requires Frank's attention. I need to leave here just a little after noon to be at the hospital at 12:30."

There was a moment of uncertain silence before Ann spoke. "You mean Bill?" Her response threw Sarah, and before she could reply, Ann continued. "After our conversation last Saturday, I did remember him telling me about the flight instructor — a Mr. Vernon I believe — changing his name to Harry and how everyone in the Army was calling him by that name. But I don't like that name. Harry; it doesn't suit him. Please call him Bill."

Sarah wasn't sure what to say. She was surprised that her grandmother had even responded, and her odd response seemed to indicate that, since last Saturday, she had at least given some thought to him. She was emphatic about calling him Bill.

Before Sarah said anything, her grandmother spoke again. "Will you be home for dinner?" she asked, as if to change the subject.

"Yes. Do you need anything from the grocery?"

"Yes, but I'm already dressed to go out, so I think I'll run an errand or two and then swing by the grocery. Will you be home around 5:30?"

"I should be. See you then." Sarah replaced the receiver on her office phone as her thoughts returned to her grandmother's comment about Bill's name change — such a different tone in her voice since their conversation about the photo.

"Hi Bill! You ready to go home?" Sarah asked in a positive, upbeat tone after she opened Harry's hospital room door and saw him sitting on the bed fully dressed, just staring out the window.

Bill was surprised to see Sarah and even more surprised that she'd called him Bill. "Bill? I believe that's the first time you've called me that. Why the change?"

"Let's save that story for another day," was all Sarah offered in response.

"OK. What happened to Frank? How did he come to stick you with this unpleasant task of providing taxi service for an old man?" Bill was attempting to be light-hearted and put forth his best effort. He felt uneasy after their last conversation.

"And it is nice to see you, too," Sarah teased then added, "Frank didn't stick me with anything, and just so you know, I am deeply hurt that you would ask Frank instead of me. And I don't see an old man. I see a distinguished gentleman. So there!"

Bill knew Sarah was joking about being hurt, but the truth was that he really had asked Frank as a way of avoiding Sarah — at least for now. After their last conversation, he just wasn't up to facing her again so soon. He also knew Sarah would ask what the doctors had to say. Frank probably would not have.

"Let's get out of here before they change their mind about letting me go," Bill said as he eased himself off the bed and picked up a bag containing all of his belongings. "I just need to stop by Admissions to sign some papers or something like that."

Before Harry and Sarah could make it out the door of his room, a nurse's aide entered the room pushing a wheelchair. "Mr.

Weber, how about a lift down to Admissions and then out the front door?" she asked.

"Do I have a choice?"

"Now, you know you don't. It's the hospital's rule."

"Not interested in bending the rules, are you, Jean?" Harry already knew the answer and managed to stand. Then he almost collapsed into the chair. He was weak.

"And who is this lovely lady here to escort you home?" Jean asked as they left the room and headed down the hallway.

"Sorry. This is Sarah. She's the activity director at Drake and sometimes my lunch partner. She takes good care of me. Sarah, this is Jean Dawson, and she's the best aide of all, except she roots for the wrong football team." Bill grinned at Jean.

"Sarah, it's nice to meet you. Now, you just keep on taking good care of Mr. Weber. We like him here but don't want to see him back anytime soon."

"Oh, I plan on keeping a close eye on him."

Bill looked up at Sarah and smiled but did not say anything.

"First stop or should I say last stop — Admissions — before we kick you out the door." Jean parked Bill's wheelchair off to the side of the hallway and went to find the clerk.

As Sarah and Bill waited for Jean to return, an uneasy silence prevailed. Both had questions they wanted to ask but hesitated. Finally, Sarah spoke, "OK, are you going to tell me what the doctors said?"

Bill looked at Sarah and first replied, "I am an old man," intending to leave it at that, but he could see from the look on her face that she wasn't buying it. He looked away before continuing. "Several things are working against me, Sarah. My body really has taken a beating along the way, but more than anything else my heart is weak — congestive heart failure."

"What are they going to do to fix it?"

"Not much, just more medicine to help keep it going for now. I've had this problem for a while, but it's getting a little worse."

Sarah was silent for a moment and then asked, "You said the doctors are concerned about several things. What else besides your heart?"

"There are some problems with the kidneys and ..." Bill stopped in mid-sentence, not wanting to continue, but then added, "I've had a couple of bouts of cancer. It may have come back for the third time, but more tests are needed."

Sarah was surprised. Bill had never mentioned cancer in all their conversations. Before she could ask additional questions, Jean was back.

"Mr. Weber, they don't need your signature after all! Let's get you home!" And with that, Jean spun his wheelchair around, and they headed for the hospital's main entrance. When the automatic door opened, a burst of cold air whipped around them. "Would you like a ride out to Sarah's car?" Jean asked but knew he wouldn't accept the offer. Bill had already stood up.

"No, I'm fine," he answered as he steadied himself with the help of Sarah's hand. Bill had been a little too quick to get to his feet.

"My car's in the second row, so we don't have far to go," Sarah told Jean as she reached for the bag of items Bill held in his hand.

"I've got it." He was not about to let Sarah carry the bag. Then he added, "Bye, Jean. Thanks for looking after me during my stay at this *lovely place*." Bill did appreciate Jean's attentiveness and pleasing personality, but he did not like being in the hospital. During his lifetime, he had spent far too many days in one.

"You are welcome, dear. Now take care and don't come back." Jean laughed and then waved as she walked back inside.

Moving at a slow pace, Bill and Sarah made their way to the parking lot. Nothing more was said, except Sarah cautioned him to watch his step when they reached the curb.

"The blue one, right?" Bill said, after looking toward the second row and seeing Sarah's car. He knew it from the Drake's staff parking lot.

"That's it. A little dirty, but it'll get us back just fine."

Sarah first opened the back door. "Can I have the bag now? I'll toss it in the back seat." Sarah smiled at Bill as she asked for the bag. She liked giving him a hard time, and he enjoyed it as well. He knew she was referencing his unwillingness to let her carry the bag earlier.

"If you insist," was his only reply, along with a smile.

Sarah moved toward the passenger's seat, trying to help Bill sit down without appearing to offer him assistance.

As Sarah pulled her car out of the parking lot and onto the highway, she started to speak but stopped when she saw that Bill had closed his eyes. With each passing mile or so, she would glance his way, but his eyes remained closed until just before the turnoff to the Drake.

Knowing for sure that he was now awake, Sarah asked, "What's on your mind?"

"Life, just life," Bill offered as he looked out the window and then continued. "I'm pretty sure this is the same road that first brought me to Summersville. It was summer then and everything was green and the sky was bright blue. We were just sure we were coming to town to win the regionals — nothing could stop us. Now, it's nothing but grays all around and a lifetime later. I suppose this will be the same road that they carry me out on."

"Don't talk like that! You have lived quite a life between then and now, but it's important that you believe there is still more to come."

Nothing more was said until Sarah parked in front of Bill's building.

He opened his door and, with one leg out, paused to say, "Thanks so much, Sarah. Sorry that I had to bother you and take you away from work. I can make it from here."

"Not so fast, mister. You're not getting away that easily. I'll walk with you to your place. Besides, you need a wing man. The very least I can do is run interference for you if Mrs. Sadler is stalking the hallway."

"You really don't need to do that. I have taken so much of your time already."

Sarah opened her car door and made her away around to Bill as he reached into the backseat of the car to retrieve his bag. Without asking, Sarah took the bag and he offered no resistance. Though he would not tell her so, he was feeling weak.

Slowly they made their way up the walkway and into the building.

As the two exited the elevator and started down the seventh floor hallway to Bill's apartment, it became apparent that Mrs. Sadler wasn't home or at least wasn't at her post by her door keeping watch.

Sarah whispered, "I think we're safe." Bill laughed a little and nodded his head in agreement.

Once inside the apartment, he sat down in the chair nearest the door.

"Are you OK?" Sarah asked.

"Sure, just catching my breath. Do you have another second or two?

"I have all the time you need. What's up?"

"I want to show you something," Bill answered as he stood and then moved slowly toward the study. Sarah followed. As they had entered the room, their eyes were first drawn to the picture of Ann on the desk, but neither spoke.

Using his right index finger to tap the window glass, Bill looked at Sarah with a smile on his face, "There, right there in the fourth row back of that parking lot is where I met your grandmother." He chuckled slightly and then continued. "She always said that I ran into her, and I always said she was walking where she shouldn't have been."

Sarah looked out the window at the parking lot but could also see Bill from the corner of her eye. She was pretty sure she was looking at the spot he had pointed to, as well as just beyond the parking lot to the baseball diamonds and the bay. Even with all the grayness that now filled the afternoon beyond the glass, she could imagine what it looked like on a bright summer's day.

Sarah turned to face Bill and, when she did, saw a smile on his face and sadness in his eyes. "It is a beautiful view, and I am sure you enjoy being able to see it all from here." What she did not, could not do was respond with a comment or question about Ann and Bill's first meeting and the rest of their story that she so longed to know. Instead, she squeezed his left hand gently and said, "Thank you for sharing this with me. I know it's a very special place for you." Sarah paused and then said, "I best get back to the office now."

"How is your grandmother?" Bill asked without looking at Sarah as she turned the knob on the apartment's front door.

Sarah was surprised by the question and without speaking raised her eyes from the door handle to look at him. She studied his eyes briefly, both from what they expressed and in buying time, trying to figure out how to respond. But she knew there was only one way to answer.

"You'll need to ask her yourself."

Bill looked away. "I couldn't do that ... I just can't. It's too late."

"Look. There's so much I don't know or don't understand about you and my grandmother, but the one thing I do know is that both of you are still alive, so it is not too late."

"Thanks again for bringing me home," Bill replied, choosing to ignore Sarah's last comment, then added, "I'll probably see you at lunch tomorrow." Sarah opened the door to leave and Bill turned to go back to his study.

Chapter Twenty-Two

"MR. WEBER! WAIT UP JUST A SECOND!" FRANK CALLED out. Then asked as he approached, "How are you feeling?"

Harry stopped, stepped back to let the elevator's door shut, and turned in Frank's direction. "*Mr. Weber?* I thought we were past that!" He joked then continued, "Actually, I couldn't be better. Thanks for asking," he replied, putting forth his best effort to mask how he was really feeling. "How have you and Pam been?"

"Oh, we're fine. Looking forward to Matt making it home for the holidays." Pam and Frank's son — Matt— was in the Army, and what he was doing was often a topic of conversation between Frank and Bill.

"That's great! Is he still headed to jump school next year?"

"He says he is, probably in the April timeframe."

Frank wanted to turn the conversation back to Harry's health. His appearance concerned him. He looked pale and thinner than when he was last with him in the hospital. "Did you have lunch with Sarah?" Frank asked, but his real intent was to figure out if Sarah had seen him today. If he wouldn't talk about his health, maybe Sarah would know and could fill him in. Frank considered Harry a really good guy and liked sharing time with him, although it was not that frequent and usually just a chance meeting around meal time, or if he happened to be out walking, something he had not done much of recently.

"No, not today. I think she's been busy."

"Is there anything you need, anything I can take care of for you?" Frank asked.

"No, I'm doing pretty good right now, but I appreciate the offer."

"OK, but if you need anything, you just let me know." Frank watched the elevator door open for Harry and then decided that he would head to Sarah's office. He hoped she would know what was going on with him.

"I will, Frank. You've been quite a big help and a good friend since I moved here." He started to step into the elevator when he paused and stepped back out. "Say, Frank, do you know Sarah's address? Seems as if she mentioned living on Oak Lawn, but I'm not positive."

"I don't know for sure, but we could stop by her office now if you want to find out. I'm pretty sure she moved back in with her grandmother a few months ago." Frank had a quizzical look on his face as he responded to Harry's odd question.

"No, no, that's OK. I want to send her a thank-you note for looking out after me while I was in the hospital, and figured I would send it to her house rather than her office. Just seems a little more personal that way. Doesn't seem right for me to ask her for her address."

"Tell you what, I'll find out from Beth then get back with you later this afternoon.

"That'd be fine. I really appreciate you doing that for me."

Frank watched the elevator door close behind Harry, then headed off toward Sarah's office.

"Beth, is Sarah in today?" Frank asked, after sticking his head in Sarah's office and seeing she wasn't there.

"Well, yes I'm doing fine. Thanks so much for asking," Beth replied."Sorry," Frank sheepishly replied and smiled. "Actually, I'm looking for Sarah's address. Do you have it?"

Beth was a little surprised by his request but said, "Sure, but why are you asking? You know, privacy and all that."

"It's not for me. Mr. Weber wants it. He wants to send her a thank-you note for being so good to him while he was in the hospital, and thinks it would be better to send it to her home."

Beth pulled a note card from a stack on her desk and wrote Sarah's address: 1218 Oak Lawn Avenue.

"Thanks," Frank offered as Beth handed him the note card. "You know, Mr. Weber doesn't look so good. I was going to ask Sarah, thought maybe she would know what's going on with him."

"Here you go, just as promised." Frank held up the note card for Harry to accept and as he did tried to survey his appearance once again. It had taken him several minutes to answer his doorbell, so long that Frank was starting to become concerned.

"Thanks, Frank. I have the card signed. Now I can mail it."

"Do you want me to stick around for a minute and then take it to the mailbox for you?"

"No thanks, I'll just mail it when I go out tomorrow. There are a couple of things I need to do then."

"OK, but let me know if you need anything else. See you later," Frank said, then headed down the hallway.

Bill returned to his study to address the envelope. With the task completed, he turned his chair to look out the window and think. He continued to ponder a crazy idea that had been stirring in his head for the past few days.

"Where are you headed?" Mrs. Sadler asked just as Bill closed his front door. Her prodding ways were consistent — always direct and equally as nosy. This one had caught Harry by surprise. He hadn't heard her door open.

"Just out to run a couple of errands."

"Must be headed to the post office. Looks like you have letters to mail there in your hand."

Bill glanced down at his hand holding the letters, wanting to ensure the addresses were not showing. They weren't. "Yes, I need to stop by the post office."

"Where else you headed?" she asked, still probing and annoying him, but he tried not to show it. He also kept trying to make his way down the hall.

"May stop by a friend's house." By this time, Bill was at the elevator, silently urging it to arrive as quickly as possible. It did.

"Who's the friend?" Mrs. Sadler called out in an effort to gain every bit of information possible. Bill stepped into the elevator. He ignored her last question and let the door shut.

Once outside, Bill felt the cool, crisp air of an autumn day, as he walked the short distance to his car. His intended actions flashed across his mind, still not sure whether to proceed or not. Ever since he decided he would deliver the letter, the thought of doing so had been a constant turmoil for him — one moment committed to the idea and the next questioning why he would do so at all. After standing beside his car for just a moment longer, he opened the door. The stronger desire to do so had won out, at least for now.

Another pause, another questioning moment came again as Bill started his car. He looked at the letters — now placed on the passenger's seat — and again questioned his decision. He turned the car off, sat motionless for a moment, and then turned it on again. He was going to do it. Bill backed his car out of his parking space and was on his way. His destination was less than

15 miles away and a 20-minute drive, yet diametric in so many ways from the path he had chosen so long ago. With each turn he took or each mile that clicked away, he grew more nervous, more uncertain about what he was now doing. He made the final turn and, just four houses down from the corner, pulled to the side to park in front of his destination — 1218 Oak Lawn Avenue.

Bill picked up the letters from the passenger seat and began to slowly rotate the two, first placing one then the other on top. The note to Sarah could have been mailed, but the other one was different. He knew that it had to be delivered in person. It was to Ann. Bill had written this letter while he was still in the hospital; the day after Sarah asked about the photo.

Throughout the years, Bill's letters to Ann always shared a little of what was happening in his life and, when appropriate, highlighted in some way a connection to what he and Ann had once shared — hearing an old song, seeing a similar sight, a funny incident. Each letter always ended with wishing her the very best in life. But this one was different. He had written about the conversation with Sarah, how he'd learned that Ann was so close by, and that Sarah was her granddaughter. For the first time since he'd written Ann from the hospital in Germany — a lifetime ago — he repeated why he had done what he did, but how deeply he regretted his actions then and what a fool he had been.

After returning home from the hospital, Bill had started to place this letter in the wooden box with all the others, but couldn't. The words Sarah had spoken to him — *You'll need to ask her yourself* — as she left his apartment lingered in his thoughts. The envelope and its letter remained on his desk, propped up against the picture frame. Each time he saw it, he grew more certain and more frightened of what he must do.

Ann passed by the large living room window and noticed the car parked on the street in front of her house. She did not recognize the vehicle, could not see the driver, and thought no more about it as she continued her way to the kitchen. Several minutes passed before Ann's doorbell rang. She had already forgotten about the car in front of her house.

Ann peered through the door's peephole but did not recognize the man standing there. He was looking down and slightly away from the front door. She debated whether to answer the door but decided she would; the storm door separated her from the stranger, and it was locked.

"Hello," Ann spoke first, and as she did the stranger raised his head.

"Hello Ann," was all Bill could say. Struggling with what might come next, he took a small step back from the door and continued. "How are you?" he asked, just as Ann started to speak.

"May I help ..." Ann had started to speak simultaneously with the stranger, but lost her words when she recognized who was standing there. Each stood motionless and said nothing, just looking at one another — in part strangers but in part connected as much as any two people ever were.

Bill spoke first to end the silence. "Ann, I apologize for showing up like this. I don't know what Sarah has shared with you or not. I don't even know if you knew I'm living at the Drake. Sarah has been very good to me since I moved there. When I was in the hospital, I asked her to go to my apartment for some things and when she did, she saw a picture of you. The one I took just before heading overseas. I keep it on my desk."

The words of his last sentence trailed off until it was more as if he was talking to himself rather than to Ann. In frustration, he continued, "Oh God, this isn't making any sense. I am so sorry for being such a fool, for coming here today." Harry turned to walk away.

"You were always really good at that, turning your back and just walking away," Ann spoke with anger. "I have no idea why you showed up today, and I don't appreciate you doing so, but once again you decide to leave without an explanation."

Bill turned back toward Ann and raised his right hand to show the two letters. "I came to deliver these. One is a card thanking Sarah for her help while I was in the hospital, and the other is a letter to you. I wrote it while I was still in the hospital, after Sarah asked me about the photograph. In that same conversation, I told her about writing letters to you, so many throughout the years but ... never mailed. I kept them all, except this one that I wanted to give to you." Bill paused, trying to see if there was any softening of Ann's reaction to him appearing at her doorstep. There was none; she glared at him, arms folded tightly across her chest. He added, "I wanted to give you this letter in person and ask how you are."

Ann's voice was strained as she spoke, "See the mailbox?" Bill nodded. "Put Sarah's card in it, and as far as the other one, you can put it with all the others you wrote."

"Sorry to have bothered you," Bill answered, dejected, unable to look at Ann. In one way, Ann's words were his prophecy foretold: rejection. In another way, they were a shock and stung deeply.

Bill placed Sarah's card in the mailbox then turned and, with head down, made his way back to his car. Ann stood at the door and watched him drive away until his car turned at the corner and he was gone.

Chapter Twenty-Three

"I'M HOME!" SARAH CALLED OUT AS SHE STEPPED INTO the living room and shut the front door behind her.

"In the kitchen," Ann replied from a distance.

Sarah glanced down at the coffee table and noticed the mail. It was Ann's habit to leave Sarah's mail on that table. There were several pieces stacked one upon the other, and Sarah began to shuffle through them as she made her way to the kitchen. Most were junk mail, but the fourth piece was smaller and different. Her name and address was handwritten, which she did not recognize until she read the return address. Sarah was surprised that Bill sent something to her in the mail and even more surprised that it came to her home rather than the office. She wondered if Ann had noticed whom it was from.

"How was your day?" Sarah asked her grandmother as she leaned over her shoulder to see what was in the pan that Ann stirred, giving her a kiss on the cheek.

"Interesting," Ann's answered without taking her eyes off the pan.

"How so?"

"Well, I had a visitor."

"And who might that have been?" Sarah asked, as she started to flip through the last couple of pieces of her mail.

"One Mr. William Harold Weber."

Sarah's body jerked slightly in reaction to hearing Ann speak Bill's full name, let alone the fact that he had come to the house. At first, she didn't know what to say, then responded, "Wow, that's surprising. Did you know that I received a piece of mail from him today?"

"He delivered it."

"He did?"

"Yes, along with a letter that he wrote to me when he was in the hospital recently."

Sarah's heart began to pound faster as she asked, "Do you mind if I ask what he said in his letter to you?"

Ann continued to stare at the pan, her back toward Sarah. "I don't know. I told him I did not want the letter, and he could put it away with all the other letters he supposedly wrote to me over the years."

"What letters are those?" Sarah tried to ask innocently, already knowing the answer from her conversation with Bill.

Ann turned and leaned against the kitchen counter, facing Sarah. "He said that he wrote letters to me over all these years but never mailed them. How crazy is that?" She paused and gave Sarah that look — the one that let Sarah know she had been caught —before adding, "But then you already knew about the letters, didn't you?"

In an instant, Sarah's faced blushed and she stammered slightly in her response. "Well, yes … yes, Harry — I mean Bill — told me about all the letters. Letters written to you since … since whatever happened between you two." Sarah paused, hoping her grandmother would say more, but Ann only asked a question, "What else did he tell you?"

Sarah decided it was time to tell all and that, with Bill showing up at the house, all promises were off. "He didn't tell me what happened between the two of you, just said that at the time he did what he thought was right, out of his love for you. When he realized what a fool he had been, it was too late. He had received the last letter you ever wrote to him, telling him you had moved on with your life."

"So why did he continue to write letters to me? The ones he never sent?" Ann asked coldly.

"He said he did it for different reasons. He said that writing all the letters to you was like having a conversation with you, and it helped him through the tough times when he thought he would go crazy over missing you. Bill said he wrote because he had never stopped loving you."

Ann and Sarah's eyes now searched one another, seeking out more than what the words had conveyed. Then Ann turned away from Sarah, placed her hands on the counter, and stared off into the distance as she looked through the kitchen window above the sink.

Sarah waited a moment longer before asking, "Do you want to talk about it?"

"No," Ann answered.

Sarah scanned the dining room looking for Bill, but he was not there. Two days had passed since Bill's visit to Ann's home, and Sarah had not seen him since then. She had hesitated to call or go to his apartment, hoping to run into him, and then nonchalantly try to broach the subject of his visit. Perhaps Bill would have more to say than her grandmother did, but from the looks of things, she was not going to find out today.

"Hi Sarah," Carl spoke as he began to clear a table nearby.

"Oh, hi Carl." Sarah spoke then added, "Say Carl, have you seen Mr. Weber today?"

"Not yet. Is he doing OK?"

"Yeah, I think so, just thought I would check on him while he was here eating." What she had told Carl was true, just not exactly why she wanted to see Bill. She did want to make sure he was doing OK physically, but at the moment she mostly wanted to know how he was feeling after Ann's rejection of the letter he had written to her.

"You know the rumor is that Mr. Weber's last trip to the hospital was a lot worse than he ever let on. Some of the residents are already talking about when his condo will go up for sale — if you know what I mean."

"Who's saying that?" Sarah shot back at Carl. There was surprise and anger in her voice. She had not heard the rumor, whose origin most likely came from Mrs. Sadler. *That woman is so mean*, Sarah thought. "That's just not true. He's fine, just needs a little more time to recover his strength." Sarah spoke firmly, partly to convince herself.

"It came from the normal gossip mill. I'm sure they're way off-base." Now Carl was trying to reassure Sarah. He liked Sarah. She was good to all the residents, and he could see that she did not appreciate people speculating on Mr. Weber's condition. Carl wished he had kept the rumor to himself, but it was too late.

"Yeah. See you Carl," was all Sarah spoke as she walked away, deep in thought.

"Hi, Mr. Weber. Good to see you," Carl greeted Bill as he pulled the chair back in order for him to take his regular table — a small two-seater by the window. "What can I get for you today?"

"Good to see you too, Carl. I'm not very hungry. Maybe just a small salad to start, then I'll decide if I want anything else. And a glass of water with lemon."

"Coming right up." Carl turned and made his way to the kitchen. Before grabbing the salad off the ready line, he headed to the phone to call Sarah. She picked up on the second ring.

"Mr. Weber's here now, just thought I would let you know." Carl jumped right past the formalities of a greeting.

Sarah was silent for a moment, catching up with Carl's quick announcement. Then she replied, "Thanks, Carl. I'll be right over. Please don't mention to him that I am coming. I'll just surprise him."

"Gotcha. See you in a minute." With that, Carl hung up the phone, picked up the salad, along with a small bowl of Bill's favorite dressing, and headed back out to his table. As he approached Bill's table, he noticed him staring out the window, shoulders slumped, and a sullen look on his face that showed no spirit.

"Thanks," was all Bill said as Carl placed the salad in front of him.

"What? You mean you're not going to give me a hard time?" It was Bill's routine to almost always give Carl a hard time when he brought the food out, always in jest. Usually, Bill would say, *It sure took you long enough* or *That's not what I ordered.*

"Not today, Carl."

"OK, I'll let you slide." Carl paused then added, "And, you're in luck. Looks like you have company."

Bill looked up to see Sarah approaching his table. As he rose to greet her, he felt a mixture of being glad to see her and a wave of embarrassment stemming from his decision to go to Ann's.

"Hello, Bill," Sarah called out first and smiled. She too was feeling a little apprehensive, but glad that she finally had this opportunity to run into him.

"Hello to you, too. It's nice to see you. Please have a seat."

Carl had pulled the chair back for her to sit. "Sarah, can I get you anything? So far, Mr. Weber has only ordered that salad, but I'm going to see if I can twist his arm and let me bring him something a bit more substantial." Carl wanted to take Sarah's order, but also wanted her to know that Bill wasn't eating much today.

"I'll start with a salad, too. Maybe I can help you convince him that he needs more than just the salad."

"Coming right up."

After a moment of uneasy silence, as Bill fidgeted with his napkin and Sarah straightened the silverware in front of her, she spoke first. "Thank you for the card. It was very thoughtful of you to send it, but I'm always happy to be of any help that I can. You're worth the effort." Sarah gave Bill a big smile and reached across the table to squeeze his hand.

"Thanks, Sarah," Bill responded, somewhat timidly as he looked toward Sarah. She couldn't help but notice his face was thinner and appeared ashen. There was also an absence of the sparkle that was most often in his eyes. After another brief moment of silence, he added, "Did your grandmother tell you how the card made it to your house?"

"Yes, she did." Sarah felt relieved that Bill had opened the door to this conversation. "She also told me about a letter that you wrote to her."

"You mean, the one she wouldn't accept." This time, Bill's voice contained an odd mixture of resignation and slight hostility.

"Did you think she would accept it?" Sarah asked.

"Why would I go to your house if I didn't think she would?" His voice rose in anger, spoken as he had never done to Sarah before. Then he caught himself, let out a deflated sigh, and turned his head to stare out the window, avoiding eye contact with Sarah. "I'm sorry. I didn't mean to raise my voice. I shouldn't have gone. I was a fool. Once a fool, always a fool."

"Bill, look at me. Please," Sarah asked and then waited. He turned his head to look at her, then she continued, "You are not a fool. I think it was brave of you to make the effort. I'm sorry that Nana didn't take the letter. I don't know why she didn't, but I am sure she had her reasons just as you had your reasons for making the effort to reach out to her after all these years." Sarah paused again, hoping Bill would say something about his effort, but he didn't, rather remaining silent and turning his gaze back out the window. Sarah did not want their conversation to end this way, so she continued, "I don't know what happened between you two. It was a long time ago — gosh, probably when you both were about my age — but I do know that each of you must have cared very deeply for the other then."

"I still do," was Bill's only reply.

"How do you really know that? People change, lives change, and time changes people," Sarah asked, surprised that she had.

Bill was slow to answer, and before he did, he turned to look at her once again. "Sarah, I wish I could explain it better. Like I tried to explain before, when we talked at the hospital, it's a feeling that comes to live within you and never goes away. I choose to believe that there is an eternity for our souls, and that the love we feel for another goes on forever as a part of it." Then Bill caught himself, "I'm sorry. I shouldn't be saying all of this to you again. I'm just an old man being a fool."

"Don't call yourself a fool! I do appreciate you trying to explain it all to me. I have never had those feelings toward someone special, but as you describe them, I can only hope that I do someday."

"I hope you do too, Sarah. I know the way I described it isn't the best, but loving someone the way that I love your grandmother is a wonderful feeling — knowing, just knowing, and carrying that feeling with you every day of your life. At least I have since I was 17. Oh, there were certainly stormy times between the two of us, but even in the midst of those times there was that feeling."

Before either could speak further again, Carl approached their table with Sarah's salad. "Here you go, Sarah. Now, can I tempt you two with anything else today? Mr. Weber, we have baked steak."

"No, I think I'm good for now," Bill answered, then asked. "Sarah, do you care for anything else?"

"No, this will do it for me. Thanks, Carl."

As Carl moved on to the next table he was serving, Bill hesitantly asked Sarah, "Did your grandmother say anything about me?"

"No ... not the other day, or even before." Sarah hesitated then decided to share with him a little more. "When I was a little girl, I loved looking at family pictures, especially the one you have of her. I asked Nana about it — many times — but she would never talk about it. At most, she would say that it was a long time ago. A couple of times, I asked her who took the picture, and all she would say was *someone taken away from me by the war.* I thought she meant *killed in the war,* but when I saw the picture on your desk, I began to wonder if it was you who took the picture. Now, I'm not sure what she meant by *taken from me by the war.*" Sarah paused and then asked, "So, what are you going to do now?"

"Finish my salad."

Sarah smiled. "Are you trying to say that this conversation about you and my grandmother is over?"

"For now, but most likely forever."

"Bill, don't give up. Don't shut down. What you feel for her, the letters, even the bad decision you made a long time ago — whatever it was — they have all been from the heart. Do more than just let it wither away inside you."

Bill looked up at Sarah, pushed the half-eaten salad to the side, and said, "Sarah, I do appreciate your thoughts and your caring. You know, I can see and hear a great deal of your grandmother in you. She was quite a spirited young lady: smart, a wit as quick as I have ever seen, and — at times — on the stubborn side. But, even when she was being stubborn, it usually turned out that she was also being right about something. You are a fortunate woman to have her in your life." He paused to place his napkin on the table. "Now, if you will excuse me, I need to get back to the condo and rest."

When Bill stood, Sarah knew there was no sense in trying to continue the conversation. As he walked passed her, he stopped to place his hand on her shoulder, gave it a gentle squeeze, and said, "Thanks."

Sarah placed her hand around his wrist and returned the squeeze. "Please ... don't give up," she softly replied, then released his wrist and listened to his footsteps walking away.

"I thought you were going out tonight?" Ann asked when she saw Sarah walk into the family room already in her pj's.

"No, I changed my mind. It was a stressful day at work, and think I'd rather just stay at home."

"What's up at work?

"Well, lots of paperwork and short deadlines, all of which keep me from doing what I enjoy most: spending time with the residents and leading some of the activities. But I did spend a little time with one of the residents today." Sarah paused, hoping her grandmother would bite and ask.

"And who was that?" Ann asked.

"Bill. He asked about you."

Sarah looked in her grandmother's direction to see her reaction. Ann was seated in her favorite chair, and on her lap was a sketchpad. She had no visible reaction to what Sarah had shared with her, just kept her pencil moving, drawing something that Sarah probably never would see. After a minute or two of silence, Sarah decided that neitherwould her grandmother respond, nor would she pursue the topic.

Her grandmother surprised her with, "I assume you did not tell him anything?"

"No. I did not say anything about you other than you had told me about him delivering or attempting to deliver the letter."

"Where did you see him?" Ann asked, without looking up from her sketchpad.

Sarah wasn't sure where the conversation was going, but at least it kept Bill in the mix. "In the dining room. Our lunchtime conversations are where I got to know him. But, since he left the hospital, I'm seeing him less."

"Will you see him tomorrow?"

"No, since tomorrow's Thursday, it's the staff's weekly working lunch with Mr. Wilkins. To be honest, they aren't very productive, but guess I better show up."

"What time does it start?"

"At noon, which is usually about the time I run into Bill. Almost always, he eats precisely at 12:00. He says it was the military that made him so punctual."

"Good afternoon, Mr. Weber. Good-looking sweater you got on. Trying to impress the ladies today?" Carl joked as he greeted Bill.

"Thanks, Carl. No, no ladies, just trying to stay warm." Bill offered.

"What can I get for you?"

"Let's start with a salad again, then I'll try to add something to it."

"You got it! Coming right up." Carl stopped to remove a couple of empty plates from a nearby table then made his way to the kitchen.

"Here you go. One *delicious, homemade* salad for you," Carl said as he placed the salad in front of Bill.

"Now, Carl, you know and I know that the salad comes out of a bag and the dressing comes out of a bottle," he teased Carl in response.

"You got me, but I bet you'll still enjoy the salad, especially since it was delivered with such *impeccable* service," Carl joked. He was glad that Mr. Weber was up for a little bantering. Before Bill could respond again, he continued. "Are you expecting company? She seems to be headed this way. May I introduce you to this lovely lady, or have you met before?" Carl knew the approaching guest. She had visited the dining room several times over the past few years, but always with Sarah.

Bill did not immediately look up. His first thought was that Sarah had returned for another lunch visit, and that Carl was just teasing him about an introduction. Then he began to swivel slightly in his chair, intending to rise and greet her. In that same motion, he looked up and was surprised to see it wasn't Sarah. Bill collapsed back into his chair and stared at his approaching, unexpected guest.

It was Ann, and she offered an answer to the question she had heard Carl ask. "Hi, Carl. No introductions necessary. We met a long time ago."

Chapter Twenty-Four

WITH ANN SEATED AT BILL'S TABLE, CARL ASKED IF she would care for something to drink. He also studied the two, trying to put the pieces together. He knew Ann through Sarah and had waited on them a number of times over the years. But Carl had never seen Ann with Mr. Weber.

"Just coffee for now. Thanks, Carl."

Bill looked at Ann sitting across from him but, for now, her eyes avoided his. He was having difficulty coming to grips with her presence. It seemed almost surreal to him. While this was something he had wanted more than anything else, he had come to believe that it would never happen — a feeling greatly reinforced by the outcome of his brief, unannounced, and disastrous visit to Ann's home just a few weeks ago.

"How are you?" Bill asked in an effort to break the silence.

Ann made eye contact with him and then the two interlocked their gazes before she answered, "I'm here." Ann paused, as if to catch herself, sighed slightly, and continued, "To be honest, I'm not quite sure why I did come, but I'm here now. And, since your *unexpected* visit, I have been thinking of returning the *favor*." As her words referenced his uninvited appearance at her home, Ann offered — for the first time — a slight smile that came across her lips.

Bill grinned and chuckled slightly. He had always loved to see Ann smile and was delighted to see it again after so many years. He was also trying to imagine what other thoughts she was thinking but not saying. "Well, for me to be honest as well, I'm shocked that you're here, but very pleased," Bill offered.

"Honesty, is that a new trait for you?" In an instant, Ann's words cut to the heart of the matter and collapsed all the years apart, as if Bill abandoning her had just happened yesterday. "Sorry, that may have been a *little* abrupt, but you know me."

"No apology needed, you speak the truth and your mind. You always did." This time, Bill looked away and his voiced seemed to fade.

"What are you doing here, Bill?" Ann asked, in a tone that mixed urgency and irritation.

"Not sure what you're asking," Bill responded, still not looking at Ann but at the table, turning his fork over and over.

"Let's see. Why Summersville? Why now? Why the Drake? And, oh yes ... why were you such an ass to just walk away from what we had?" Ann paused then quickly added, "Just thought I would throw that last one in for good measure."

Bill looked up as Ann's last question shot through him. Her lips were drawn tightly shut. There was no smile. He didn't understand why she'd asked it. He had explained it all in *the* letter; the one she responded to — saying she was moving on with her life.

Before Bill could begin answering Ann's questions, she added, "By the way, I hate that you now go by Harry. As you may recall, I told you when it first came about in flight school that I did not like it, still don't. It just doesn't suit you." Bill took Ann's add-on as a way for her to slightly soften her last piercing question, but in no way to take it back.

"Can I start with the easy questions first?" Bill asked.

"You always did. It's the *avoider* in you," Ann shot back.

"Do I not get partial credit for showing up at your house and trying to give you the letter I wrote?" Bill asked, but knew what

Ann's answer would be. He was also trying to lighten the mood just a bit, or maybe he really was trying to avoid answering her bigger questions.

"You really don't want me to answer that," came Ann's quick response.

"OK, sorry," Bill answered, only to be cut off in an instant by Ann.

"And quit apologizing. Save your apologies for when you *really* need them."

Bill continued. "I don't know what all, if anything, Sarah has shared with you about how I got here." He did not want to repeat what Ann might already know, but he was also interested in trying to learn what the two of them might have discussed about him.

"Doesn't matter. I want to hear it from you." Ann caught herself then added, "All I know is that Sarah talked about a resident named Harry and something about him being so nice to her friend, Helen, and her husband, Ben."

Bill took a deep breath, let out a shallow sigh, and gazed out the window as he began to speak, "For a lot of ..."

Ann cut him off. "Hey, I am over here. Look at me."

"Sorr ... " Bill caught himself before he finished *sorry,* then started again. "Well, for a lot of years, I thought about moving to Summersville but never did more than think about it. Then one Sunday, about a year ago, I saw an article in the newspaper describing the Drake and all that it offered. As it turned out, Sarah had actually written it." Bill paused in order to try to get a read on Ann.

"I'm listening," was all she offered.

For the next hour, Bill shared with Ann the unfolding of events that brought him to Summersville and the Drake Living Center. Little of what he shared dove deeper than a couple of years past. He told of buying the place sight unseen, but did not mention the view from his study. He spoke kindly of Frank helping him unpack the car and being the one to find him when he "took a tumble." Bill told of his first meeting with Sarah and how the connection with her friend, Helen, had come about. As Bill talked, Ann mostly listened, not attempting to redirect the conversation or influence it, even if Bill continued to avoid the most difficult parts of what needed to be said.

Bill was surprised at how freely he was speaking and how easy it was to share all of this with Ann. At times, he would have flashes of conversations with Ann from long ago. Ann always had a way of getting Bill to open up and speak freely, something that was not in his normal character. As he was drawing near the end of answering the *easy* questions, he twisted slightly in his chair and, in doing so, could see the person now sitting at the table behind him: Mrs. Sadler. Bill had no idea how long she had been sitting there; however, he was very sure she was trying her best to hear every word of his conversation with Ann. He assumed Mrs. Sadler did not know who Ann was, but then quickly decided that might be a bad assumption. She made it her mission to know as much about everyone as possible.

"OK, so you have answered the easy questions. Now, tell me the rest of what I'm waiting to hear," Ann stated with the first hint of any impatience.

Bill looked at Ann and, with a roll of his eyes and a slight backward head nod as well as lipping the word *nosy,* made an effort to indicate to Ann that their conversation had an eavesdropper. Ann understood his message, nodding in acknowledgement.

Bill spoke in a whispered voice, "Ann, I will answer the hard question, but can we go back to my apartment and continue this conversation?"

Ann looked at Bill, studying him and his invitation, then stood and moved closer to his chair, which also placed her near Mrs. Sadler. "Sure, but don't think you are going to get *lucky*." Ann's response was spoken loud and clear, enough for the eavesdropping neighbor to hear without any difficulty. Bill grinned as he stood to follow Ann out the door.

The two walked to Bill's apartment, side by side; a feeling of uneasiness prevailed and they didn't speak. Bill wondered what Ann was thinking and exactly how he would answer *the question*; would he stick to the lie that the letter contained or would he now tell her the truth? Thinking of the only options, he felt tension and apprehension building up inside. Neither one was good, and both could produce further disasterous results. He did not want this to be the last time he saw Ann. Bill also thought about the many times Ann and he had walked hand-in-hand. There was a time when it would have seemed so natural for him to reach out to take her hand in his, but he dared not now. Bill was grateful for the recollection of those fondest moments. Being able to pull them out of memory had helped him through the years, but he also knew this was a very different time. When they reached the apartment, Bill turned the key to his front door lock and stepped back as a gesture for Ann to enter first.

"Nice place you have here. Who's your decorator?" Ann spoke, as she stepped into the living room, seeing its sparse contents.

Bill smiled; he knew Ann's first comment was sincere and the second was taking a playful jab at his decorating efforts, or lack thereof. His condo had tall ceilings with ornate molding as well as tall, beautiful windows — original details from when the building was first erected over a hundred years ago. However, the living room definitely lacked any decorating efforts. What was present was more mishmash than a collection of complementing pieces.

Ann surveyed the area a bit more, then asked, "So, where is the picture?"

It took a second for Ann's question to register with Bill before he answered. "Oh, it's on my desk in the study."

"I want to see it."

Ann followed Bill to his study. He stopped at its doorway and stepped to the side, gesturing for her to enter first. Ann made her way to the middle of the room, looking one direction then the other to survey its contents. In stark contrast to the living room's appearance, Bill's study appeared rich in color, nicely decorated, and filled with mementos of a lifetime. Ann stepped to the bookshelf, picked up the baseball mitt, and as she did, confirmed that it was the one she had autographed. "Oh my God! I can't believe you still have this glove!"

Bill laughed and replied, "And I still can't believe you autographed it."

"Hey, I was just letting you know my name. You kept asking," Ann answered as she looked at Bill, and he saw a twinkle of mischievousness. For just a moment, the two were again sharing that summer's day from so long ago. She returned the glove to its place on the bookshelf and walked toward the wooden boxes sitting on the floor beside the desk. "What's in the boxes?" Ann asked.

"I thought you knew," Bill answered.

"Maybe, but tell me anyway," Ann said as she kneeled to take a closer look at the boxes.

Bill tried to speak but, at first, the words wouldn't come out. Then in a weak and broken voice he said, "Letters, all letters to you. The first one goes back to when I was in the hospital in Germany after the helicopter crash, and the last one was written a couple of days after I paid you that visit — trying to deliver a letter to you. Guess you could say I got shot down with that one, too." Bill paused to see if Ann reacted to his attempt at humor.

She did not, so he continued, "All the letters in-between record my life as I lived it and shared with you."

Ann stood quickly and wheeled around to face Bill, her hands on her hips and anger in her eyes. "Shared! Shared! You mean the life you wrote about and shared with a piece of paper that got stuck away in some damn box." Ann's words and the look in her eyes spit fire at Bill.

Bill stammered as he tried to respond, "Yes ... yes, I mean ... yes, you are correct. I did not share them with you, of course not, that is not what I meant to say. I ... I meant that I wrote about my life, and what I wrote often reflected on moments and feelings we had once shared. The letters were for me. They helped me tie the present that I lived to the past that we had shared."

Ann offered no immediate response or acknowledgement of what Bill had said, but some of her anger had been appeased by his response. She stepped to the window, looking outward at its view. "When you described your condo to me, you didn't mention that you could see the bay from here."

"It certainly is beautiful to look at, but it wasn't the bay that I bought this place to look at. It was the ballpark."

Ann continued to look out the window as her hands nervously played with the edge of the drape. "Why the ballpark?" she asked, knowing the answer.

"Because that's where we met," Bill answered.

"Met? You tried to kill me, tried to run me over when you charged off the bus!" Ann responded as she turned toward Bill; her eyebrows raised and just a hint of mischievousness danced in her eyes.

"You and I will just never agree on who was at fault," he offered in response.

"No, because there is only one right answer." Ann shot Bill a quick glance and a half-smile to emphasize her point. She then walked to the desk and picked up the picture. "This is such a terrible picture of me."

"You always said that about every picture that was taken of you," Bill protested then continued, "I love that picture and that it forever captured all that we shared that last day."

Ann returned the picture to its place on the desk and then moved back to stand by the window, not looking at Bill. After a moment of silence, she spoke with a sad tone. "I hated that you were leaving. My heart was breaking. I remember an incredible feeling of sadness that seemed to be swallowing me, but I didn't want to show it. I wanted to put on a brave front for you. From my expression in the picture, I didn't do a very good job."

"Ann, I hated to leave you and never wanted that weekend to end. I never wanted our lives together to end," Bill offered and then instantly realized his words struck at Ann rather than sooth her.

Ann's eyes flashed with anger, and her words came quickly, "But you left and, oh yeah, never came back. So much for not wanting our lives together to never end." Ann's comment struck hard at Bill, because he knew that Ann spoke the truth.

Bill waited to see if Ann would add anything further. She did not, seeming to be now absorbed with reading the inscriptions on the plaques and citations displayed. He asked, "Do you want to go into the living room to talk?"

"No, I think I want to stay here for now," Ann said as she sat down on the chair by the window.

Bill followed Ann's lead and took a seat at the desk chair. They each looked at one another without speaking, waiting for Bill to answer *the question*. He began. "Do you remember Bill Estep? He was my stick buddy in flight school, and after graduation, we were in Vietnam together."

"I remember," was all Ann offered.

"He's the one who wrote the first few letters from me to you after I ended up in the hospital and couldn't write on my own." Bill paused, looked down, and then barely audible continued with the truth. "The last one he wrote was the one that I lied to you, the one that I said I had found someone else — an Army nurse at the hosptial. He was furious at me, said he would write it so I could get the craziness off my chest, but at first, said he wouldn't mail it. But, he finally took the letter to mail when he left the hospital that day. That was the last time I ever saw him."

Ann jumped to her feet, and Bill saw anger flash in her eyes again. "What are you talking about?" Her voice was raised, almost shouting. "I did *not* receive a letter from you telling me you found someone else! Believe me, I would remember *that* one. Why would you lie and write such a terrible thing?"

Ann's response threw Bill and confused him. "But — but you wrote back. You wrote that you accepted my decision and was moving on with your life."

"I did no such thing!" Ann's lips twitched as she fought to hold back the tears and a torrent of anger that swelled inside her. Her words came fast and furious. "This makes no sense! I wrote you lots of letters — almost every day — hoping and praying that you would respond. Your letters just stopped coming! Bill, I told you that I loved you, over and over again. That I didn't know what was going on or why you had stopped writing. After weeks and weeks of nothing from you, I wrote to say that if you continued to not write, all I could do was assume you had stopped loving me. I waited, Bill — and nothing from you! Do you know how I felt? Every day going to the mailbox and praying that there would be a letter from you and every day nothing! I was a wreck. Finally, I did write that I was moving on with my life. It was that or die from heartbreak, and that was not an option." Ann wiped the tears from her eyes and in a softer tone, spoken not from conciliation but from emotional exhaustion, added, "At least I tried to reach out to you. You just unilaterally chose to cut me out of your life! Why? What is the truth?"

Bill tried to speak but choked on his words. He cleared his throat and began again, telling her — for the first time — the truth. "I couldn't give you what you wanted." His head hung low and tears filled his eyes. Bill looked up, and their eyes met. "Annie, almost since the day we first met, you always talked about having a big family — five or six children — and when you did, you would just light up. I always thought that they would be *our* children, but then the injuries from being shot down and the crash took all of that away for me. I knew if we stayed together, I could never be the father of your children." Bill paused briefly and added, "You were born to be a mother." Bill paused again. Ann sat motionless on the edge of the chair, tears streaming down her cheeks. She no longer looked at Bill but out the window at the ballpark. He continued.

"After the doctors told me I would never be able to father children, I had one hell of a pity party. My insides were all messed up, but my thinking was even more messed up. I decided that if I told you the truth, you would fight back — try to hold on — but if I lied and told you I had found someone else, then you would see it as having no alternative but to go on with your life."

"You are one selfish bastard, Bill!" Ann snapped, turning momentarily toward him, then back to looking out the window. Her voice rose sharply to add, "You had no right to think for me or make decisions for me! You even lied about your injuries, trying to tell me that the accident was no big deal. Who do you think you are?"

"Then … I thought I was being so noble, giving way to your desires for a family, sacrificing all in the name of love. But, not too long afterward and to this day I know that I was a foolish, foolish young man. That decision — made as much out of self-pity as love for you — has haunted me for years. Writing all

255

those letters, later, helped me cope some with a life without you. Hell, sometimes they just helped me cope with life itself. The only things that have stayed true for me are that I have always loved you and that I wanted you to have what I couldn't give you."

"Bill … it just makes no sense … throwing me away … holding onto some naïve thought of love … just no sense … none of it," Ann said slowly as she moved her head slowly side to side.

"Maybe not, maybe it doesn't to you. And, being honest with you, there have been times that it made no sense to me. But, most of the time, and especially in these latter years of life, I have come to peace with it all. What I did was wrong, and it couldn't be undone. I could only hope that life had brought you the very best. As for me, the love I felt for you then has remained with me all these days, and I am convinced that it will be with me *forever* —'eternally,' as we used to say."

Ann responded, her voice not as loud but still filled with anger. "It sounds to me like you threw us away and then did the same with your life. You could have had love, but you threw that away too by holding onto — oh, I don't know — just some thought of me, and some youthful, dreamy idea of love. To me, love without any connection is just not love."

"I know I did wrong in lying to you and, yes … because I did, I did throw us away. I did it — or so I thought at the time — because I loved you so much but that was the not love. It wasn't an act of love at all. But, I did not throw my life away. Maybe it makes no sense to you, but the love I have for you has been there since the day we met — right out there by that ball field — and it has been with me every day since. Maybe me writing the letters was naively seeking that connection you believe is essential, but I know it really is possible to love someone when they are not in your life just as much as it is when you are side-by-side. I have done it; I have felt it. And, if that love for you has been with me this long, I am convinced it just doesn't stop. It goes with the soul into eternity.

Ann said nothing more, standing by the window and looking out at the bay, the ballpark, and the hint of blue sky trying to break through the clouds.

Bill wanted to change their conversational focus to Ann's life. He had to know. "What about your husband and your family? Sarah has not told me anything except that her mom died when she was just a baby and that you raised her. She has never mentioned anything about aunts and uncles."

"She doesn't have any. Her mom was my only child," Ann responded coldly.

Bill was surprised; almost stunned that Ann had had only the one child. "I'm so sorry that you lost your daughter. I can only imagine how difficult that was for you and your husband."

"I never married. It was just me and Eileen — Sarah's mom. Eileen was a beautiful, wonderful, loving daughter. She had Sarah when she was just 18. Sarah's father was never in the picture and gave up his parental rights not long after she was born. When Eileen was killed, I thought I would die too. It was Sarah and caring for her that kept me going."

"Was Eileen's father at least around when she was growing up?"

Ann sat down again, almost collapsing into the chair. She first looked up at the ceiling then back down at Bill. "No, he wasn't. He left us, before Eileen was born."

Bill could not believe what he was hearing. First, he had left Ann and then another man that Ann had loved abandoned her, too, except he also abandoned his unborn daughter. Bill struggled to find words, any words that would convey his feelings and thoughts. Finally, he spoke. "How could he have done that? How could he just leave you and his unborn child?"

Ann stood, walked to the study's door, then paused to face Bill one more time. "Guess only you can answer that question." Her words crashed against Bill's mind as he tried to comprehend what she had just said. Then she sarcastically spoke, "Don't get up. I will show myself out."

Bill was stunned; the room spun. Two competing, circular thoughts pounded in his head: He was a father! And how could Ann not have told him? After a few moments, a third thought entered his mind; he had not heard the front door open and close. Bill stood, saw the picture of Ann on his desk, and looked at it in a way he never had done so before — with anger. The woman in the picture was the mother of his child he had never known because she had never told him until now.

Bill made his way to the living room. Ann was sitting on the couch, motionless, tears streaming down her cheeks, looking straight ahead with a stare that took her far away from the room but to exactly where Bill did not know until she spoke. "She had your eyes and smile."

"How could you not tell me!" Bill shouted in a demanding voice.

Ann's snapped back. "You bastard, you abandoned me!" Ann's lips were drawn tight and anger filled ever word. "If you didn't want me then, I knew you sure as hell didn't want a child."

"You knew! Now who was deciding for whom? Don't you think that was my decision to make?" Bill yelled.

"You didn't give me that *luxury*. You see, you weren't communicating with ME, or did you forget? I wrote you telling you how much I loved you, over and over again. I called the hospitals — both overseas and stateside — but the calls would be disconnected, or I would find out that you had been transferred, or be told that you weren't taking calls. Did you once call me? No! In every way, you were rejecting me. I had no choice. I would not use our child, the child we created, as a bargaining chip to draw you back into my life."

Bill eased himself down onto the couch at the opposite end from Ann. As he did, he said nothing more, struggling to come to grips with the truth, but holding onto Ann's words of *our child*. Finally he spoke, but in a hazy way, as if mostly just thinking to himself. "What now?"

"What do you mean?" Ann questioned.

"Does Sarah know any of this?" Bill asked.

"No," Ann replied.

"I want to know about our Eileen," Bill stated with firmness.

"You mean the daughter you never knew because you abandoned us," Ann snapped back.

"Damn it, Ann, stop! You had no right not to tell me, to keep me from knowing and loving our daughter! You owe it to me," Bill insisted.

"I don't owe you a damn thing!" Ann stood, grabbed her coat that was draped across the arm of the couch, and moved past Bill, headed to the front door.

Still sitting on the couch, Bill reached out and grabbed Ann's wrist, circling it with a firm hand, in an effort to prevent her departure, not in violence or anger. As he held tightly to her wrist, he was looking down at the living room floor, and his shoulders jerked up and down as he sobbed. Finally, he spoke. "Annie, I am so sorry; sorry for hurting you, for abandoning you, and for being such a fool. You're right; you owe me nothing. I can only hope that one day you will find it in your heart to share your memories of our daughter."

Ann stood motionless and offered no response. Then she turned more in his direction and placed her free hand over his hand that bound her other wrist. The touch was not in an effort to loosen Bill's grip but a gentle, soothing one. She rubbed the palm of her hand across the back of his hand as it still held her wrist. As he opened his grip, Ann used her two hands to hold his hand in hers. He took her hand in his, then reached up with his other hand. Now their four hands intertwined, holding tightly to one another. She stood above Bill and looked down at him. He did not look up at Ann, but pulled their hands toward his head so that now his forehead was pressed against her hands, against Ann's belly — where Eileen had once been. His shoulders continued to heave as sobs filled the air and tears rolled from his eyes.

Finally, Ann's words broke the silence. "We'll talk again," she offered." Then she added, "Promise."

After moments of silence, each softly and somewhat reluctantly released the other's hands. Ann continued toward the door. Bill heard the handle turn and the door open then close. She was gone, and he was left with the knowledge of a daughter he'd never known, of a granddaughter that he had come to know only through her work at the Center, and desperately clinging to hope offered in Ann's single word, "Promise."

Chapter Twenty-Five

"HELLO." BILL ANSWERED THE PHONE WITH RELUCTANCE. His phone did not ring often, and he wasn't expecting a call. More times than not the incoming calls were trying to sell something or sounded like a probable scam.

"Bill, this is Ann."

Bill was surprised that she was phoning and pleased to hear her voice. He recognized it as soon as she said *Bill*. A week had passed since their time in his condo. For some reason, Bill thought that if Ann kept her promise, she would knock on his door one day or show up again in the Drake's dining room. He wasn't sure how she got his number.

"Hi, Ann. Nice to hear your voice. How are you?"

"I'm OK, just been busy, and doing some thinking about things you and I discussed."

"Me too. Well, not so much the busy part but definitely the thinking part."

"Do you want to come to my house tomorrow, around 2:00 or so?" Ann asked.

"Tomorrow sounds fine, and I appreciate the invitation. Have you said anything to Sarah? I haven't seen her since you and I talked."

"No, I haven't said anything to her, and why don't you save all the questions until tomorrow."

"Sure, *sor* ..." Bill caught himself, then continued. "I look forward to it."

"See you tomorrow." Ann hung up the phone without saying anything more.

Bill held the phone to his ear for a second longer, then placed it back on the receiver. He was grateful to hear from Ann; it had just been a long, difficult week as he had waited. As the days had passed, Bill worried and started to wonder if Ann would keep her promise.

Ann hung up the kitchen phone and then leaned against the cabinet, releasing a deep sigh. It had been a difficult decision for her to reach — to keep her promise to Bill. She would do so, but she still wasn't sure how far their conversation would go. Over the last week both poignant and treasured moments from their past had played out across her mind in vivid detail.

Ann recalled the deep anger she had felt toward Bill. Though she had moved on with her life, the anger would surface at unexpected times. Ann could not deny that at other times, she missed Bill so very much and her thoughts were about the life they should be sharing. As the years progressed, the intense anger surfaced less and less, but a love for him remained within her though Ann rarely acknowledged it to herself and never to others. Maybe it was because Bill was the father of her child, maybe it was because of all that they had shared during their years together, or maybe it was simply because there would always be a presence or semblance of love for Bill in her heart.

Now, after all these years, all of these feelings — especially the anger — were beginning to stir within her, and what for? Why allow Bill even a peek into her life? But she had opened the door with her promise and now an invitation to him. In a little over 24 hours, their past would be cast into the light of a present-day conversation and those long dormant feelings might be awakened.

Precisely at 2:00, Bill rang Ann's doorbell. He was feeling both anxious and grateful — the latter from Ann's invitation but anxious because of the uncertainty of the direction their conversation would take.

Ann had been pacing, watching the street from the living room window, and saw his car pull up in front of the house. She hesitated for a few seconds before she answered the door. "Hi, Bill. Please come in."

"Thanks. I appreciate your invitation."

Ann moved away from the door as she spoke. "We can sit here in the living room or go into the family room."

"Whichever you prefer. Where do you spend most of your time?"

"Let's sit in the family room. This way," Ann said, then turned to walk down the hallway. Bill followed. Once in the family room, Ann sat down in a chair near the fireplace. He took a seat in a matching chair on the other side of the fireplace. It was there or a large couch on the opposite side of the room. As he glanced around, Bill noticed the warmth of the room and figured that Ann and Sarah probably spent a lot of time there. Ann asked. "Would you like something to drink?"

"Not right now, thanks. Maybe later."

"You might not get another offer or maybe you won't be here long enough. Better take it while you can," Ann offered in a matter-of-fact manner; there was no teasing in her voice or twinkle in her eyes.

"Just a glass of water, thanks." As Ann left the room, Bill's feelings of trepidation spiked. He thought Ann had appeared nervous and not at all at ease. Bill started to wonder if it would turn out to be a very short visit.

"Here you go," Ann said as she offered Bill the glass.

"Thanks," Bill answered, noticing that Ann did not have anything to drink. His heart sank further. Apparently this would be a short visit.

Ann took a deep breath, let out a sigh, and spoke. "Bill, even though I made a promise to you, I really struggled with whether to keep it or not. I know you want answers to all the questions you must have, but do you have any idea how hard this is for me? There is a very large part of me, I mean a very large part, that has no desire to give you the time of day, let alone share any of my memories, those difficult and painful memories after you left me."

Bill answered, trying to remain calm but feeling panic inside. "Ann, I do understand, and I want you to know that I'm certainly grateful for that part of you that has agreed to invite me to your home as well as anything you decide to share with me."

Ann did not acknowledge Bill's effort at expressing his appreciation. She looked at him and then began to speak again. "I was so very angry with you when you just abandoned me, just stopped writing at a time that I needed you so much." Bill's instinct was to interrupt Ann, to say that what he did was not an act of abandonment but misguided sacrifice, but he knew better than to do so. Ann went on, "Not only was I angry, at times I really did feel as if I hated you — you and everything about you. I wished we had never met. Those feelings ate at me like nothing else in my life ever had. I almost let it destroy me before I was able to move on with my life. Now, for the first time in a long time, I feel that anger within me again, and I hate it."

Bill looked at Ann for just a second and then hung his head, avoiding further eye contact. "I am so very sorry."

"Really! That's all you have to say, 'I'm sorry'?" Ann's response was loud and filled with exasperation. She pounded her hand against the arm of the chair. "You son of a bitch! You can't even look at me. And the best you can do is mutter *I'm sorry?*"

Bill had never heard Ann so loud, so angry, and his hopeful ideas of how their conversation might go evaporated with her outburst. He looked up at her, struggled to find the right response without success, and then slowly stood. "Ann, I know you don't like to hear me apologize, but I will, I must. I am truly am sorry for all the pain that I have caused so many years ago *and* for upsetting you today. I was wrong then and wrong now for asking you to share your memories. I'll show myself out and not upset you any more." He turned and took his first step toward leaving before Ann shot back.

"Leaving, huh? Just like you! It's always the easiest thing for you to do. Doesn't matter the mess you leave behind or how you have hurt those who love you, you just leave. Nice, real nice!"

Bill stood at the family room doorway, his back toward Ann, and without further movement. Her words pierced his heart. He turned, looked at Ann — each stared at the other with intensity — and then spoke. "Ann, there has not been a day since I lied to you in that letter that I have not regretted it more than I could possibly ever explain. Even though I knew you would be hurt, I could not and did not imagine the depth of that hurt. In my crazy, mixed-up thinking then, I thought you would quickly move on, away from me and toward the life that you wanted and deserved. As selfish as it was then, I did come to understand that actions at the time were more about me and what I had given up, rather than on you and what you had lost." Bill paused and slowly, hesitantly, returned to his chair. When Ann said nothing, Bill continued. "Ann, in my eyes you were always the strong one. So self-assured, so focused, so determined. I thought that strength would make it easier and quicker for you to move on with your life without me."

"Well, it didn't!" Ann snapped at Bill. "I needed you, Bill, and God only knows how much I loved you then. I moved on because I had to. There was no other choice. A baby on the way — I couldn't let the anger destroy me. Having Eileen, holding her, loving her, that all helped me more than anything to release the anger." Ann paused, chuckled slightly, a soft but ironic laugh, then continued in a softer tone, "I hate to even say this, but every time that I looked at our daughter — from the day that she was born —I could see you in her eyes, her smile. I realized then that I couldn't look at her and still hold onto my anger." Ann again paused for a second, hesitant to share her next thought. "But I was really surprised when I would look at her and a piece of me would feel some sort of love for you. I rarely acknowledged it or even tried to understand it, but it has been with me everyday, first in Eileen and then in Sarah."

Ann wiped away the tears that flowed down her cheeks. "Eileen ... after the accident that took her, I was so angry — at the drunk who caused the accident, at God, and even with you again. But I also had a grandchild to care for, and just as with Eileen, I had to release the anger. Holding Sarah as a baby, I could see so much of Eileen in her, which included her eyes and smile. The ones she got from you."

The room was silent; neither spoke. Both sat motionless in their chairs, staring not at one another but into memories of days long past. Finally, Ann said, "There are a few pictures of Eileen on the desk. One is of Eileen, Sarah, and me. It was taken just a week before she was killed."

Bill walked to the desk and picked up the photos. There were four. He examined each one carefully. The photographs opened a window on the past that offered Bill both a feeling of completeness and one of immense sadness from all that he had missed. He would never know how it felt to hold his daughter, to live life as a family, to be with Ann just as they had wanted when youth fueled their dreams and their future together looked so bright. When Bill looked at the last photo, he let out a soft laugh.

It was of Eileen with Sarah on her lap, probably no more than a couple of months old. The backdrop of the black and white photo was a grassy field, a few trees, and the bay off in the distance. Eileen was sitting at a picnic table looking down at Sarah. The photo captured her beauty and the love she had for the daughter she held. But it was the multiple crayon markings across the photo that had led Bill to chuckle. He asked, "Did Sarah color this one picture of her and her mom?"

Ann answered. "Yes, that was Sarah's work. She had just turned 5 and was starting to ask more and more about her mom. When she did, I would use the photos as I talked about her mom and how much she loved her. Sarah decided that photo would look better in color, and started in with her crayons before I could stop her."

Bill returned to his chair, sitting more on the edge, as if he was unsure if he was staying or going. He looked at Ann, "So, is this it?"

"What do you mean?" Ann asked.

"Well, you shared with me the anger you felt, your reluctance to meet with me again, and the photos. All of which I'm grateful for. But I get the feeling that you have said what you needed or wanted to say and have given me a glimpse into the past. Beyond this, you can't or won't be offering anything else. Like you said, and now I understand, there really is no reason for you to share with me more or offer me more. What you have done is gracious, and I appreciate it."

When Ann said nothing in response, Bill continued. "You have a lifetime of both wonderful and tragic memories. I have two boxes filled with letters that were never shared. It was my decision, my actions that set each of us on our course. One life lived to its fullest and the other never really lived at all — just words on pieces of paper."

"How do you know that my life has been lived to its fullest?" Ann challenged.

"A daughter, a granddaughter. Those make it seem full to me. Am I wrong?" Bill asked.

"Having Eileen and Sarah certainly made life worth living, but I had dreams." Ann paused then added, "Life would have been more complete if I'd had someone to share it with."

Bill looked at Ann as she spoke, listening intently and studying her expression before asking, "Why didn't you marry?"

"Why didn't you?" Ann snapped back.

"Because I knew what was in my heart."

"And that got you what? Oh yeah, two boxes full of letters," Ann retorted.

"Ann, I made that choice not to marry, and I have never regretted it, not even for a single day. Now, are you going to answer my question?"

"Why do you want to know?"

"Just seems that you would have married. Probably stems from my deeply misguided notion that once I was out of your life, you would go on to live a complete life — the wonderful dream that you had."

"And what wonderful dream of mine are you referring to?" Ann asked.

"Why do you keep asking me questions instead of answering mine?" Bill paused to see if Ann was going to answer. When she did not immediately do so, he continued. "Having a large family is the dream I'm talking about. You never talked about a career or adventure. You always talked about lots of children in your future."

Ann rose from her chair, stretched a little, and then asked, "Do you want some more water? I think I'll have some." When Bill handed his empty glass to Ann, she held it up in an exaggerated fashion to emphasize the fact that the glass was empty. "Looks like you stayed longer than I thought you would — needing a second glass of water."

Bill looked at Ann and could see a slight twinkle in her eye. This time, her words were teasing him. Ann looked beautiful as she smiled a little and teased about the water. "So, now you are reverting to drinking water in order to avoid my question?" he asked.

"No, avoidance is your suit. I'm just thirsty." Ann continued the banter as she left the room. When she returned, Ann set Bill's glass down on the table beside his chair without saying a word, and then sat down in her chair. After taking a sip of water, she spoke. "I came close — twice."

It took Bill just a second to register what Ann had just shared, that it was in response to his question. "What kept you from it?"

"The first time just wasn't right. I think I was rushing into something, maybe trying to prove a point. The second time … the closer it came to us setting a date, the more certain I knew that I could not marry him. Deep down inside there was a feeling that I fought, but in the end, I knew what was in my heart, and it would not have been right to marry someone without loving them completely."

"I'm sorry that you did not find the right one to share your life with," Bill offered, not sure exactly what else to say.

"Oh, I did find the right one, but he abandoned me!" In an instant, Ann showed anger again.

Ann's heated response caught Bill off guard. It was as if those feelings were just lying under the surface, ready to burst forth with the slightest remark or provocation. "Ann, if I say I'm sorry a thousand times, it won't change what I did to you." Bill waited to see if Ann would respond, but she did not. "There is a song that describes love and how people deal with it. It says that some hold onto love and some let go. I guess I did both. My head let go

— thinking I was making a sacrifice out of love — but my heart held onto you ... and still does."

"Is all of that supposed to make me feel better?" Ann asked.

"No, I guess not. Maybe what I'm saying is still a way to make myself feel better," Bill offered.

"Somehow, I'm not too interested in making you feel better at the moment."

"So, what are you feeling?" Bill really wanted to know.

After a moment of not responding, Ann spoke. "Do you really care how I am feeling?"

Ann's question irritated Bill. "Yes, of course I do."

"Just like you cared when you walked out of my life?"

"Annie, I can't do this. All I am doing is upsetting you and making things worse." Bill stood, ready to leave.

Ann looked at Bill with anger in her eyes and started to speak, but was suddenly silenced by the sound of the front door opening and Sarah's voice.

"Nana, it's me!" Sarah called from the front hall.

"In the family room," was all that Ann offered in response.

Ann and Bill looked at one another, their expressions showing surprise and bewilderment. Ann took a quick glance at her watch. Sarah was home early — something that Ann had not expected.

Chapter Twenty-Six

SARAH WALKED INTO THE DEN AND WAS SURPRISED to see Bill sitting there. "Oh, hi Bill. I didn't realize that was your car parked out front." When she turned toward her grand-mother, Sarah could see that she had been crying.

Ann wiped her cheeks then said to Sarah without looking directly at her, "You're home early. Everything OK?"

"Everything's fine. I had a few hours of comp time and decided to leave early. Thought I would surprise you."

"That you did," Ann answered.

Sarah did not know what to say next. The three of them shared a moment of awkward silence: Bill still standing, Ann trying to dry the last evidence of tears in her eyes, and Sarah glancing at first one then the other, trying to figure out what was going on. Hesitantly Sarah spoke, "Should I leave you two alone?"

Bill looked at Ann for the answer and then started to tell Sarah that he was just leaving. Before he could speak, Ann responded while still looking at Bill. "Tell her." Ann's words were not loud and sharp but firm.

Bill was not expecting to hear Ann say those words. He asked, "Can we do it together?"

Ann did not reply to Bill's question. He was relieved that at least she had not said *no*.

271

Bill offered Sarah his chair, the one nearest her grandmother, and then moved across the room to sit on the couch. Sarah eased into the chair, first glancing at Bill and then her grandmother, wondering what was about to unfold. She had no idea what was going to be said, feeling more concerned that Ann had been crying, something that did not happen often.

Ann and Bill each looked at each other, then Bill looked at Sarah. "I'm not sure where to start, Sarah, but I'll try. The picture — the one you saw on my desk — the one you have here in your home — I took that picture." Bill paused to gauge Sarah's reaction. She did not appear too surprised, and Ann gave no indication that she was going to add anything. He continued. "You see … I loved your grandmother very much. I loved her for years before the photo was taken and have ever since. We first met when she was 16 and I was 17, but that picture was taken almost six years later. On the day of the picture, we talked about spending the rest of our lives together. Even though we had talked some about it before, that day it felt as if it was going to be. I just knew that we would marry as soon as I came home from Vietnam." Bill lowered his head and added, "It was what we both wanted very much."

Bill looked first at Ann and then at Sarah. Ann said nothing; her eyes again filled with tears. Sarah was slouched to the back of chair and had a conflicting, quizzical look on her face.

"That day — the day of the picture — was the last time I saw your grandmother until I showed up on her doorstep, trying to deliver the letter. The day after the photo, I left Summersville on my way overseas. I had orders to Vietnam that took me away from your grandmother and into that terrible war. Within days of being there, the helicopter I was flying was hit by enemy fire and crashed. The other pilot was killed, and I had severe injuries that forever changed my life." Bill again paused to look at Sarah. Her expression had not changed. He couldn't look at Ann.

He now had tears in his eyes. "Sarah, I made a terrible decision. I was a fool. Because of the injuries and the impact that they would have on the rest of our lives, I decided your grandmother's life would be better, more complete, without me."

Sarah looked at Bill, over to Ann, and then again to Bill. She said nothing, feeling dazed by what Bill had shared, yet with a feeling that there was much more to the story.

Bill went on. "I wrote or had a friend write for me — I couldn't write because my right arm was messed up — a letter to your grandmother." He swallowed hard; it was difficult for Bill to continue. "The letter told a lie, a lie that I came to regret soon after I wrote it and every day since then. In the letter, I told Ann that I had found someone else, that I was moving on with my life, and that she should do the same."

Suddenly, Ann interjected in an agitated, hostile voice that startled Sarah. "And I never got the damn letter! All I got was *nothing:* no letters, no phone calls, just silence from a man who had *decided for me* just how I should live my life!" Bill winced when Ann spoke. Sarah had never seen her grandmother display such anger.

When Ann said nothing more, Bill continued telling Sarah. "Soon after I wrote the letter to Ann, I was evacuated to a hospital in Germany and then moved again before I ended up in the hospital in Washington. It was there, not long after I arrived, that I received the last letter your grandmother ever wrote to me. By then, my wounds had started to heal and the bitterness, self-pity I was feeling had lessened. And, I had come to realize what a fool I had been. I thought more and more about writing Ann, to tell her the truth and beg for forgiveness, but then I received her letter. After I read it, I knew she had moved on — just as I had previously wanted. It was too late."

Ann spoke again; this time not quite as loud and angry. "I wrote you nearly every day for weeks and weeks, the whole time never hearing a word from you. I begged you to write, to call — but *nothing*." Ann turned more toward Sarah to add, "Finally, I wrote Bill my last letter. It didn't say much, just that I had accepted his decision and was moving on with my life."

Bill spoke up. "That final letter … When I read it, I believed she had accepted my decision — my lie about someone else in my life — and would go on with her life. I have no idea why more of her letters never made it to me, probably due to me being transferred to different hospitals and even different wards within the hospitals. The military postal system wasn't the best during those days."

The room held an awkward silence as Bill took a longer pause and Ann added nothing more. Finally, Sarah spoke, "I don't understand. Well, I understand that you lied to my grandmother in a letter — one that she never received — and that you received her letter about moving on, but what I don't understand is about the injuries. It is terrible that you were hurt, but soldiers are wounded — many severely — and they come home to their families, their loved ones. Why couldn't you? Why were you so different?" Sarah asked as she felt herself becoming angry with Bill.

Bill took a deep breath and then exhaled it before he answered. "In all the years we were together, leading up to the time when the picture was taken, your grandmother talked about having lots of children, five or six. When she spoke about it, she glowed. Having a big family was all she ever wanted in her life."

Ann cut in, "Except you! I wanted you." She said nothing more, but her words struck hard at Bill.

"Because of the injuries, the doctors told me I could never father children. That's when I decided I had to let Ann go. I couldn't give her children, a family. I thought I was doing so out of love for her, but it wasn't. It was a very selfish thing to do. I figured if I told her about the injuries, she would resist, but if I said that I had found someone else, she would have no choice."

Sarah looked at Bill as if she could not believe what she was hearing, but said nothing, simply left speechless for the moment. The three sat in silence for several minutes, each exhausted by the emotions that had filled the room. Bill and Ann knew that what was unfolding before Sarah was not yet complete. Sarah wondered if there could possibly be more.

Finally, Bill leaned a little forward, looked at Ann, and said, "Should I continue?"

"Yes, she needs to know," Ann answered.

"Everything?" Bill questioned.

"Yes, everything."

Bill looked at Sarah, to Ann, and back to Sarah. He was finding it almost impossible to speak, but he finally began again. "Sarah, not only did I give up your grandmother ..."

In a flat, dejected tone Ann interrupted, "You mean *abandoned.*"

Bill lowered his head and continued, "Not only did I abandon your grandmother, but I now know that I also abandoned your mother."

Sarah struggled to absorb what Bill had just told her. His words made it feel as if the room had collapsed around her, impossible to focus on any one thing or person. A wave of heat engulfed her body and, at the same time, numbness swept across her, making her feel as if it would be impossible to move.

Ann could see Sarah's reaction and asked, "Are you OK?"

Sarah did not answer her grandmother, but hearing her voice helped Sarah regain control of her thoughts and senses. "Are you saying that *you* are my mom's dad, my grandfather?" Bill did not speak, just nodded his head. Then Sarah pivoted in her chair to look directly at her grandmother with an expression of bewilderment. "You always said that the *war* took my mom's dad, my grandfather. You wanted mom and then me to believe that he was dead. How could you do that?" Sarah had tears in her eyes.

Ann's lip trembled as she started to reply. "I was so angry with Bill. I was pregnant and alone. At first, it was the loneliness of him being away from me, off to Vietnam, but there were occasional letters, and they helped to keep me going. Then — just like that — no more letters, no phone calls, nothing. I wrote and pleaded with him to write, to explain what was going on — but nothing." Ann paused to look at Bill then continued. "There were times when I wished he was dead, but that hatred was destroying me and, if I was going to make it, I had to move on, let go of the anger. Having your mom started me on the path of doing that, of letting go of the anger, but she also reminded me of Bill — his eyes and smile — and eventually of the love that we had shared to create her. Sarah, you have those same eyes and smile. I have seen Bill in you every day since you were born."

Sarah and Bill looked at one another as soon as Ann made the comparison. Each could see what Ann had known all along.

No one could say anything more. Finally, Bill spoke again. "Ann showed me a few pictures of your mom and you, the ones on the desk." With tears streaming down his cheeks, he continued. "Your mom — *my daughter* — was a beautiful woman. I see her in you. I am so sorry that she was killed when you were so young ..." Bill began sobbing, his shoulders heaved up and down as he gasped for his breath and struggled to continue his words. He was barely audible when he added, "... that I never knew my beautiful daughter."

Each sat in silence, tears streaming down their cheeks. Then Ann rose to her feet, walked across the room, and sat down beside Bill. She placed her arm across his back and her head on his shoulder. "Your daughter was beautiful, just like your granddaughter." Ann rubbed Bill's back and then added, "I am so sorry that I kept Eileen from you. I was wrong. I am truly sorry."

Sarah wasn't exactly sure what had just happened when her grandmother crossed the room to sit beside Bill and apologize, but with those actions, the tension that had filled the room seemed to evaporate. She let out a sigh of relief and then stood, going to the desk to look at the pictures. Holding one picture in her hand and then moving across the room to sit on the other side of Bill, Sarah asked, "Don't you like my artwork? I think it adds so much to the picture."

All three gently laughed.

Chapter Twenty-Seven

"WHAT WOULD YOU LIKE FOR LUNCH TOMORROW?" Ann asked as she watched Bill pull on his coat, headed back to his apartment for the night.

"A smile from you," Bill answered then wrapped his arms around Ann to pull her close.

"No problem, you can have a double helping," Ann offered as she moved closer to Bill and placed her arms around his waist.

"Would you like to go out to lunch instead, maybe invite Sarah to join us?""I don't think so, at least not tomorrow. I really want to spend the afternoon here. Who knows what kind of mischief we might get into?" As she spoke, Ann looked up at Bill to give him a big smile and a wink.

"I do like the way you think, Annie." Bill pulled her even closer and then they kissed, kisses with softness and passion. Finally, Bill pulled away reluctantly, straightened his jacket, and gave Ann another quick kiss. "OK, I best get going, but I'll see you at noon."

"Drive safe and sweet dreams."

"I'll be dreaming of you," Bill said with a smile and a twinkle in his eye.

"You better!" Ann watched him until he backed from the driveway and then drove away down the street. She turned out the lights and headed to bed, still thinking of him. Another day coming to close in what had now become a daily routine: not just the meal, but Ann and Bill spending hours together.

Three months had passed since the fateful day when Bill had gone to Ann's home, an emotional, life-changing visit that had transcended from Bill wondering if it would be the last time he would ever see Ann and then Sarah's unexpected arrival home to the start of a healing process that had brought the two of them to what they now shared today.

When Bill left Ann's home after that fateful visit, he had hesitated to ask but did, "When can I see you again?" He felt hopeful, from what seemed to be Ann's change of heart, but he was also felt anxious. Would Ann feel as if all had been said that needed to be?

Ann's short reply was more than he could have possibly hoped for. She said, "How about day after tomorrow for lunch. Come at noon." Bill did and after that lunch the two talked the entire afternoon and into the evening hours. At times, emotions flared but were worked through rather than permitted to take over the conversation. This pattern was repeated over and over. The tension and focus of prior conversations gave way to sharing: their pasts, stories of Eileen, and the joy of being together in the moment. Bill loved to hear Ann laugh, and as days passed, he heard more and more of it from her. It was her laughter that often carried his thoughts back to the first days of his love of Ann, a love that had lasted a lifetime.

Ann looked at the kitchen clock again. It was almost 12:10, and Bill had never been late. She was a little worried, especially since he had not phoned. Maybe it was traffic or road construction, she thought. When 12:15 arrived and still no Bill, Ann called Sarah.

"Hi, Honey, it's your Nana."

"Hi, Nana, what's up? Thought you and *Gramps* were doing lunch again today," Sarah teased.

"We are, but he hasn't showed up, and I'm worried about him. He hasn't called either. I tried his phone and cell phone. Both went to voicemail. "

Sarah could hear the worry in Ann's voice and wanted to assure her that everything was OK. But she also knew Bill, and it was not like him to be late. "I bet everything is fine, and he will show up any minute. You know, he turns off his cellphone all the time and forgets to turn it back on. But I will run over to his place to check. If he is still there, I will tell him to get a move on."

"Thanks honey; call me back just as soon as you can," Ann said.

"I will and please don't worry." Sarah hung up the phone. Even though she told Ann not to worry, she could not help from doing so. She grabbed her sweater and called out to Beth, "I'll be right back."

Sarah rang the doorbell for the second time — still no answer. *This is not good,* she thought but would not let her thoughts go darker. She had hoped to draw the conclusion that her grandfather had left and was on his way to Ann's, except that his car was still parked in his spot in front of the building. Sarah pulled the front door key from her pocket — the one that Bill had given her after his last hospital stay and insisted she keep — and inserted it in the lock. She opened the door, paused, and listened for any sounds, nothing but silence.

"Anybody home?" No reply. "Are you here?" Still nothing. Sarah waited a minute longer then started toward the study. Maybe he had fallen asleep in his favorite chair. She froze in mid-step and let out a startled gasp! There he was, lying unconscious on the bathroom floor, his body in such an awkward position, looking like a crumpled heap of clothing.

"Bill!" Sarah screamed, as she ran the few steps to the bathroom. "Are you OK?" She knelt down beside him and saw the source of the pool of blood that surrounded his head: a large gash above his right eye. Her first thought was that he had fainted and had hit his head on the sink or tub. His breathing was shallow.

"I'm going to call an ambulance. I'll be right back!" Sarah almost shouted to her grandfather as she jumped to her feet and dashed to the phone in the study to call 911. With that call placed, she debated for a second whether to call Ann but did not, rather racing back to Bill after opening the front door to give the ambulance crew entrance to his home. Sarah knelt beside Bill again, one hand on his shoulder and the other holding a towel against the open wound on his forehead, all the while talking to him, telling him over and over that everything would be OK. He remained unresponsive.

As the paramedics assessed Bill's condition and prepared him for transport, one asked, "Will someone be coming to the hospital?"

"I'll be there just as soon as I can," Sarah responded. "I just need to make a phone call first."

"Nana, it's me." Before Sarah could say anything more, Ann burst in with, "Did you find Bill? Why didn't he call?"

Sarah did not want to say the words. "He's on his way to the hospital. I found him unconscious in his apartment. The ambulance just left. I'm leaving now and will stop by the house to pick you up in about 15 minutes."

"I can drive. I want to get to the hospital as quickly as possible."

"No, I don't want you to drive now, please. I'll be there just as quick as I can," Sarah pleaded.

Ann did not argue with Sarah, just replied, "Hurry, please hurry!" then hung up the phone. Thoughts began to race through her mind, but the one that played over and over was *Please God, don't take Bill from me now.*

By the time Bill was discharged from the hospital, two long weeks had passed. His fall, as a result of losing consciousness, had taken its toll on him as well as brought to light other serious health matters that he had tried for so long to ignore. As a stipulation for his hospital discharge, the doctor insisted that Bill could not be left alone. When Ann learned of this, she volunteered and began to stay with him around the clock, rarely leaving his side. Likewise, Sarah wanted to do whatever she could to help; she wanted to offer assistance and to be close to her grandfather and grandmother. To do so, she spent most nights sleeping on the couch in Bill's living room. During the workday, she would leave her office a couple of times and come to his condo to check on them both.

Each passing day that Ann and Bill now shared in his apartment brought about a mixture of emotions and concerns. At times, Bill experienced pain that gripped him tightly until it finally succumbed to the drugs circulating in his body. There were moments of sleep, sometimes restful and for longer periods, but frequently fitful and in small amounts. There were periods of quietness: Bill saying nothing and Ann left to wonder what he was thinking. But, regardless of the changing moments, two things remained nearly constant: Ann by Bill's side and holding hands.

Ann and Bill shared moments of wonderful conversations, often with one of Bill's letters to Ann being the catalyst. Though somewhat reluctant at first, Ann joined in with Bill taking turns to read aloud the letters Bill had written to her over all the passing years. As they read letter after letter, Ann's feelings about them began to change. She came to enjoy discovering what Bill had done over the years and how he had often associated it in some way — big or small — with something that the two of them had once shared. The letters gave Ann greater insight into Bill's life and understanding of the love he felt for her then and now. Likewise, the letters offered a reference point of time that Ann could use to recall events from her life, the life she, Eileen, and Sarah had shared.

"Hey you," Bill softly called out as he opened his eyes to see Ann sitting by his bed, her arms and head resting on the blanket that covered him.

"Hey you, yourself. Did you have a nice nap?" Ann asked as she looked up then stood by Bill's bed to fuss over the cover.

"Not bad, just a few crazy dreams that made no sense," Bill replied with a smile, as he looked into Ann's eyes.

"Can I get you anything? Maybe something to eat?"

"No, nothing to eat. Just sit here by the bed, if you will, that's all I need."

"You know I will." Ann pulled the chair a little closer and reached for Bill's hand.

Sarah heard the latest exchange between the two and knew Bill was now awake. She walked into the bedroom, stood at the end of his bed, wiggling his big toe ever so gently, and said, "I think I'll call it a night, but anything I can do for you before I head that way?"

"Honey, would you mind getting one more letter for your grandmother to read?"

Before Sarah could answer, Ann protested. "Bill, you're tired. Why don't we save the next one until tomorrow?"

Bill looked at Ann, then answered, "No, I think now's the right time to read the one that has been on my mind for the past couple of days. I don't want to wait any longer."

"Which one is it?" Sarah asked.

"It's from May or June 1981, should be on the second shelf in the first box, and it has a little extra something inside. It's the only one that does. You'll be able to feel it through the envelope. That's the one I want, please."

"Be right back."

With little difficulty, Sarah located the requested letter. She saw three were written around that time, but only one had something extra placed inside the envelope. With letter in hand, Sarah returned to the bedroom and handed it to her grandfather as she bent over to kiss him on the forehead. She looked at him and laughed. "You look good wearing pink," Sarah joked in reference to the outline of her lips now on his forehead. She then made her way to the other side of the bed, kissed her grandmother, and said on her way out the door, "Good night you two. Try to get some rest. See you in the morning."

Bill held the envelope in his hand, using his fingers to feel its contents one last time before he handed the envelope to Ann. "Will you read it, please?"

As she opened the envelope to remove the letter, the object that had been sealed away for so very long inside dropped onto the bed sheet. When Ann saw it, she looked up at Bill with a quizzical expression. The object was a simple golden wedding band that showed the wear of age long before it had been placed in the envelope decades before. Ann looked at the ring, then at Bill, and then at the ring again as he picked it up to hold between his index finger and thumb.

Ann unfolded the letter and began to read.

My Dearest Ann,

As luck, good fortune, or perhaps fate would have it, I decided to go to an estate auction today. Several pieces of my furniture and other household goods were damaged with the move to Fort Hood, so I thought I would be able to find replacements at the auction. Besides, some of the stuff was what I bought not long after I went on active duty. Hard to believe almost seventeen years have passed since then. But what I came away with from the auction turned out to be very different.

With no real forethought or investigation, I found myself bidding on a small cardboard box filled with assorted desk items: pens, pencils, an old ruler, and a broken watch were all that I could see as the auctioneer touted its contents. For just six dollars I took ownership.

This evening, as I looked closer at the contents, I discovered this ring hidden under the inside bottom flap. It has no markings, no initials or design, perhaps all rubbed away by the constant wearing over the years. First, I thought about whom this ring might have belonged to and wondered why was it no longer with the woman whose finger it encircled for so long. Then I began to think about the ring itself, which has no identifiable beginning or end; To trace it with your fingers the edge of the ring seems to go on and on, a simple but clear representation of the love that I have for you.

As van Gogh so beautifully captured it, "Love is something eternal; the aspect may change, but not the essence." Years have now passed since we were last together and life has brought about many changes, but the essence of my love for you remains steadfast. For that, I am grateful.

Eternally,
Bill

Ann's hands had begun to tremble as she finished reading the letter and then she let them fall onto the bed, still clutching the letter. Neither spoke, they just starred deeply at one another through tear-filled eyes. With no words spoken and as if guided by the unseen forces of destiny itself, Ann arched the fingers of her left hand upward and Bill slid the ring onto her finger. As their fingers intertwined, each could see and feel the gold band that Ann now wore. The embrace of their eyes conveyed a measure of love that no words could ever capture.

Moments passed and then Ann spoke in a cracking voice, "I need to check on Sarah, make sure she has an extra blanket, but will be back in just a minute." Simultaneously, they both squeezed the other's hand just a little tighter and said, "I love you."

Ann made it out of Bill's bedroom before she began to sob with gasping breaths filling the air. Standing at the edge of the living room, she could see that Sarah had not gone to sleep, but sat on the couch with her knees drawn to her chest and a pillow held close to her face in an attempt to muffle the sounds of crying that emitted from her body. She had heard the letter read. She had heard the "I love you's" spoken in harmony.

Sarah left the couch and went to where her grandmother stood, wrapping her arms around her. Ann collapsed into Sarah's arms, burying her head in her chest to dampen the sobs that flowed from her.

"How that man has loved you so," Sarah softly spoke. That was all she could say, all that needed to be said.

Catching her breath, Ann uttered in response, "Yes … yes, he has, and how I have loved him as well." Wiping tears from her face, she stepped away from Sarah to return to Bill's bedside.

Ann paused at the bedroom doorway, her eyes fixed on his closed eyes and his chest, searching for the rise and fall that would assure her there would be more moments for them to share. Reaching his bed, she bent over to kiss him on the forehead, leaving an imprint of her lips just above those of Sarah. Ann sat down, looked at Bill, and looked at the gold band on her finger.

Without moving a muscle or opening his eyes, Bill said, "Well."

His one-word statement startled Ann; she thought he had dozed off again. "Well, what?" she replied.

"Will you marry me? I just gave you a ring." Harry opened his left eye as if to peek at Ann and her response. A slight grin came across his lips.

"Why would I marry you? Besides, you didn't ask me. You just managed to slip this ring on my finger; I might add — totally unexpected."

"So, you're looking for a formal proposal, where I get down on my knee?"

"Maybe and maybe not. But, if you get down on a knee now, you would never get back up."

"Guess I best get a move on with getting well and back on my feet." Still eyeing Ann and displaying a widening grin, he added, "Do you want to give me back that ring for now? That is until I ask in a proper fashion."

"No, I am going to hold onto it."

Pushing his bantering luck, Bill said, "I bet you're holding onto it because you just can't bear to part with it."

"Wrong again," Ann replied. "If you try to walk out of my life again, I want something close at hand that I can throw really hard at you."

Bill chuckled slightly as he offered, "Annie, you still have those snappy comebacks — something I have always loved about you." He also thought to himself that her words offered a glimpse into embers of anger. The two of them had come such a long way since Bill's first visit to her home — unhealed wounds exposed, then the first layers of forgiveness and greater understanding applied, and now the beginning of wonderful feelings of love reunited.

They had more to discuss, to examine, and to heal. Bill was confident that they would, and as Ann held tightly to his hand with both of hers, he seemed to know that Ann wanted the same.

Epilogue

IT WAS A PICTURE-PERFECT SUMMERSVILLE DAY.
The few morning clouds had dissipated by noon, leaving blue
skies arching over the bay. The slightest of a gentle breeze stirred
the water only slightly, just enough to further heighten the color
of the sparkling bay that shimmered a brilliant turquoise. The
temperature was pleasant, reflecting both the warmth of the
afternoon sun and a slight hint that the arrival of fall was not
too far off.

Sarah paused ever so briefly to take in all the natural beauty
that surrounded her and to let her eyes survey one more time
the setting in a small corner of the bay's park that she had
worked so hard to bring about. Chairs with their backs draped
in white cloth were arranged in a gentle arc to seat the invited
guests — 40 in all. In front of and centered on the chairs, stood a
decorative archway, constructed by Frank for just this occasion.
Billowing flower arrangements in whites, yellows, and blues
began on each side of the archway and in a descending fashion blanketed the surrounding area. The arrangements were
from the florist as well as pots from Ann's flower garden. Sarah
had meticulously placed each one — arranging and rearranging
them to create the perfect complement of colors, heights, and
fragrances. Everything Sarah had undertaken in preparation
for this day was done with an immense feeling of joy and love,
which now shone through brightly. The setting encompassed

simplicity, graceful elegance, and above all the natural beauty of the bay just 50 feet or so beyond the archway. But, reaching this minute of final preparation had not been without a few points of resistance — coming from both Ann and Bill. While both had agreed on the setting, Ann had initially resisted increasing the guest list. What had first been seen as just a very small gathering of three or four grew from Sarah's persistence. She knew in her heart that more than just a few should come together for this joyful celebration and through tenacious efforts convinced Ann that she was right. When Sarah first suggested that Bill wear his uniform, he was adamantly opposed to it. "I am only wearing that uniform one more time — that's when I am buried." Bill's strong resistance succumbed to Sarah's playful pouting and when Ann simply stated, "I have always loved a man in uniform."

On this day, at 2:30, Ann Marie O'Connell and William Harold Weber would stand before gathered family and friends to celebrate their love and bear witness to its power — the power to prevail, to heal, and ultimately to guide life's journey. Music would play and the two would speak their chosen words of love for the other as testimony to what they shared: in the past and in the present, as well as destined for the future. A love ignited one summer's day long ago that had weathered the greatest destructive storms that life might have to offer.

Taking their temporary positions near the ball field — the same one where it all began so many years ago — and just out of sight of the assembled guests, Ann and Bill stood in silence and held hands. Then the first notes of music began to softly play.

"Sounds like it's about time for us to join the others," Bill said as he beamed a giant smile, then added, "Ann, you look beautiful. And thank you."

"What are you thanking me for?" Ann asked.

"For everything. For loving me ..."

Before Bill could go on, Ann cut in, "Yeah, that has been tough. I should get sainthood for that." Ann smiled and her eyes twinkled with love and mischievousness.

Bill grinned at Ann's playful retort. "Like I was saying, thank you for loving me, thank you for your forgiveness, for raising our beautiful daughter and granddaughter, for opening your heart once again, and for the love that we will share." Bill paused then added, "Shoot, I even thank you for autographing my ball glove. If you hadn't done that, I would not have known your name, couldn't have written those first letters, and well ... you know how the story goes."

"Yes, I do know, William Harold Weber. I know it well, and may I say that you are welcome. Bill, I love you."

"Ann, I love you. And, that love will go on for all eternity."

"You mean *forever,*" Ann said then squeezed Bill's hand, kissed him on the cheek, and added, "Now, let's get this celebration started."

Ann placed her arm through Bill's and the two slowly walked together toward the assembled guests, the sparkling bay, and life anew — together.

Acknowledgments

I BEGIN WITH THE LAST FIRST THAT IS MISSION POINT
Press whose collective, herculean efforts proved invaluable in
shaping, polishing, and producing this novel. The process began
and ended with Doug Weaver, whose continuing encouragement
and advice were greatly appreciated and needed. In between,
the tireless efforts of John Pahl – editor extraordinaire – helped
smooth the jagged edges and disconnects; Ruth Campbell shared
her valued expertise as the copy editor; and Heather Shaw lent
her creativity as the graphic designer in presenting Coming
Home to Yesterday in such an inviting package.

As a life-long learner, education has helped shape the writer
that I am. It began with my high school English teacher, Miss
Judy Lanier, who quieted a rowdy spring-fever fueled senior class
by reading aloud my first short story and, in doing so, planted
the seed of writing within me. At the end of the academic journey, it was Dr. Dustin Berna – my dissertation committee chair
– that both challenged and encouraged me to dig deeper and
work harder than I ever had before. In addition, I have greatly
benefited from the writing wisdom of noted Michigan mystery
writer Elizabeth Buzzelli as she informed and encouraged aspiring writers in her class offerings at NMC. Likewise, through the
Creative Writing Workshops held at the Interlochen Center for
the Arts I have learned more about the craft. With each work-
shop attended, I have been privileged to meet budding authors

eager to share their works-in-progress, fears, and aspirations as we were gently and skillfully guided by inspiring and talented authors such as Mary Kay Zuravleff, Patricia Ann McNair, and Katey Schultz.

I sincerely appreciate the support from family and friends. Family members – Drema (sister), Rilla (aunt), and Frank (uncle) – patiently listened to an excerpt reading from an early draft and, along the way, offered their encouragement and support while refraining from the question everyone wants to ask, "now, when will your book be finished?" Whether by actual experience or inspiration, moments of many friendships shared have found their way into *Coming Home to Yesterday*. A special thanks to Dr. Marilyn Fitzgerald for her support and encouragement as the story of Ann and Bill slowly made its way onto the printed pages.

Finally, to the "one" of my life, the one that makes it so for me: "If there really is an eternity that takes us beyond the life we live, then it must be possible to share it with the love of your life and that love, my dear, is you."

About the Author

STEPHEN (STEVE) G. TOLLEY, PH.D., IS A RETIRED ARMY officer and helicopter pilot, whose nomadic lifestyle has led to residences and adventures in eleven states and seven countries. With each stop along the way came invaluable friendships, indelible experiences, and wisdom of the heart. In one-way or another, all contributed to the writing of this book.

Work on his second novel is now underway. Set in the bustling city of Philadelphia just prior to the United States entrance into World War I, a small guild of old-world inspired craftsman carve blocks of wood to create majestic carousel horses. Rows of these horses form the merry-go-rounds that fill the night air with their accompanying lights and music to attract young and old alike. An unlikely couple first finds common ground in their love of carousel horses and ultimately in one another. Yet, it is the city, the war, and the carousel horses that ultimately collide to test the young couple's love to the greatest depths imaginable.

S. G. Tolley currently resides in Traverse City, Michigan. When not writing or thinking about writing, his activities include restoration of an old home, hot yoga, carving a carousel horse, and enjoying northern Michigan.